For Linda
from The C...
L...dsey
with love

MARY FLORIDA

A ROMANCE

Lindsey Erith

CRANTHORPE
MILLNER

First published by Cranthorpe Millner Publishers (2022)

ISBN 978-1-80378-094-8 (Paperback)

www.cranthorpemillner.com

Cranthorpe Millner Publishers

For John Boyden, my husband and (non-fiction)
romance

Chapter I

A bang on the head and a set of cracked ribs proved that when his Sovereign King Charles demanded loyalty, John Blackavise had delivered. No white flag had been raised by him. He had not surrendered but been carried off unconscious. His recovery at home set him back on his feet. At this point he wasn't the man to be told he was unfit to travel, especially not by his stay-at-home son and his miminy-piminy daughter-in-law. He was healing up now.

"Look at you; no ways fit," reiterated Susan her mouth a buttonhole. No lips, he thought, how could Simon bear to kiss her, if he did. Blackavise couldn't see the incentive. He'd have preferred a minx for a daughter-in-law; who wouldn't, faced with Susan? While he had been away, the house in which he used to relax had been taken by an enemy, in petticoats. The wider world had been captured by the Parliament. What could he do, faced with the increasingly bleak alternatives? Either get himself killed, or throw in his hand and be publicly reduced to parent in the wrong, the parrot in the family cage? He was too young and too vigorous for a half-life as a prisoner.

"Will you stop marching up and down like an army?"

Caught at relieving his feelings, he halted abruptly, trying not to eye Susan as if reviewing a bunch of his troopers. He couldn't admit aloud that King Charles's Royal cause was dead. He must sustain his defiance by supporting the King's rightful cause which must live, so he might survive.

But even he admitted to himself that the cause could live and still prove hopeless. Blackavise was reduced to the two troopers, the plain young woman and his earnest, pink-faced son; a small force but one capable of harrying him considerably. Simon joined the chorus.

"Rejoin the troop, father? What troop, in the name of reason?" Simon complained, "you are only with us today by virtue of a thick steel helmet. Just look at you."

"I am fit enough now," Blackavise growled, annoyed with himself, feeling that he had rather overplayed his hand. I'm resolved to go back."

The troopers spread their hands, told-you-so-ing; they would do this once too often, and today was that day. Blackavise had backed himself into a corner. What else could he do now, but gird up and go, with a sinking feeling?

He, of all people, a realist, knew he would find ten mixed colonels, majors and captains, all wounded or crazed, for every willing soldier now remaining to King Charles in Oxford. They had a derogatory name for such cannon fodder: 'Reformadoes', meaning dregs lumped together. There had been a winter without hope in Oxford. Would he rejoin that rabble? Was he for suicide?

Never take up an attitude, he told himself, bluff called, next morning, with his leg athwart the saddle, the warm horse beneath him blowing herself out as he heaved on her girth. He hid the pain of his mending ribs with a sharp intake of breath. Now you have burnt your bridges. You can leave this ungracious pair in Sussex and be gone.

It was Susan who gave him the strength to kick on, though. "'Tis selfishness, 'tis perversity," she pronounced from the porch door. He acknowledged inwardly this might be true; worse still, she might be right. But when she added, "May God forgive you" in a tone of piety, he could not wear that, and he glared round the garden, his eyes striking a glancing shaft upon the pair of them.

Why did she stand there like Moses and provoke her

father-in-law? He was a strong man in the prime of life, and she a know-all of twenty. The very cap she wore annoyed him, snagging her ears in a pancake the colour of unbaked pastry and she too mean to crimp the edges.

"Good fortune," he called crossly to Simon, as the mare strode towards the open gate. Did people murder daughters-in-law? Having overheard them plotting to encourage a Widow Clarence to take an interest in him, he felt he was sparing the family an unnecessary crime. The hideous widow rose in his mind's-eye, and like a horse with its ears flat back, John Blackavise baulked and bucked inwardly. He would not be reduced to hoping God would forgive him, nor to consorting with widows yet. They were an intrusion; the widow Clarence with her brass voice would have likely practical effects, unlike prayers.

His ribs twanged rhythmically as he rose to the trot of his mare, whose hoofprints left their trail of crescents in the mud-and-suck lane. The bare oak branches of the woodland thinned out in fan-vaulting above his broad-brimmed hat. He could look up at the calm sky. Goodbye to Sussex.

They were out of the wood. He clicked to the mare. The blue-grey line of the North Downs encouraged him onwards. Fresh air, a clean inn and a sleepless night informed John Blackavise that freedom was sweet, spring would shortly be softening the blackthorn buds, and as yet his heart was not in the business of stepping off the quay into the Royalist sinking ship. Half a day's hoofmark crescents led further, and the inner voice told him that going for Oxford was wilful, hopeless and, if he would persist, he would only have himself to blame, not even Susan. It was not her fault the King's fortunes had been laid low.

The fact he had seen no soldiery at all, no new wheel tracks carved deep in the mud by the baggage wagons, not so much as a Royalist flea, struck him as the beneficial reality of his new position. An escape plan rose in his mind like a treasure map from a long-drowned wreck. As if from the deep, an eddy released a giant bubble which rose to the surface of his awareness. A plan had burst upon him. Where might he yet be welcome? He turned Hetty's chestnut head towards the fingerpost pointing towards a trail he knew: one that did not lead to the no-hopers in the city of Oxford. He reined Hetty in, for soldiers keep in mind a better place to be, away from injury, campaigning and surrender. A haven, that's the term. In five miles this lane would lead him to tread a quite different dance into an older world, with no need to sacrifice himself, not yet. Why not go to see that jolly, rumbustious woman, his godmother, where the sand in her hourglass had seemed not to run since the disgraceful court of old King Jamie? No-one there had heard of Naseby, Bristol, retreats, treaties, brave men and sorrows. His heart cheered at a silly, ironic fancy. Suppose that someone in his godmother's disorganised and isolated household had been fool enough to believe that America had been discovered; it would almost certainly be rejected for a rumour spread by Royalists to persuade the starchy Puritans to sail off the edge of the flat, old world.

In this good humour he clip-clopped past the Three Tuns at the ford's slop-bowl of mud and overflow, the ducks leaving hastily as Hetty trod their glass and broke up the reflections. His heart beat up martially, for here came the first neighbouring gateway, that of the big house of Aynescote, looking as if it were occupied at last, for the pillars at the entrance stood clear of their old, strangulated undergrowth. Hetty scrunched by and he turned to stare at the gleaming gold of the windows in candlelit squares and arches.

Well, well; but he passed this peepshow, bent on landfall, suddenly urgent to reach the best of moments, coming now, at the ironwork of his godmother's entry entangled by ivy and brambles far more than he remembered, as if it were Hercules beset by serpents. Had the gaps between his comings and goings grown so long? What with life and limb at hazard and the blood-smeared crises of war, Black House had not seen his footmark these two years. But his godmother's stone-built stronghold lay snug in the back of beyond, didn't it?

The tired horse and rider rounded the curve of the approach. The long shadows of sundown formed them into a creature, as if they became a centaur wearing a wide hat. The familiar roof-slopes, the weathervane, the pattern of windows reflecting sunset, revived Blackavise with the memory of happier times as he approached. The old house was titled from her surname, which she had given to him, standing ochre coloured for all its sombre title, hewn from the local quarry, safe as Arcady. Nobody answered the door, but perhaps he had not banged loudly enough with the butt of his pistol. He was sparing his still sensitive head. The second time, just as disquiet began to stir, there was noisy unbolting before his head had finished resonating, and then scraping noises as if they'd put a bar up besides. Then he was worried. Black House didn't have doors barred up.

But here was Bessie, her solid sets of curves taking an upward turn once she identified John standing with his back to the sinking sun; and here was her boy Ginger, in jerkin and raggedy breeches for which he had grown too long.

"Yes, it is me, Bessie - how are you? What's amiss, why is the drawbridge down?"

"Missus has had a turn, sir," she said simply, "times be worrying."

"What? Is she bad? A turn?"

What's a turn? wondered Blackavise.

"Has she had the physician? What does he say?"

"Oh yes sir, and lawyer came. I am glad you stand here indeed. It seems you must have smelt we had trouble, sir."

Blackavise, thoroughly disquieted, followed as she led him, and mounted the stairs paying unnatural attention to the linenfold and the carvings of stiff, heraldic-looking sheep atop the door frames. He felt the grain of the oak banister under his trailing fingers, counted the treads - anything to avoid concentrating on calamity. But his cheery heartbeat had sunk plummeting to his boots, where it banged away defying anatomy.

It was so dark in his godmother's bedchamber after the outdoors. The tester bed loomed, he advanced, unable to stop himself flinching at the sight of the prone woman. It is always a shock to see a familiar figure in bed for the first time, and to see disaster. That she was stricken could not be gainsaid, it was fact. He had made a journey, one of many, and came to find her at the end of her life's journey. His heart ached to see her shrunken, beached by infirmity. When had he ever beheld her less than clumsily animated, a great charger and gesturer, indifferent to the fate of small ornaments, a big, rosy elephant?

As he reached out to take her hand, two large cats moved against the bedhead. For a moment, before his eyes adjusted to the gloom, it was hard to make out his godmother, her bonnet on the pillow casting shadows. Then the cats' eyes reflected in unison like silver coins because Bessie behind him was fiddling with a tinder box, succeeded and lit a candle. No; there were three cats, six pennies reflecting, adding to the tally of the coins in the half light. It was a very strange reality: his godmother's hand lay in his, as limp as bones in junket. He turned his head in dismay.

"Bessie - doesn't she know me?"

"Oh sir, she comes and goes."

What could he do? Bending forward, he put the hand he held against his shirtfront, over his heart, in an instinctive gesture towards her.

"It is John Nameless," he told the cats, told the bonnet lace, "John Nameless come to see you." John Nameless, that said it all: the name he had been called when he was a rebellious little boy, in his first pair of breeches. She'd been his mother's confidante, hadn't pilloried her for getting the bastard. When his mother died, she had hauled him off, dusted him down, and set him up, in that order. Promising she'd lend him her name, if he'd have it, and then no bully bigger than he would ever dare to call him John Nameless again. After that, he'd been John Blackavise, and although one or two got a sore nose and a watery eye for trying 'Nameless' after, it lost its power to hurt. Sticks and stones. He was now a King's officer, an adult man. It was years and years since he'd admitted the old nickname aloud, but he knew if the poor lady could recall that, she could recall … ah! The hand he held had gripped and faded.

"There," he cried, "praise be, you know me."

"Don't go," she mouthed at him.

"That I won't," he vowed.

He was so anxious about the old lady that two days later he was still sitting there, notwithstanding meals with Bessie in the kitchen and nights in the comfortable raft of the tester bed in the guest chamber. His life ran with that of the poor lady. While she breathed, he breathed, while the blue network in her wrist pulsed, his pulsed. It was an over-reaction, but sincere.

"You can't stay there," whispered Bessie, tutting.

"May I advise you, sir," said the physician, unable to refrain from the professional pleasure of inspecting the scar on Blackavise's head, "spare yourself. That's a neat bit of healing, if I may say so. How's the ribcage?"

"Well enough," said Blackavise hastily, fending off the doctor's probing fingers, "but the poor lady - what do you have to say about her?"

"I fear I can do nothing," and here the doctor hesitated, "she may linger, she may not."

"But she knew me, I swear to that."

The kind little goblin sighed and looked at the example of soldierly strength and convalescent health before him.

"I could interfere all I might, and yet I fear I would but sorely try her. The outcome would not change. You don't want her leeched, do you?"

"No, no, please leave her be. Let Bessie tend her out of life."

"Just so," assented Master Goodman, "but how long you must wait I cannot say. Don't chain yourself. Walk abroad, whatever; restore your own vitality."

He could do with some fresh air, if only to stride about as he got used to the tidings. He had to grip sorrow by the throat and master the keenness of it. But when the doctor left, John Blackavise still sat at the bedside, when to his surprise he heard approaching clumping of heavy boots on the staircase, and Bessie's warm country voice quelled by a harder tone. There was

11

a minor skirmish in the doorway, as Bessie sought to defend it, lost, and was bested by a travel-stained man in a cloak and muddy turned-down boots. He also wore an unfriendly expression.

"Who the devil might you be?" was his greeting.

Blackavise was taken aback. Concern for the invalid kept him from immediate, *fortissimo* outcry: he rose to his feet and eyed the newcomer with disfavour.

"I am godson to Mistress Blackavise; what's that to you?" he responded, tersely, "Kindly keep the Devil to yourself."

The blast of Blackavise's eye halted the stranger's advance and prompted the newcomer to attempt to regroup his features more acceptably. But the effort came too late. A strong suede-complexioned face under wet-straw-coloured string remained marred by the tetchy blue eyes. Who was this man, and why on earth was he angered to find Blackavise sitting peaceably at a sickbed? The man spoke, as if in riddles.

"You can't be."

"I can't be what?"

"'Tis I who am the godson."

Thus far, this wasn't a conversation for clarity. Blackavise had met better manners from those who were his Parliamentary enemies. He wouldn't stand much more of this.

"Sir, I care not if you be the Pope of Rome," he said in his best military tone, "but you do not raise your voice in this sick-chamber. You shall address me civilly in the parlour below, or not at all."

He brooked no argument, and such was the power of his approach upon the traveller that he had his way, and various civilising factors such as the parlour fire, and cushioned chairs and a wooden figure of a little black boy offering painted fruit on a platter, gave him something with which to subdue the seething gentleman.

"Now sir, pray acquaint me with your purpose," John demanded, trying to conceal how taken aback he felt. He made for the fireplace to occupy the high ground, as it were, and stood deliberately at ease, placing his forearm along the shelf. He took heart from the warmth of the fire as he casually crossed one boot over the other and turned a forthright eye on the newcomer.

"I'm damned if I like your pretence of owning the place," quoth the other.

Blackavise had to keep his elbow from jumping on the mantelshelf to seem unaffected.

"I own nothing here," he told him, "I but lodge here to see how my godmother fares, and I hazard I've had as bad a fright as you, to discover her so ill. I am her godson, certain; I had not heard she had others, but, as I live, I've heard no law against it."

"Mayhap I spoke too precipitate," the traveller allowed, biting his mauve lip, "I nonetheless have to say you are mistaken, sir, I am the godson, and that's that."

What an intransigent man! And a strange point to insist on. Unless Blackavise had begun to get a spark in the darkness as to what had got the newcomer so riled up. Was that comment about 'owning the place' an assumption that he would be the sole beneficiary of her will when the poor lady died? But that was distasteful. And what did such things matter?

"If we stand here as godchildren together, then we have a bond, not a division," suggested Blackavise.

"I am named as the godson, and know of none beside myself, and in that case, take you for a pretender."

Blackavise, perhaps mercifully, laughed. If this were all about a challenge to the uniqueness of his standing, why be angered?

Bessie's well-risen cake of a face appeared round the door to determine how the interview might be developing, and he hied her in. "Come, Bessie, give an opinion. Have you seen me once a season here, these many years, and is not that anniversary feted as my old Christening day?"

"Oh yes sir."

Her eyes darted like pale blue fish, one way to John Blackavise, reassured to see him smiling, darted back to the uneasy presence facing him.

"'Tis undoubted: May the twelfth," she declared.

"I'd get Parson up to vouch for it, only I see no need whatsoever to pursue such a trifle," said Blackavise.

He remained more intrigued than angry. The stranger's pettiness contrasted to the depths of the hostilities when King's and Parliament's forces took to the field. Blackavise was pleased to see Bessie's assertion had made its mark. The man took her for a simpleton who had truthfully confirmed what he didn't like to hear.

"I am John Blackavise, sir; as plain John, my name was flung over font and the good lady upstairs stood sponsor. Now it is your turn to introduce yourself. As yet, you have the advantage of me."

"Flynn Gerard, of the county of Hampshire, sir."

The courtesies had recalled him - so he wasn't a madman, he knew he had been rude.

"Then at last we have exchanged names, we share, it seems, a godmother, and perhaps Bessie would fetch us a glass, that we may discuss whatever it was brought you hither."

Bessie reluctantly quit the range of earshot, and Blackavise, wondering if the cross-grained Gerard

15

would take it as mortal insult, offered him the courtesy of bidding him pray be seated.

"I had a letter, bidding me come. I came at once despite the state of the times, in some danger I'll have you know – did it reach your ears Parliament's rebels are even now a-chasing some spymaster of the King's up and down the county hereabouts?"

"I hadn't heard that," said Blackavise, interested and noting that Master Gerard seemed united with him in the conflict, if not in their relationship with the godmother upstairs.

"I'll have you know that letter was signed by Mistress Blackavise's man-of-law, one Pettijohn, and it plainly states, I was the godchild and even after all these years I was to come at once."

He bit the dark lip again, for Blackavise visibly brightened at the giveaway.

"Er, 'All these years'?"

"So, I admit there had been a ..." he baulked and then pulled himself together, "My family did not approve of what she had been. They did not know at the time all that had gone on."

All what?

"They liked the connection at the time, I suppose," Blackavise suggested.

Whatever had his poor godmother got up to? What

more than the peccadilloes inevitable at the masques beyond the reach of candle lighting? She'd been a jolly girl, that was all – he supposed that was all – what a train of thought! He returned to the attack.

"You thought you were the only godchild?"

Gerard gave a giveaway pat at the brown pouch hanging from his belt, saw Blackavise notice, shot a tetchy glance and pulled out the booty, a single folded sheet with the seal hanging off.

"Look for yourself."

"This letter of yours comes from Pettijohn and he says nothing about there being only one godchild," remarked Blackavise, "although it does seem possible that if she had the taste for it, we could be but two of half a hundred." He was joking, yet it crossed his mind that it was seriously possible there could be half a dozen, all pending, and all set to give him difficult mornings. Would the inn house them all? Would half of them be Parliamentarian colonels he would be compelled to fight? He had come by chance without a letter and he was in possession, so to speak, of the high ground, for he was in the house and not holding court to any Toms, Dicks and Bothersomes. He'd had enough of this one. Gerard gulped down the last of his wine, threw back his chair and announced he would get him gone.

"I shall be at the hostelry," he pronounced to

Blackavise's relief, "and wait on the event."

The word 'event' reminded John of what he had been pretending not to know. He'd rather say, himself, he'd come to be near his godmother whilst she wasn't yet an event, but breathing.

"The Red Lion's preferable to the Tuns," he made himself say.

Gerard, at the door, reared round yet again displeased.

"I've already settled my traps at the Three Tuns," said he as if it were personally John's fault. Blackavise made a mental note to keep the man off the guest list for any gathering he wished successful, should he feel the urge to sparkle in local society.

"Good Lord, Bess," he said after the footfall, clap of the front door and the resultant peace took their sequence, "did I conjure that man up? Was I visited by a dark dream?"

"No, certainly," Bessie turned the blue goldfish at the top of their bowls earnest upon him. "What a turn-up, weren't he!"

"Your mistress did have the lawyer, then?"

"Surely she did. After she had a little turn, the physician came, and she asked him to see that lawyer stepped up. An 'he did. They were shut away, hours, an' when I was showing him out she called after him "mind you send those letters, if I be stricken."

"Were there many letters?" asked Blackavise, absentmindedly rubbing the scar interrupting his spray of hair, "Did you know?"

"Three, four, might'a been five."

So three, four, might'a been five godchildren. If one was for him, that made two, three or four others. Of whom he had met the first already.

"Then she had this seizure, sir, must'a had a foreknowing."

"Yes."

"But did you get no letter, sir?"

"I've been off a-soldiering," he said wryly, "where would she send it?"

A letter might be mouldering in Oxford city this moment or arrived and be unopened at Simon's after he'd left. He knew, comforted, that it was he she'd wanted. "Don't go." She'd been able to tell him. What was the animosity of one scratchy fellow? He laughed at it, now the man was gone. Only a slight misquiet that his desert island had been violated sent a cloud across the half-strength early season sun.

Chapter II

Then John Blackavise took to a fit of curiosity. Two hours sitting by the inert old lady called for a mental flow, to avert thoughts of doom. King Charles's fortunes were sufficient, in that line, he told himself. So he thought about the godchildren. His childless godparent had given herself comforts; he was surprised only that he hadn't known, that she'd not held open court for them all, encouraged the house to ring with cries and laughter and unchecked high spirits, which he'd enjoyed on his own. But were these the results of what Gerard had let slip? "All that had gone on". What an intriguing thought. Gone on, when? Not in his time here. But hadn't his own mother disgraced herself when she got with child at the time the two were at Danish Queen Anne's court together, years back? What if they'd both had good times and only one of them was caught out? His godmother had a near squeak, perhaps, and near squeaks provoke whispers. He hadn't heard them, wouldn't have heard them: and if he had, wouldn't have cared; he loved her. Perhaps the patronage of her good name to the Gerard family of Hampshire might have lost its appeal. He'd go to this lawyer fellow Pettijohn and see what else he knew. For an adult man, an Army officer (what army?) and unsuccessful father to an adult son, he felt oddly innocent.

Master Pettijohn belied his name. He was a large, unfit looking man like a succession of pears melted together, and his godparents, whomsoever, had named him Frank. He had books, ledgers and the usual paraphernalia of moulting quills and wax sticks and little penknives littering a table, upon which wax blots interfered with the polish.

"Did I write to you, Master Blackavise?" the top pear furrowed, he brightened and hauled a note covered in scratchy drowned-fly writing from a folder. "Indeed I did," he answered himself.

Trying to make out the other names upside down, John Blackavise enquired where he had sent it. Discussing his precise billet in Oxford didn't unknot the upturned handwriting either. He was unwilling to ask outright and receive an outraged rejoinder that it was

Mistress Blackavise's business, not his; so they sat discussing the invalid's decline.

"Of course one forgets her age," Pettijohn was saying, "she was ever active, ah me! The picture of vitality, young at heart."

"A gentleman called Gerard called," John told him, hoping to circumvent actual questioning.

"Has he? Ah!" The lawyer bent his gaze on his list, and as the name he looked for was last, he turned the paper tantalisingly in front of Blackavise to check it, found it and re-aligned the paper before Blackavise could do more than get the outline of a name resembling Blorraskins. Or Blossapin. Hopeless! He'd have to abandon subterfuge.

"I'm puzzled at this business of other godchildren. That's what this business is all about, isn't it? There's myself, there's Gerard, and from what I understand, maybe three others. I don't understand why I never met a one of them. I suppose they don't live locally."

"I think the Corrydenes are still at Overhill, but no-one sees aught of them. Of course his fortunes have taken a tumble in the war," said Pettijohn unknowingly helpful.

Was it a secret, thought Blackavise. Was it common knowledge to all but he? Better be open, then.

"And the others? May I know their names, in case I

am put to entertaining?" The desirable paper turned like a weathervane, Pettijohn was handing it to him. He grasped it, it was his. Forewarned was forearmed. Radlett, it said: Corrydene, Pragg, Lyons. He was pleased to see the name which he had misread was his own, and first on the sheet with Gerard over the page, last. He didn't know the new names, and there were no addresses. Pettijohn presumably only jotted names as an aide-memoire until he returned from Black House to his office.

"Thank you," said Blackavise allowing himself a wry smile at his godmother's lawyer, "it comes as a surprise to find I am not so singular as I'd thought myself."

"We are all singular, in this life," said Pettijohn gloomily, "singular we come into this world, and singular we depart. Unless we are twins, of course," he added rationally, brightening.

"Do you know any of these people, at all?" asked Blackavise, fidgeting with the hilt of his sword.

"Not a one, barring I have heard the name Corrydene. But I know of you, sir, I know of you."

Which remark, calculated to disconcert people newly introduced, ricocheted off Blackavise, for another question had dawned on him. "By any chance, do you know the name of the new people who have taken the great house of Aynescote? I saw signs of life there when I rode up this week. None of them is a Radlett, Pragg, or Lyons, are they?"

The old lawyer leaned back in his chair and raised his eyes to the ceiling searching for inspiration.

"I've heard the name – now what was it? None of those, I'm sure. Seems the young man's inherited from a string of relatives. Ah! Lacey. Aeneas Lacey! That's the name. Seems he has a young wife everyone's keen as mustard to see, word is she's a beauty, cheers life up, that, and he's set about poor old Aynescote with dusters and spider brushers and paint-lickings. I haven't heard her name. Should be Dido." He smiled at his own joke.

"It should be," Blackavise allowed a smile in return, "but I trust not, as her fate was settled so miserably, what with the aftermath of the antique old Trojan Wars."

"And now we are in the aftermath of our dreadful Civil Wars, which I am delighted to see you have survived. Happily Aynescote has been not savaged by the Greeks. The Laceys have been settling in scarcely a fortnight. You must go and call. Open house, I hear. Mistress Blackavise would wish you to welcome them on her behalf, that sort of gesture."

I could do with someone welcoming me, thought Blackavise, remembering his meeting with Gerard. "And so I shall, in her stead, you're right, she'd wish it.

24

Time hangs heavy for all of us while my godmother's in her half world. But first, I'm for Overhill, it's time I met Master Corrydene."

*

The first hurdle in that journey saw him dodging Flynn Gerard, who appeared next morning red-eyed, having found the inn's bedstraws full of ticks, the ale thin, and his temper not improved, just as Blackavise was thinking of starting out. He had to waste an hour indoors forced to exchange small talk in the parlour, repeating the sweetener of wine. He didn't want Master Flynn here latching on to his visit and turning the milk sour in the next godson's porridge. Gerard was not anxious to elaborate upon his family's disfavour towards Mistress Blackavise, and he sat there on the carnation sprays of that lady's erratic embroidery, determinedly telling John where his army manoeuvres had been ill-planned, where Rupert had been wrong-headed, where Ireton and the bunch of King's enemies had got themselves better trained, supplied, and paid. All of which Blackavise knew too well.

"And did you participate, Master Gerard?" he enquired, hoping to land a blow. But Gerard had the answer even there. His brother had fought, and got himself slain upon the field of Chalgrove (irony, that, a Royalist success) and, from what he now told Blackavise through clenched teeth, had beggared them as well.

"'Tis those who see to matters at home that have to pick up the pieces," he said accusingly to his temporary host. Was he at last rising to take leave?

"I'll be back tomorrow. I'm waiting for the event," he declared.

This Parthian shot removed the pleasure John had been allowing himself at Gerard's retreating rear view, but at least it cleared his path to Overhill.

The sun, pale but hitherto genuine, lost heart as he rode Hetty over the roll of the hill, skulked into a cloud as he sighted rooftops, and then the cloud cried tears as he enquired of a housewife rescuing her washing. She mumbled to him through her mouthful of clothes-pegs, spat them out and directed him more clearly.

"I thank you, good wife," said Blackavise, and sure enough, behind the square-towered church, behind the yews, up a lime avenue, was a dreary little manor house crouching amid a run-down topiary garden. He determined on the hail-fellow approach. Any lack of conviction could only give away the uncertainty of his right to ask about this link he had with Master Corrydene. It was as bad as if he were a foundling

26

trying not to embarrass decent kin. The right to hold his head up had been his godmother's gift, apart from the four apostle spoons, and he most keenly wanted a look at the batch of them, these godchildren, if only to prove Flynn Gerard was not typical. Where their godmother's house was amber stone, with some life in it even on dull days, this one was ditchwater grey, its stones hewn from a quarry of donkey colours. The roof of heavy slabs sent the hat down over the oblong eyes of the first-floor casements. A stripling came to the door, yawning. Blackavise, improvising, hatted.

"I would pay my respects to your master, is he at home?"

Politeness was something the youth recognised, even though he was not able to reciprocate. He half opened the door, failed to convert his yawn and continued to breathe through the vent thus created, but stood aside. Blackavise strode forward, his heels ringing on the flagstones. In the poorly illuminated hall, the immediate danger came from walking into the furniture: what was this pile of stacked boards and clutter? He inhaled a rich and pleasant set of notes on the air. He'd smelt this before: it was when his Colonel had sent for him to promote him – the moment had happy associations – and he'd been shown into Jackson's presence to find him there having his portrait taken by that marvellous catcher of likenesses, the King's Sergeant-painter, William Dobson, standing there with a brush in his hand. The aroma he remembered, transported him, as smells often will, the artist rose in mind's-eye, he saw the paraphernalia of pestling and grinding and whatever painters did to pigment and, behind that, the living Colonel and his image half-completed on the easel, a popping good similarity, sashed, lobster-breastplated and posed with a map on a drum before him. Who was painting Master Corrydene? Not poor Dobson, already dead; some journeyman painter, probably, but commissioning a portrait was unusual, in times when down-at-heel little manor houses had owners to match. Corrydene might be a Parliamentarian, of course, but it was unlikely in these parts. Blackavise told himself not to go creating divisions in his own mind between himself and his fellow godchildren, before they'd so much as met. Impatiently he sat in the deep-sea gloom of the hall, on the knobbly chair traditional for unannounced guests, his sore ribs twanging after the ride. Eventually a stout inner door opened, throwing an oblong of cheese-coloured light in perspective down the flagstones. It illuminated Blackavise sitting there with his hat on like a figure in a Dutch painting, his turn-down boots extended and crossed. An emaciated young man came padding into the hall, making a dive for a bag beside Blackavise's chair, fumbling in the dark contrast to the raft of light from the open door. A folder spilled leaves of paper, and charcoal sticks tumbled and broke. Blackavise, his eyes now accustomed to the gloom, bent, gathered them up and handed them back.

"Oh, thanks," said the young man, who would have shaken hands had his palms not been smeared with oil paint like Joseph's coat of many colours. He began rubbing at the mess with a cleanish rag from his sleeve. Released from rag and man, the aromas grew stronger.

"Master Corrydene's having his likeness taken, I presume?" Blackavise suggested, accepting the rainbow hand.

"Ah, would that were accurately true," responded the other, "Francis Pye, your servant, sir, likeness taker of sorts. Have I kept you waiting? I do apologise. He's all yours. The daylight's failed today. I've given up."

He rubbed anew. Blackavise thought of Lady Macbeth. Francis Pye rolled the rag up, sighing. As was often the case, chance comers who he did not have to portray struck him as having greater possibilities than his sitters. Sideways lit, Blackavise displayed a strong-boned three-quarter profile, a straight nose, meshing of face-planes from hollowed cheek to play of interested expression at the mouth. Had I this one as a subject, the artist thought, I could catch the spark in that eye, even in this light.

"Confound it," and he threw the crumpled rag at the maw of his leather bag, missed, and grovelled after it, growling. The ideas in his mind of these portraits of his were always one thing, the canvas, too frequently, another. Corrydene's was a disaster.

"Master Corrydene's in yon chamber?"

"He's inspecting the likeness," Pye said, drooping, and talking to a stranger because it delayed the return to his patron and the canvas.

"Do sitters recognise themselves?" asked John Blackavise, "After all, one does but see one's face scraping the bristles once a day, and back to front in the reflection, at that."

"That's true," cried the painter, "what I show them isn't reversed. No-one ever thinks of that." He awarded Blackavise half a mark. He wished to clutch at straws to delay his return to his easel. "Art thou urgent upon audience with Master Corrydene?" He lowered his voice. "Please do not let me keep you from him. In truth I would value a diversion, while I hide my head."

"It can't be that bad," said Blackavise tactlessly, "I ought to get that boy to announce me, but he's fled."

"Oh, I'll stand in. Your name, sir?"

"Master Corrydene should know my name:

Blackavise, of Black House, though as yet he don't know me."

"Is that the Black House beyond Aynescote?"

"'Tis. D'you know Aynescote, then?"

"I'm bidden there, after this."

"Are you really?"

"Yes. I know I was fortunate to obtain the commission; but there's no-one else these days to hold a brush, now that Dobson's died."

"I did not mean to slight you! No, I am interested, that's what." Blackavise declared.

"Spare me a word, later, then?"

"Why not."

Pye led him into the further room, to announce Blackavise's arrival.

"O Lord, there he is looking at it," the artist dropped his voice before leading Blackavise forward. "A visitor, Master Corrydene. Master Blackavise of Black House.

"Who?"

No-one says that to Colonel Cromwell, thought Blackavise, lifting his hat with a flourish, repeating his name louder, and advancing blinking like an owl after his sojourn in the mineshaft of the hall. He was confronted by a framed painting of a miserable man with grey hair, by another painting in its naked state upon its easel of a miserable man with white hair, and by the subject himself, wearing the same well-rehearsed expression. Blackavise felt the immediate urge to rustle up old Holbein, the master of likenesses, from the great heyday of King Harry's court. Corrydene's presence, and his own tact for the sake of the living artist shifting from foot to foot next to him, stopped him from voicing this thought aloud, but only just in time. But the old man was already a Holbein in himself; the crafty beetle brows, the delineation of cheekbone, beneath which some teeth had perished, and he was enfolded by a big wrap hiding his modern sleeves and collar to suggest the identity of a Tudor grandee. Writ small, thought Blackavise. He postponed the details of his visit by a feint, to approach Corrydene via the paintings, rather than make a direct enquiry into Corrydene's start in life at the font.

"My word! Your likeness, sir!" cried Blackavise in his usual manly tone.

"Ah, yes," said the patron earnestly, "I am having this taken in order to show the cruel difference these last years of strife have wrought in me. Look, how blithe and carefree I was then! Now I'm a wreck." he shuddered, "do you think Master Pye has done me justice?"

It was one of those questions where either yea or nay could be construed as an insult, but Blackavise weighed in with a confident affirmative for the painter's sake, and he hoped nobody would ever be in the position to unfurl one of the masterly drawings of Hans Holbein under his nose to dissatisfy him. Beady-eyed, the old crow nodded, as if that did away with the courtesies usually wasted on the weather, or the state of King Charles.

"And what can I do for you, sir; what did you say your name was?"

"Blackavise," he bellowed, and launched on the introduction that he had honed in the dark night of Corrydene's hallway, and nor he did falter despite indications that the name had not called forth rapture. The big wrap tossed like the moulting of spread wings, the hitherto complacent old bird flapped and hopped, as if the perch upon which he had arranged himself had been blown by a passing tempest. Blackavise was continuing, "So I took the course of a call upon thee, as a fellow godson. I conceived it my duty to let you know how she did, as it looks as if the world and she must soon part."

Corrydene had become more animated than the portraits. He was now vigorously hopping up and down, and Blackavise, interested, paused to discover why.

"Blackavise! The by-blow!" spluttered the old man, "How dare ye walk in here!"

33

"Oh," cried Blackavise, the bastard, confounded: "I merely brought word, I would have thought not untimely."

"The presumption of this," quoth Corrydene, forced to stand on tiptoe in an attempt to look Blackavise in the eye, "that I would wish to be reminded of that woman's household, with all its history – and added to that, you, sir, the by-blow, comes to plague me! Get you gone, sir, and take to heart that this is a God-fearing household, with no wish to hear again from a past connection which I for one have long considered dead and forgotten."

Blackavise, dumbfounded, stalked off through the dark cold hall, and then, with considerable relief out into the broad day. Chilly spring drizzle cooled his hot brow. He dashed a glove over his ear as if to shut out the righteous tones of his fellow Godson. As he stood on the weedy gravel unhitching Hetty, he caught a glimpse of Corrydene about to shut his own front door upon him, and there at his shoulder a little woman peeped, shawled, capped; an open-mouthed gargoyle. The lady wife, he could but guess, of his uncharitable host. He threw a leg over Hetty, and even with her warmth beneath him, the trudge down the lime walk seemed endless. Then Hetty baulked and her master collected himself with a soldier's instinct, for the painter lurked

34

behind the last slim tree, a human stalk in out-of-breath haste.

"Master Pye, you surely do not wish to take a sketch of such a bastard as you heard me, rightly, called."

"Look, I am to quit this household forthwith; I didn't wish you to think I willingly heard what Master Corrydene had to say."

"I've been called worse," said John Blackavise, reviving, "but you're civil to say so."

"He was abusive to you."

"I wonder why? Not as regards myself, but my poor godmother who deserves better. She has ever been kind to this ill-favoured godson. Damn it, I don't know what he meant by 'that woman's household with all its history'. What history? None, but being open hearted. Perhaps old Corrydene thinks she ought not to have given me her protection. What the devil does he know of being a bastard, isolated here in his fool's paradise and passing judgement? He is not, I take it, a by-blow himself." Blackavise astride his mare made a gesture of exasperation to the younger man standing by the horse's head in the drizzling spring rain.

"Don't tempt me to an opinion on his mother," agreed the portrait painter.

Blackavise, ever the soldier, remained controlled, but furious and seething.

"Corrydene's cut me to the quick. He may not have the actual bar sinister, but he deserves the descriptive term." He had even brought the rain on, too. The scudding clouds delivered an unnecessary extra baptism on Blackavise, who shook himself like a water spaniel, his flag of hair dripping and his hat-brim guiding overflows.

"Don't stand there in shirt sleeves and get a wetting for courtesy's sake. Be off, but thank you."

"I'll see you at Aynescote, no doubt," said Francis Pye, "are the roads clear? There's more talk of Parliament's hounds out after the spymaster, I wondered if 'tis safe to travel."

"They're chasing a fox. A reynard used to bolt-holes. Your brushes come from a different animal, Master Pye, they won't be after you. Your portfolio is your safeguard."

"Ah well, good; see you at Aynescote, then." Francis Pye, a watersprite in wet-sail linen shirt, turned and loped away under the lime trees, and Blackavise, the combatant, reflected on milksops who dared not travel in broad day. He was up to his teeth in godsons, he thought to himself, trotting homeward. Why not visit Aynescote, come to that? Change the run of sour faces. See the Beauty.

36

Chapter III

John Blackavise reflected that to call upon new
neighbours is a palatable chore, they ought to be
interesting, even though he might fail to like them. He
was absolved from the burden of reciprocating by the
illness at Black House, so he could not be blamed, which
would make a pleasant change. He stood twitching a
white cuff and wishing his boots were newer. His ribs
had ceased complaining and his reflection in the dusky
sky of the mirror surprised him by looking not only
authoritative but alert and bright eyed. He viewed
himself critically enough: clearly not new hatched, but,
thank the Lord, not old. His hair was thick tabby brown
mixed with silver, his shoulders broad; his torso and
legs would support a Tudor court cupboard. The active
life of soldiering had kept him muscular despite the
interval after the wounding, and if he had got up and

about too soon his strength had supported him. The two other godsons were older than he. So had his inclusion had been an affront to their families, allied to whatever they had discovered about his godmother? Why had they abandoned her? What was the mysterious history alluded to by that creature Corrydene? Most likely it meant nothing more than the failure of these people to keep up with an aged spinster, to the disadvantage of their own horrid offspring. Blackavise had spent an hour brooding by the invalid's bedside, his hands clasping her cold fingers. She knew nobody today, not even him, which hurt his tenderness for her. But he could not live in limbo, waiting. He trod down the broad stairs in search of life in the kitchen, and announced his intention to visit Aynescote.

"Ooh yes, do you go," encouraged Bessie, checking her copper pots and pans upon the iron cooking range, newly bright after hasty burnishing following Blackavise's arrival, "we all be a-dying to hear about the newcomers."

Bessie turned to concentrate on the incoming Blackavise; the bouncing copper lids announced her inattention as she focused on him. Great clouds of steam formed rivulets down the windowpanes. Ginger was hovering at her elbow while sniffing the aromas of his dinner.

"There's a proper show a-going on," Ginger butted in, "half the county's coming in at Aynescote gate. There's wagons trying to get out an 'people trying to get in, I been down to see."

"Oh is there, master big eye," said his parent cuffing at him.

"Missed me," said he, dodging.

"Get him cleaned up a bit," said Blackavise, "and next time, I'll consider taking him with me, then you can light me back up, rascal."

Hetty and he ambled down the hill, through the coppiced woodland full of the rising saps and smells of springtime; her neat half-moon hoofprints marked the violets and the celandines and bruised the anemones. The trail of crescents oozed and filled from the damp of the woodland path after the rain. It had the stillness of the Garden of Eden.

Not until the roofs and chimneys of the house of Aynescote formed a man-made mountain range above the fringe of trees, did John Blackavise scent trouble. He heard a rustle in the undergrowth and a twig snapping. Alert, he swung Hetty round. He had seen them coming in his half-glance behind. But he was caught awkwardly with his sword half-drawn, they had his knee, heaved, unhorsed him, he crashed, and as he tried to recover from the impact, they were upon him.

He punched somebody in the ribs, feeling the thrust from his fist shoot up his arm. He drew his boot back, kicked, but it did not save him, he had no answer. He was aware of Hetty plunging and crashing off. Something was going very wrong, and night swallowed him.

*

Night lasted, then pain arrived in a thunderclap upon his already tender head. Something was indeed very wrong with him: chiefly moss and ditchwater. Blackavise surfaced sufficiently to choke vigorously on muddy water, spat, and withdrew his face from the eighteen inches of running water which can drown a child, or an unconscious man. The shock of inhaling a faceful of this liquid distracted him from the pain of the blow on the head, and enabled him to sit up and feel for the old wound delivered by Parliament's men last autumn. Bemused, rubbing the familiar scar, Blackavise realised he was rubbing the other side of his skull. He wasn't back on the field of conflict. There were no cries of hurt men and horses, no acrid smell of powder, nor eddying smoke. He was all on his own, extricating himself by painful degrees from a ditch into which he had evidently been thrust headfirst, either for dead or to drown. That sat him up straighter, whilst he held the newly injured side of his head and groaned aloud. As he did so, light footfalls came down the wood, and crashings beside. Before Blackavise had time to wonder if his assailants were coming back to finish him off, the clearing of his vision enabled him to see a boy leading a dishevelled horse by a broken rein. It was Ginger and Hetty, and he was weakly overjoyed. Ginger bent over him, goggle eyed.

"O Lord," said he, his new man's voice breaking back to a squeak in the crisis.

"I'm not that bad," whispered Blackavise, "surely. Is Hetty sound?"

"O yes, barring she's cut her heel; but a scratch."

"I had better try to stand. Give me a haul."

"One, two,"

All he managed to do was pull Ginger off his feet on top of him. They untangled, and reconsidered.

"Could you mount Hetty? Half on? Let her pull you?"

"No," said Blackavise, "confound it."

"I'd best go to the big house," said Ginger, "that's what."

And he left Blackavise to the ringing noise in his head and the threat of returning private night. A struggle, amid concerned voices and some sort of united tug-of-war, got Blackavise to his feet, and thus supported, brought him most painfully down the last of the hill and to the house. Its bulk to his disordered awareness seemed to pulse and tower and cave in upon him, high from its eaves and pinnacles; it mopped and mowed and lowered, and the blessed night had got him again. Then lucidity, no nightmare, but dawn, or something; here he was, lying down in a strange anteroom, himself again, under a blanket on a daybed. Had he stormed the gates of Aynescote unawares? And then he remembered, in a rush, the alarms and blows of his approach, and the fortune of it that he was not drowned in that ditch. He tried himself for dampness, and discovered they'd had his breeches off, and he was not wearing his own shirt. What a way to arrive a-visiting. Now it was permissible to lie here and gather up. He would ask questions later. He heard music. Was he hallucinating? No: that was a wrong note. Wrong notes are reassuringly real. Here came a shadow with a cool hand and a basin. The water soothed his sore head. He thanked the owner of the hand.

"Lie still, sir."

"What time is it?"

He'd been here two hours. Then dozing made it three, perhaps. Came to, feeling better, and in the half-light sat himself up to test his head and limbs.

The girl who had tended him had not latched the door
properly. In sitting, he had turned, and through the door
which had whispered ajar, could behold the world. He
was in a little side room leading off a great oak panelled
chamber, with a gallery at the further end. A handsome
staircase ascended out of his view. He glimpsed candles
haloed in sconces against gleaming woodwork.
Frisking in and out of his view a group of young people
were dancing; someone out of sight was plucking a lute
as if the house employed a private nightingale. He saw
coloured clothes, skirts and little half-cloaks and lace
embellishments which would have made a flowerbed in
Spring dreary. When had Blackavise last beheld apricot
and carnation and cherry tints, or set eyes on decorative
maidens, lately?   To his fevered eye, the house of
Aynescote was such as a latter-day Dr Faustus might
promise Mephistopheles something foolish to obtain.
Blackavise was saved from rhapsody and the softening
of his aching brain by the attentive shadow of Ginger
slipping into the room, blocking his view and then
shutting the door upon it. He had a candlestick in one
hand and Blackavise's breeches over his arm, newly
dried out and cleaner than their owner had thought to
see them again. Somewhat restored, he glared at Ginger
for shutting out the peepshow. Ginger was looking
three sizes bigger for the glorious success he had been

having, including outdoing Blackavise by neither getting a bang on the poll nor being shut away to recover from it. His master had the opinion that Ginger would next be requiring a shilling for the privilege of his account of the new world out there, all dancing and merrymaking and behaving as if it were Christmas in good King Charles's vanished heyday. He hauled on his breeches. When he had his second foot in, the floor tilted like a ship in a light breeze, before the floorboards steadied and he looked for his boots. Ginger watched as if expecting him to crash like a felled oak. He would have hurt himself had he been wearing a pair of ill-fitting breast and back plates. But at least he was up, and it was time he thanked his host for having him tended with such consideration.

"How closely did you follow me, Ginger?" He thought, I'll wager not too close in case I saw him and sent him packing. "Did you see what happened? Who did it?"

"I weren't that handy," said the boy, "what alerted me, was ol' Hetty coming back stumbling about in the brambles, silly like. I caught hold o' her, and o'course, then, came after to see if you'd got thrown."

"I did not get thrown," cried Blackavise, incensed, "I was set upon." Shouting hurt his head. He wished he hadn't.

"O well," shrugged Ginger, "mayhap you were taken for that spymaster, sir, perhaps you bear a likeness."

The attack hadn't looked like Parliament's usual crew of efficient, ants' nest scurriers searching out some poor end-of-the-road cavalier, thought John.

"Haven't they caught him yet?" He failed to attend to Ginger's re-hash of pot-room gossip, for he was trying to remember more of his assailants than a pair of shadows, one with a raised arm and the other with a weapon. But he was facing a blank, because of the blow to the head.

"I must go and thank Master ... er?"

"Lacey, he's Master Lacey, sir."

"Right. I'm rehearsed. Now open that door."

Ginger frowned, and Blackavise reaching for his headache met a bandage, and patting it and finding a candle sconce to distort further his likeness, recoiled, and reconsidered. He could see what Ginger meant. He couldn't show himself and alarm the party, out there innocently at their pleasures.

"I'll not come out," he decided. "I'd hate to fright the Beauty. So get you to Master Lacey and request him hither. I want the loan of a couple of men of his to light me up the wood, I want Hetty brought round so I can get me gone; but first I'd be civil to my benefactor. Go on, boy. I'm well enough."

All of which saw Blackavise homeward, sore, a wary campaigner prepared for more trouble in the wood. Ginger, concerned for his master's safety, looked left and right as he led Hetty by a hand on her bridle. The torches of Lacey's men cast shadows that came and went on the trunks of trees and striped the slim arms of coppicing. At Black House, over the front door, a lantern like the moon hung on a bracket. Blackavise mumbled his thanks to Lacey's servants, after which he heard Ginger aping his master's manner in an echo. He told the boy to look to the mare and check her scratched heel. Then he staggered into the kitchen, grabbing at the door frame for support. Bessie rushed to him, frightened by his state.

"Whatever's happened to you, sir? You look all done in. Come through to the parlour, I'll poke up a fire," and then her face registered another concern: "What have you done with Ginger? Is he all right? Has he been with you all this time? What on earth have you been up to?"

"Ginger's well, he's seeing to Hetty. I was caught up in an ambush, Ginger found me afterwards. Here I am safe, if not sound. I've a bloodied bandage, that's all." He realised he could go no further; the parlour and its fire were too far to reach. Why was she pushing him in that direction? Bessie didn't want to leave him in the kitchen, but he was insistent. He wanted warmth and peace and quiet and the kitchen fire with a pot hissing on its hook above the glow. Bessie was still trying to tell him no, with the three round 'o's of her mouth and eyes, and a wagging finger.

"Let me be," sighed John Blackavise, and he flung himself down in Bessie's chair, let his strength gather, feeling the blessed warmth, and drowsiness come flooding over him. In a half-doze he let the candle burn away until it drowned the wick in a puddle of wax. He didn't want empty cold sheets upstairs. He didn't want to think about people he didn't know who wanted to kill him. He might be dead in a ditch. It was enough for the moment that his head ached diminishingly, that his strong arms were still his own, and after a very near squeak, he was extremely glad to be back in his own hole. The dreamy vision of the young people enjoying themselves at Aynescote swam before him: maidens with slim stem waists, young men carefree and at ease. Every glimpse proclaimed an oasis in Blackavise's desert. The innocent vision of Aynescote made his heart ache, the place was a nest of butterflies. His own house, wherein he had left his only living kin, Simon and his daughter-in-law, seemed as grey as yesterday's mutton, as straight-laced as poor Susan in that fearsome cap.

Army life, with its brawlers and drunkards, and, increasingly no-hopers, had been nothing but a temporary hell-hole. And here, in what had been his golden childhood castle, his godmother, the one person in life he really loved, lay dying. He glimpsed Aynescote like King Tantalus. Wryly, he blamed the headache. Had his eyes closed again? The fire had subsided, the pot hissed no more, and the candle had long died. But Blackavise started, sat sharply forward in his chair.

Was he mad, from the blow on his brains? The fire darkened, a shadow intruded. His neck hair was prickling. Thank God I'm not prey to sprites. Perhaps I'm dazed yet from that blow. But I do see this – Johnny, you're not deranged. That flagstone is rising. How is it possible for this rectangle to rear up in front of my very eyes between me and the embers? He heard the scrape of the stone upon its fellows, accompanied by laboured breathing, and he waited. Grabbing the poker, he saw an Atlas unequal to the struggle, and when the flagstone slipped, it had pinioned a neat little man with a hat on. The hat had softened the impact of the heavy flagstone. Blackavise, finding the ring on the upward surface, was able to give the single pull needed, and then to secure the captive whilst the breath was still knocked out of his body.

"I suppose thou art a godson, too," quoth Blackavise, motioning with his poker.

"What are you rambling about?" panted the creature, looking up at Blackavise with intelligent, rodent eyes.

"I would hear what business you have beneath my floor," but in a flash he knew. "I'm a King's man, so you'd better tell me; the spymaster, of whom we hear so much – art thou not he?"

"Then I shall discover if you are a true King's man, or no, I see."

"We need not discuss that," said Blackavise tersely, and his angered dragon's eye impressed his prisoner, who nodded.

"That's a relief," said he, "I'll try not to trouble you long. I have, unfortunately, a cruelly sprained ankle."

Blackavise reached for his headache again, and sat down. It was a nightmare. Here he was, crawled home after footpads or worse had left him for dead, and he was fronted by the fugitive that half a regiment was out chasing, who had the nerve to announce that he was not staying long. It was worse than discovering one's mother-in-law surrounded by her packing cases unannounced in the hall. Neither did this wanted man, this spymaster, in any way resemble him, which did away with the comforting theory that the roughs who'd attacked him had mistaken him for this very fellow. He was small, neat and bandy. Two of him might make up one Blackavise. When he had needed information he had made use of spies, was alive now, possibly, due to good old forewarned is forearmed.

"You're safe here," he said, "that I tell you. I've used many a tuppenny spy in my time. How close are you pursued?"

"The scent ran cold by Underhill. I felt hounds a mite too close for a while. They're beating the bushes up and down. I have a man or two yet planted. I am anxious not to be taken, in case they make me talk."

Blackavise nodded, taking the point. There was a limit when pain made the dumb speak, and it was a point best not taken for granted. What armaments a man carries within himself, only extremity will disclose.

The kitchen door heaved and Bessie's and Ginger's heads protruded like two tortoises out of the one shell.

"Come in," ordered Blackavise, "I can see from here that one of you knew and one of you didn't. Bessie, did you let this man in?"

"Yes, sir, whilst you and Ginger were gone." She looked woebegone and guilty. "I thought he could slip down to the cellar and be away in the morning, an' nobody'd know. I'd feed him later, when you'd gone to bed. Didn't think you'd stay here in the kitchen, sir; you don't usually. I didn't know you'd get hurt."

"I, er, fear it might take a day or two," put in the refugee, "My ankle won't carry me. I've contacts to make, I've a man to get to the coast, I would best succeed if I keep my head down whilst the scent goes stale and the hounds go back to kennels."

"I've a sick lady upstairs," Blackavise pointed out.

"I'll stay in the cellar."

Right: he was for the barrels and the rats for a day or two. No-one must know he's there. The girls who came in to help Bessie, Plain Jane and Sarah, went home of an evening. And if it were himself in need of a safe place to hide?

"Then in secrecy," he conceded, "feed him, Bessie. Then to ground."

Thus John Blackavise, his mind whirring, took a counter-irritant to his cold bed, to solve the question of who had attacked him. As sleep came to his rescue, he realised that he now knew how it felt to be a papist and keep a priest up the chimney.

Chapter IV

The siren song of the different world at Aynescote surfaced. Blackavise's sore head mended, and he told himself his ill-wishers had chosen a thick skull to thump and failed to drown him. This was positive. His godmother, inert, had sunk no further. The spymaster under the floorboards quickened John's pulse and kept his Royalist sympathies throbbing.

"Thought I'd look in," said Flynn Gerard, and there he was, again, a limpet by the parlour fire, complaining that the Three Tuns had been crawling with common soldiers all morning: "Thought it might prove quieter here."

"I hope it does so," said Blackavise fervently.

He fumed till Gerard left, impatient to get on with his little plan regarding Aynescote. He couldn't put it in motion until Gerard got him gone. He would wander back down to Aynescote to thank Master Lacey for his kindness, and he'd already smartened himself up, with his hair brushed sideways to hide the bruise. He didn't intend to have prickly Gerard attach himself to his coat tails and follow him to sneak an introduction. He'd keep Aynescote for himself. Like a child saying a new toy is not for sharing. He made Ginger put on an out-of-date coat from a closet. Two more inches, and it might fit him, thought Blackavise. Give him a fortnight and his knuckles will emerge from the cuff.

"That's better, boy. Now pull your stockings up." He was on the verge of asking the child, "Will I do?" He shook his head at his own foolishness. If he wasn't careful he'd soon be joining Ginger who was already delving into this closet full of old masque costumes and moth-eaten fancy hats. Ginger, cavorting, had now got himself into a mask with ribbon knots on either side. Hopping up and down half-blinded, he knocked down a box from which a cornucopia of party favours spewed forth.

"Calm down, boy," John sneezed as the dust rose, "take that thing off. You're uglier without it."

Ginger saw him grinning, amazed to see him human. These masquerade costumes had been put carefully away. He'd poke about and have a thorough rummage once he had time. Oh, the vanished show of feather plumes, the headdresses of crescent moons like this one now shedding its tarnished silver flakes on the floor! He tried to conjure up the substantial figure of his godmother prancing about in it when she was almost as new as the tinsel now beneath his feet. She had to have been slimmer in those distant days, when torchlight had sparkled on the Diana with her toy bow and arrows, or on Juno in her chariot drawn by fowls. Well, that was for another day. He'd play with the memories later. There was a great silvery scallop shell, the sort which one might have in the garden with a fountain playing into it, were it made of marble. This one was of carved wood, a lovely thing.

"Come, Ginger, playtime's done with."

Aynescote sang to him as the sirens had sung for Odysseus. Ginger would have to serve as his master's talisman against ruffians in the woods. Blackavise refused to be deterred by a single assault, although he knew he must sharpen his wits to keep himself alive and kicking. Had the assailants been deserters? There were herds of them about these days, wanting what they could filch from a man's belt. But the chinking silver coins still in his pocket reminded him that he had not been robbed.

Aynescote's newly laid gravel awaited him. Handing Hetty to Ginger and shaking himself down

54

after dismounting, John saw three workmen in the entry porch. They were fiddling with leaded lights which held little glass lozenges. A ray of sunshine claimed his attention when it transformed the dull lights into shafts of amber and gold. At the crunch of horseshoes the men had looked up and were clearing the way for him, hastily shoving tools into a large leather bag. There was knuckling of foreheads to the gentleman. They were on the point of leaving. He marvelled at the pretty little glass pictures. In these troubled times, who had the time and imagination to flaunt a set of sporting pictures to beguile visitors such as he? In soft ochres and golds and browns, men took aim at wildfowl, spanielly dogs pulled ducks from bushes; men in hats sat fishing at a golden river's brim. The door opened, even as he was bending to admire the detail, but it was not that his arrival been noticed, merely that the new owner of the house had emerged to assess the progress of his hirelings.

"Flemish work," he said, recognising Blackavise and waving the men off for the day, "a fancy I had. How do you, now? I'm relieved to see you back upon your feet."

Lacey was a man of perhaps thirty summers, dressed in over-embellished silks. Sleeves and pantaloons, the latest of modes, swelled in full sail. His sleek moustache above a frilly smile was worthy of King Charles; no doubt a loyal act, thought Blackavise. But he was grateful for Lacey's interest in a new neighbour's welfare.

"I'm come over to thank you," replied Blackavise, "My previous attempt to bid you and your household welcome, as a neighbour should, was hardly a credit to me – to be carried in like a battering ram, feet first, and laid out for dead, seems impolite, to say the least."

"Put it this way," said Lacey, "we lack the diversions, in these Puritan days. You provided us with the best of plays, for you now show us that the chief character can be nine-parts slain, and yet reappear, as you do this day, to take a bow at the groundlings."

"I'd have made a better shot at it, with rehearsal," said John ruefully, half ashamed for letting himself be armed in, made welcome and hearing himself say, yes, he would be pleased to dine; even though he had been hoping for it. Why would it be wrong to accept all this merely because he wanted it? He wouldn't carry scruples that far. He mentally threw off the hair shirt comprising his assailants in the woods, Flynn Gerard, miserable old Corrydene, and of having a spymaster in his cellar. Here was another world, and he would enjoy a festival away from all the pinpricks and sorrows, so he would, away from the everlasting long faces of Royalist misfortune. For once, Blackavise was about to overlook a non-combatant. It seemed this man Lacey had drawn aside from involvement, and had not risked life or limb. Well, if he, Blackavise, had risked his, where had it got him? For an afternoon he'd pretend he agreed with his host, or at least keep his views to himself.

"I chose to live out of the way," Lacey was over-explaining, "I could not find a desert isle that had comforts, so I have retreated here. The wider world has less to offer me. I do not care to have my style of life altered; I care for my cook, a rag to my back, and music and so forth. Do you agree that suchlike things don't line the road to hell? So I have watched the way the wind is blowing, and am removed hither, the better to continue. My last house was too close to a nest of bigots, I don't care for hostility; certainly not from that crew. They got too much pleasure from it."

Lacey was bestowing the smile upon him again. It was the first time in weeks John had met someone who was neither cross nor upset. He found he was smiling firmly back at the man wearing silver bobbin lace on the rag to his back. Lacey showed him with obvious pride into a huge room lined with linenfold panelling. A shine highlighted each wooden upright down the perspective. Optimistic early spring sun slanted through the mullioned windows. In front of a mighty fireplace a stylish handful of young people stopped milling about to stare at the newcomer as he strode in with their host. There was a clear contrast between the military man in his buff coat and Aeneas Lacey in silks. Blackavise realised that these were the same souls who had seen him carried in, at Lacey's music party. That man now spoke.

"Allow me to introduce my wife to you. My dear, this is our neighbour, Master Blackavise. You recall, he was unfortunate in meeting trouble on his way here the other night."

His wife wafted near and joined the circle gathering around the newcomer. Blackavise felt expectation beginning to reward him, would have progressed his formal bow, but for two earnest young men of military age who put themselves forward wanting assurance they would be safe in broad day on their pending return journey. He passed this off as shortly as politeness and his natural ire at their attitude permitted, but they had baulked him of the chance to follow his bow with a pleasantry to the lady. He looked around at the gathering, all the while hell-bent on catching the Beauty's eye. He found the other ladies wanting, even though they appeared as a group of fallow deer, full of early grace, suppleness, and active eyelashes. They were the herd. But when the Beauty had trailed a turquoise glance at him at their formal bow and curtsy, it had given him a jolt. Had she been properly animated, that glance would have struck him by lightning. As it was, she had made an impression, and he was happy to welcome such a new picture to his mind's-eye. He found himself wanting to know what lay beneath her surface. He had registered that she had the smallest waist in the room, that her melon sleeves were the fullest and her skirts a cloud of sea blue. But now she'd moved on, so Blackavise swam on round the roomful of people like a goldfish in a warm new pond, essaying music with the lutenist he had heard offstage the night when he lay hurt, discussed shooting with two wild-fowlers, and, when stuck for a topic, he fell back on the amazing refurbishment of the house, and when asked, he passed off the fading bruise on his temple as a trifle.

"Some houses are glum old things," Blackavise heard himself declare, "like maiden aunts, they won't cheer up. I admire this place, indeed I do. Do you realise Master Lacey rescued the house from years of decay? It had been boarded up for far too long, you know."

"Aeneas would feel slighted if we weren't green with envy," said a set of fair ringlets and a dimple, "that's why he invited us so promptly. Now we've seen it all, he's tired of us."

The saying was that after three days, fish and guests are past their best. Well, I've used up but half an hour, said John to himself.

"I admire the little glass pictures in the porch as one comes in," he told his audience, continuing his good-mannered impromptu.

"Oh, Aeneas always has the latest trick!" the ringlets replied, "he has been known to fling people into the street who have failed to appreciate his latest enthusiasm. He hath had the little glass pictures put where no-one can miss them."

"I believe I fell over the men adding the finishing touches. Never saw such quality. Sporting pictures are my taste."

The Beauty, about to float by again upon those billowing skirts, trawled him into the net of her sea-blue eye, and backed up her sails to anchor at Blackavise's elbow. Caught by his marine simile, he instantly wished his stiff boot leather hadn't prevented the waves of her hem lapping his human, sensitive ankle, with breaking waves of petticoat beneath. Heavens! But the tide ebbed as she paused, the skirts subsided and she veiled the coloured eyes, at which he bowed sternly. No mountebank, he.

"I apologise for missing the glass pictures the first time I arrived."

"Seeing as you had the misfortune to be carried in past them, we will excuse you."

"I regret the discourteous arrival. I suppose I came in like a hunting trophy, in which guise I might have made a subject for another pane in your husband's porch window."

"Wish you to be featured by my husband in his next glass picture? Which part did you think of playing?"

He smiled at the sharpness of her question.

"I require no painted window. But God alone knows I came close to providing the kill in this adventure, had I not been slow a-drowning." He made a deprecatory gesture. "Playing the kill at the hunt wouldn't suit me, not even for the best window picture."

She murmured while lowering her eyes, "Who wants to see horrid everyday men out hunting? Although I know that fighting men such as you prefer prosaical subjects."

Indeed yes, but he wasn't going to say so. She was calm and self-assured. What could he do to provoke a wave of interest on her tranquil ocean?

"Had I been asked to set Master Lacey's fancy windows, perhaps I would have chosen Diana the lady huntress, with her crescent moon."

Such antique treasures as he had at home in Black House, so recently discovered in his attic. Half a mark,

John: that got me a second glance. She's lovely, she's deep; could I but stir her depths. She had liked the idea of Diana and the moon.

For all he'd dragged the idea out of an abandoned closet, where the old headdress showered its silver rain, it had worked, for it had caught her interest. But hang on, Johnny, she belongs to someone else. The colours in her complexion of apricot and rose on peach, were part of the daily bounty which had come to Lacey with her wedding band. John experienced a passing pang at the thought of free spirits, unrestricted by the need of gold rings. He had never forgotten the fascination of looking into a map-maker's window, where the hints and tints of exotic islands were surrounded by images of fantastic sea creatures from a world of dreams, in a life free of constraints. But this was her island and he voyaged offshore. No matter the sudden rush of attraction, he must not startle her. Returning mentally to the shores of reality, he decided on a different metaphor. She might be chestnut filly in her spring coat. He never saw a mane like hers with the curly tresses on her forehead, so neatly tied up behind. She broke into his inner fumblings.

"Don't trust that moon you mentioned, she's inconstant," she ventured.

"I should rather you'd said, don't trust Diana, had I

been Acteon."

The pearls round her neck glimmered, she turned to Blackavise.

"For no more than looking at the Huntress, she turned her hounds loose upon that man and they hunted him to death. Merely for watching her bathing." What a punishment, for no more than looking.

Mary Florida studied the man before her. He didn't look a poetical figure, unlike the lutenist, or outdoor bores like the wild-fowlers. But he was infinitely preferable to the maunderers and numbskulls of her recent guests. Her eyes told him that she found him an unusual soldier, for all that his weaponry of sword and pistols were resting in the entry room and she encountered him unarmed.

Charmed by her glance, he thought there's more to me than ever you might think, lady. I'm full of surprises. Did you but know what I keep in my cellar, with spymasters and bats and what-not? By the time I get home there'll also be three mad magicians and a man who's King Charles's double, just to confuse me.

How delightful now that Madam Lacey set aside a little formality by accepting he lead her by the hand. Sensing her living arm against his cuff, he held her passive, tapering fingers, upon one of which shone her wedding ring. Her various textures appealed to him. I enjoy pearls and silk and peach tinted shoulders, he thought fervently.

"Alas, poor Acteon," she murmured, "such an unexpected fate."

"Ah! Naught's unexpected," he remonstrated, "look at soldiers such as I. Remember every one of us began as a private gentleman with our sundry ways and pastimes. All most of us want, is to resume those paths. Your husband is as we, he differs only in that he hath not seen fit to give up his personal enthusiasms." Blackavise, you've let that out too forthrightly. The man's just bidden you welcome. You have been drinking his sack, now you are chatting with his wife, and you are about to eat his dinner. So there it is; I am not sufficiently emollient. It probably comes from spending too much time with fighting men. Here comes that very husband, Aeneas Lacey, easy, smiling, marshalling his score of guests to come and dine. Had he overheard? Should he smooth his plumage? Mary Florida had withdrawn her hand, turned to face the chimney breast. Was that disdain? It was the back of her neck, certain. Blackavise was faced with her husband's welcoming manner.

"Did you say what I think you said? That I'm giving nothing up? Let's show you a Lenten dinner, then, and prove my austerity."

Ah, a charmer, an easy tongue, and he took no offence. Blackavise's idea of a Lenten dinner was a salt fish rejected by the cat. Happily the presence of his invalid godmother in Black House had given Bessie the excuse to waive the Lenten strictures, and when the invalid sucked her beef broth, attendant parts of the beast had been nourishing Blackavise. He wasn't going to admit as much, however. Here they were advancing into a dining chamber lit by a run of more mullioned windows, already dull as a lowering day began to spit arrowheads of sharp spring rain at the glass. He stood back against the panelling waiting to be signalled forward to take a seat at the long trestle, displaying the usual platters and cutlery. It was as if everyone else had set to partners and he was the miserable wallflower left over. Opposite him was propped one of those painted cut-outs of a lady, keeping the old custom of issuing a substitute should a guest arrive without a partner. The glossy painted face smirked at him. This was dismal. He was alert to the need to make a good impression. Instead he had been over blunt, ever his failing. Had he offended his host and hostess? He could not keep hiding behind the excuse of being a soldier. Neither did he forget the generosity shown him when this household took him in after his disaster.

A hunger pang brought his attention to the table,

laden with fresh fish, a salted salmon, oysters on sippets strewn with whiskers of orange peel. Further along, a pastry latticework showed church windows of candied cherries, and there were the usual preserved fruits in pyramids, and nuts prettied up with little green leaves set between them. These did not quite distract Blackavise from the empty eyes of the painted face on her board opposite him. Therefore he looked left and right. But because of a subterranean forest of table-legs by his knees, he was not well placed to turn and converse with either the bonny maiden to one side, in ribbons and twiddling curls, or a fading matron whose nimbus of front hair extinguished any chance of catching her eye. Two serving men saved Blackavise from these difficulties. They came each side of the cut-out lady and grasped it as though they were heraldic supporters. Up came the wooden guest, and revealed Mary Florida behind it. She slipped into the vacant position, cool as cowcumber, skirts subsiding as if she were once more a cloud. Forthright Blackavise smiled. He took her arrival as good news, indeed, a gift.

"How do you have these heaps of sticky plums and orangadoes all bright as day, when you are but moved in five minutes since?" he essayed, "I thought all such were unobtainable till summer's done and the cooks stir themselves."

"This poor old house was empty bar the work of spiders. Aeneas had to bring every one of our hundred casks and jars with us, and set the maids a-packing until my husband judged it safe to risk the roads. But if your taste really runs to wrinkly plums or a dead walnut or two, I will have them sought out. We could feed an army."

"Please don't feed either army, because ours is fled, and Parliament's is far hence, I do trust."

"So I hope, too. My husband is anxious about those Parliamentary soldiers who chase the spymaster, 'tis the talk. They are not hence at all."

"That talk's a week old, mistress. Pay no attention, there's always tuppenny gossip. Soldiers like me must keep an ear to the ground. I heard but yesterday that particular fox had run back towards Overhill and the scent's gone cold." He felt his neck hairs prickle as any man's will, who harbours that very spymaster in his cellar and is telling lies to sooth an anxious household and put an end to the topic. He wished Mary Florida's neck hairs to lie undisturbed.

"Aeneas hath reacted too strongly. He hath the ambition, he will tell you, to be the man attending the play, not the player. Not even the player King. I do truly say that we have not seen one blow struck, nor sighted one trooper, in our bid to avoid the blood of conflict. Aeneas hath removed house to thereby avoid living by the high road of life."

Blackavise considered this way of thinking. He was in the act of shaking his head and she noticed, so he gave her his straight gaze and straight view, for better or worse.

"One of my failings," he asserted, "is going up to an event and trying to shake it by the collar. I've often regretted it and I've forsworn it, but I still do it. I bear the scars to prove it."

He shrugged and pulled a face. He couldn't grasp Lacey, but was prepared to make an effort to think him through, and tried again. "Perhaps he hath created an oasis for us all," he suggested, "we come up parched and panting, and he gives us a fresh camel, and dates from his tree."

She laughed, safe and charming in her husband's oasis, and her laughter made her dragonfly eyes sparkle. People rose from the table to help themselves to the jolly candied orangadoes, and Aeneas Lacey came up and took Blackavise aside to ask how the aunt did?

"Godmother," Blackavise explained, "poor soul. St Peter will let her in without more inquiry than announcing that she was expected. But when that will be, he knows and I do not. I hate this waiting. I hate knowing that she hath the half-world come upon her;

she ever made my world good for me."

"St Peter nearly welcomed the two of you," said Lacey, "what was behind that business which got you hurt in the wood?"

Blackavise lowered his gaze to the thumbscrew nutcracker he was manipulating, and tried to answer.

"I'm still in the dark, I'm still wrestling with it," he shrugged, tossing nutshells in a cannonade at the fireback, "I've cheated no-one at dice, pulled no-one's nose, hardly set foot out of doors since I got me hither."

"Army business? Or should I say, does enmity in arms lead to private troubles? I wouldn't presume to press you, but I have this full household and therefore I do ask; with apologies."

Blackavise glared at him feeling like a Barbary pirate invading a nursery, but the glare faded as he mastered himself and he laughed.

"Nay, what cause have you to apologise? I'd not bring trouble hither. I have seen fine feeling between men with no regard to allegiance, believe me. As far as I know I brought no trouble with me. I was set upon by faceless men, and must now look the twice over my shoulder. What puzzles me is whether I call it the work of a cutpurse, or a deserter now leagues from your door?"

I wish I knew the truth behind it, he thought, so I shall

pass it off to Lacey, whilst I continue to debate in the small hours as to its meaning.

"My wife was fearful as to how you were doing … She saw you muddied and bloodied that night."

She saw me, like that? He recoiled at the thought of being carried past her in his darkness: he'd no idea she'd seen anything so concerning.

"What a way to make an impression on a first visit," he said ruefully, "and I'd come to bid you and your family welcome. Yet as matters turned out it was you who looked to me. I can't even reciprocate your hospitality at the moment."

But he couldn't have made altogether a bad impression, for when he slipped out to go home, careful not to outstay, and had bowed and hatted Mary Florida, his host shadowed him to the door where the glass pictures had the blinds of night behind them, turning them invisible, and there Lacey chatted with him until Ginger brought up his master's mare. The evening air was fresh and clear after the rain, with a star or two above in jewellery upon the blue.

"Piers and Jesse will light you up the way," said Lacey, "I believe a pair of torches will keep off any species of gnat or wasp."

"There's really no need."

"Look down again, won't you? Not tomorrow, when

the cousins pack, nor Wednesday, when they will get them gone with ado and uproar. On Thursday? I've a taker of likenesses arriving, if that might be a small interest."

"Francis Pye!"

"D'you know him? I've been rash enough to have taken him up upon a chance mention. How did you know it was he?"

"O, I met him just lately, he mentioned his destination."

God send Lacey would not ask if his work had merit. Blackavise allowed himself to smile in the dark. This promised to provide him with a much needed diversion.

"I'd be pleased to look in. And let me say, how much I have enjoyed your hospitality this evening; this time I was awake to relish it."

Two serving men armed with torches came trotting on foot round the corner of the house, the tarry-scented rags casting sudden zebra shadows. In their company Blackavise, his boy and the mare were sent home in style, and the wood was illuminated round them as if they travelled in a lantern.

"Goodnight and thank you," called Blackavise at the gate with its strangulation ivy outside Black House. The outward show of affable farewell was undercut with the awareness of the wanted man beneath his kitchen flagstones, and his attention was on that, with a heady topping of the colours and courtesies shown him at Aynescote, so he did not give more than half an ear to Ginger's prattle. Ginger had been constrained by the presence of Aynescote servants all the way, and was fairly bottled up.

"S'funny thing, when I led ol' Hetty round the back, they've grand stables, sir, with harness horses in, and a couple of fairish riding horses, one's a big grey, that's the first yard, see, an' I had to hitch Hetty, didn't know where, was having a look, an' there's this second yard behind. Their man came out an' took Hetty, an' he said to me, 'You get in the kitchen, they'll give you a sup of ale: don't you go poking about the back here, there's no horses in that yard'."

"So?" said Blackavise, dropping from Hetty with a crash of his boots, "you can take her in, now."

"Yes, sir, but there were horses in that yard, I'd put me ear to the gate before he came, an' I heard someone bang his hoof."

I wish that was all I had to worry myself over, thought Blackavise, preparing to visit his flagstone.

*

Mary Florida, in the privacy of her solitary bedchamber,

had done with being on show for the day. She had her bodice off, and stepped from the wide blue pond of the skirt she had let drop onto the beeswaxed floorboards. Untying her hair and tossing the resultant fall was a gesture. If Aeneas downstairs at cardplay sent back for her, Dorcas would report that Mistress hath taken her back hair down, Sir, and that would be that. Dorcas was now bearing away the sea-blue bodice and skirt, dead and deflated over her arm, leaving Mary Florida in her petticoat feeling undressed and unprotected. Large in her mind's-eye she saw John Blackavise and he refused obstinately to waft away. There he stood, in his considerable masculine strength and determination, an imported oak amidst saplings. There he was, with arrow-shot glance, falcon's head of hair with the untidy spray where the blow had raised a bruise, unselfconscious, positive, and she ached because she wanted him. It was a strange way to discover that the blind boy's arrow had transfixed her.

No outcry was available to her, cousins had ears, Dorcas had ears, Aeneas below at the card table had ears, so she burned silently in a powder keg of denial. She felt a slow-match inching up an endless fuse. Blackavise had popped the illusion of her contentedness. Dorcas had left a heap of cambrics neatly centred on a side table. Although there was silence, the room burst into life as Mary Florida gave vent to her feelings. Lace collars flapped like great moths about the bedchamber, and came to rest, wings crumpled or spread, upon her dressing-table, or extinguished the cheerful gleam of silver pots, snuffed the nosegay of violets, rose to the mirror-frame, drunkenly; fell to the floor, dead. Constrained by the need for silence, burning within, Mary Florida wrote 'I am trapped' in calligraphy of fire across the darkness of her inner eye.

Chapter V

Waiting for Thursday, keen to repeat the welcome he had received at Aynescot, Blackavise funnelled his thoughts as if on the full twelve days of Christmas, a swirl of imagined company and pleasantries. He was sternly denying his fool's urge to dance with Mary Florida under the candlelight. As an afterthought, he looked forward to furthering the acquaintance of his host Aeneas Lacey, who had generously admitted him, prone and hurt, on his arrival. For the next two days he wished it Thursday, mainly because Flynn Gerard appeared betimes, complaining before he'd so much as doffed his hat.

"I found you forth yesterday," he said accusingly, "why was I not informed? I wasted the whole afternoon in coming up."

It is a good thing you do not keep a dog, thought

Blackavise, the poor creature would spend his time having his fur rubbed up the wrong way.

"Sit with our godmother, did you?" he asked, to annoy him.

"Hmph," said Flynn, "certainly not, as you ought to know, she is in no state to receive visitors."

So he continued to sit in the parlour, as yet unsupported by the restorative he was hoping Blackavise would pour out.

Every morning John spent time with his godmother, holding her hand, disturbed by watching her slide into the hereafter. So long as her fingers clasped and weakened upon his grasp, he sat firmly. So long as she derived comfort he'd offer it. When she dozed, he tiptoed away, but not before. And while he sat at her bedside his mind drifted to picture the brighter bauble of Aynescote, to the long dining table, the rattle of talk, the informal beards-wag company. Someone had supplied a naughty little cousin with candied violets with which he pelted his three affronted sisters and caused his mother to lead him by the ear to bed. The innocent parties, smug as lambkins, had won ten minutes' shuttlecock and squeaking, while their betters dodged the resultant rockets. And this had made him laugh. He hadn't wanted eyes-down card play, but to participate and feel alive-o, enjoying telling a circle of big eyes the story of how he unhorsed a heavily plated member of Haselrigg's regiment 'the Lobsters'.

"After the crash," he related, "he could but sit there, purple, cursing, and able neither to rise nor to run away. Friend, I said, the good Lord hath armed thee, now let him raise thee from the dead."

The memory set him laughing, and they laughed with him, and one way and another it had been an easy victory.

In the past two days the spymaster's ankle had recovered only slowly. Bessie wrung out the third cold poultice of the Wednesday and they had put him back in his hole with the instruction to put the tight, puffy football up on one of the smaller casks, upon a cushion. There was no hurrying the process, unfortunately. Blackavise, a realist, made sure the hatch was well battened down while Gerard favoured Black House, and continued to watch the hands of the clock inch towards Thursday. He discovered Ginger to be doing the same, and in due time found himself and the boy unnaturally smartened up ready to go visiting. Blackavise's anticipation of gracing the house of Aynescote featured Mary Florida, a talking point as the Beauty and the general pleasure she was. He played with her image all the way down the hill; he was working out how Francis Pye would choose to paint her, but received a setback when he arrived and began on these speculations to his host.

"Nay," Aeneas interrupted, shaking his head and his lace collar in surprise, "'tis I who is having my likeness taken."

He was dismissive, while Blackavise felt foolish for having made the wrong assumption, an error that snagged a thread in his mental tapestry that she, the Beauty, should be captured for posterity. Why not? He was overwhelmed with sympathy towards the neglected Mary Florida. Where was she? Blackavise decided to test Aeneas's knowledge of pictures, if he had any.

"You must be a connoisseur. There's no doubting you have an eye for a picture."

Lacey used his most confidential tone in reply.

"I was always going to be a collector, of course. Now my uncle's inheritance has given me the chance, I can't wait to see myself hanging in a frame over my fireplace."

What a starting point, thought Blackavise. And he is to begin upon himself. Well, there it is! A child in a toyshop. I know he's young; he'll have to be careful he doesn't get soft. He is soft. I am older than he, with seasons of campaigning behind me. Too many pretend the war gave us a meaning for living. What nonsense. Nothing but hardship makes us the men we are.

Blackavise sighed. It would be delightful to announce that he, too, was about to start collecting. One advantage he'd have over Lacey, is that he would never employ Francis Pye. Perhaps he, Blackavise, had an eye for a portrait; but alas, he had no money.

"I delight in paintings," said he, "the toys of a grown man."

"More than that, surely," Lacey missed the irony: he led his guest through a half-formed library, with bookcases ready ranged but empty, save for a lonely shelf-and-a-half of odd sizes of binding. A room as yet some way, thought Blackavise, from the atmospheric cell in which men read and ponder for slow-ticking hours. One has to start somewhere, though. "I absolutely yearn after paintings," Lacey continued, smiling at everything a-brewing in his fancy, and added as an afterthought, "and books; a pity I must send miles to the binder, but as I won't live in town, what else is there for it? And, what say you to this?" He had reached a window and gestured outwards at a flagstoned terrace girt with balustrading, at the glimpse of Mary Florida sauntering at its further end and at a vista of untamed parkland. Unsure which delight Lacey meant him to admire, Blackavise waited.

"There!" gestured Lacey with a hand emerging from his big cuff. He had not chosen the compass point with his wife in it; the paving and the balustrade were beneath the elevation of his rhetorical movements, so Blackavise looked out at the view.

"Ah yes," said he, generally.

"Once I have come to grips with clearing the tangle, I shall have a perfect site for a banqueting house. I have it in mind to erect a beautiful little building to rise just there, on that swell of ground. So I can lead my guests there to the marchpane and the suckets. Don't you think a fountain should play somewhere? We could lay pipes."

Blackavise thought he saw Lacey swell larger before him.

"It all sounds full of promise," avowed Blackavise, wondering how long the Lacey fortune would last, and whether pipes would run uphill. At least Lacey was not facing sequestration, as were so many of King Charles's defeated supporters. He'd have to pay up himself, and was not looking forward to scraping it up. Lacey's man Jesse came clumping up and coughed for attention.

"Excuse me, sir; a gentleman's downstairs."

"Oh, is he come? Excuse me," said the master of the house, and with the eagerness of shifting his attention he left Blackavise marooned. It did not seem the moment to start a solitary perusal of the volumes on that shelf, so he opened the door to the outer day to join

Mary Florida. How would he describe the elusive shade
of green she was wearing? There were more shades of
green than of any other colour, a nicety Francis Pye
could confirm. Could he assume it was Pye who'd
arrived? Probably. What green, exactly, was she
favouring?

"Good-morrow, lady."

She turned and acknowledged him, so as she curtsied
and he scraped the flagstones with his hat, their eyes met
somewhere on the halfway mark. Her sleeves today
seemed to be composed of stiffened, broad ribbon, tied
at intervals by rosettes. There was a matching floret at
her waist. The effect of melon sleeves and full skirts
reminded Blackavise of an opulent fruit, which he might
peel and eat. Eat? What was he thinking? She turned
her glance to one side, as though she might have been
sleepwalking. Yet he watched the swell of her bosom
rise and fall. She breathes, therefore she lives, he told
himself. Now, Johnny, dazzle her and wake her up.

"Frog colour," he said firmly, "becomes you."

This did the trick; she liked the unusual compliment.
She had never, it seemed, been told she wore the green
of a frog before. He'd caught her attention. He smiled
at the turquoise eyes.

"I hear such plans," he said, "are you out taking the
air, or do you have a mind to influence Lacey's ideas for

81

his banqueting house?"

"That is for Aeneas to decide," she said, "he loves diversions above all things."

"Must prove exhausting, after a spell."

"His grandfather was given to mounting extravagances. He was one of the last gentlemen in England to keep a household jester."

"How dreadful! The cap and bells leaping out at any moment to force a lame joke on one."

"The same one, moreover. When he became an old man, his memory limited his repertoire. My husband's grandmother referred to his jokes as no laughing matter: I felt for her, whenever she had a headache."

Mary Florida watched his straight face for a reaction until he posed an awkward question.

"Are you saying Master Lacey hath inherited his grandfather's wish to avoid tedium? 'Tis clear he hath joy in pursuit of his diversions." Had she nodded, or had the breeze blown the mane of her chestnut ruffles? Why was she facing away from him at the grey balustrade? Its texture was as rough as old cheese-rind against the smoothness of her skirts. He had no wish for her to turn away from him. All he could see of her was the nape of her neck and seven excellent pearls above the lace collar so fine that the frog colour showed through, diluted: tint of frog. He thought she was wrapped in calm in front of him, unconcerned by the gone-to-seed park. Urgency did not grip her to have the bushes cut down, or to slash at the nettles, let alone do battle to master the wilderness. She detached herself as if she were the sphinx. But he'd forgotten at least one possibility. Her husband hadn't chosen her to sit for the painter. He could hardly blame her if she felt affronted. He sternly set about denying that fool's urge that pounced upon him to dance with her under the candlelight the next time there was music of an evening. He comforted himself with the hope that she would cheer up once the inept Francis Pye took a brush to the easel. Revenge on her husband was coming.

"There you stand, like a mariner looking out to sea," he told the pearls and the back hair, "holding on to what do they call it? The taffrail."

"This is a ship that would sink, then," said Mary Florida turning round and looking up at him suddenly, giving the lie to her sleepiness. Placing her elbows on the rail of the balustrade, she leant back; the gems of her eyes brightened.

"A stone ship, a plummet," her hand trailed, indicating downwards. "Sailing a brambly ocean."

"What was it, hitherto? Such is the state of its innocence, the Garden of Eden. Pick no apples, lady."

Too late, she thought, too late.

"Look, 'tis all the wreck of a topiary garden, sunk among the brambles."

She turned to look, increasingly aware of his presence. 'Tis not all pain, thought Mary Florida; just close related.

Unaware of this, Blackavise assumed her to be indifferent to topiary.

Aloud, she declared, "We need much talent if we are to rescue the park, and the practical streak you soldiers have."

This compliment encouraged him to think up a battle plan to subdue the rampant undergrowth. He gestured towards all the neglected greenery, wondering if Lacey could muster enough men wielding billhooks to win a victory over the wilderness.

"Behold that great topiary bird or some such, all grown over," Blackavise pointed, "I recognise the signs; we have a pair sprouting like those up at Black House. Our garden is not so far gone, that's all. We have a pair of topiary globes, and a peacock bird, too. My Godmother hath tried for donkeys' years to grow a horse. This is not easy. The four legs grow from the ground, she hath clipped the body and the approximately horsey head. Nobody could swear it is not a horse: but the tail is open to criticism. Shoots grow ever upward. She hath long tied a brick to the end of the tail. Take away the brick, and the tail lifts for heaven. Leave it, and it spoils the effect."

"I should let the tail swish, as if her horse were alive-o."

"I'll put it to her."

But his face told Mary Florida that the old lady was far beyond interest in horses and swishing tails.

"I fear the physician fails to be of help," and she allowed her butterfly touch to brush his coat sleeve. "I'm sorry."

The reticence of so gentle a murmur struck him. It dawned on him that he might not appear (as he undoubtedly did to Susan) to be stripped of the feelings and sensibilities of those half his age.

At this human moment between them, the library door burst open and ricocheted loudly off the boot scraper, discharging the cargo of Aeneas Lacey and the man he had chosen to found his collection of portraits. Francis Pye, decently abashed with his eyes lowered examining the stone paving, did not at first grasp that standing above Blackavise's boots was the very man he had met at Corrydene's. When he looked up to be introduced to Mistress Lacey, he recognised Blackavise, and visibly jumped.

This is as tricky as finding a godson, thought John. He felt the warmth of an advancing spring sun upon his shoulders.   Politenesses began to pass to and fro between the patron of the arts and his painter, who started to relax.   Birds sang on cue to welcome the newcomer. Blackavise, as the bystander of this group, saw the painter was struck by the beauty of the lady in green, and watched him sizing her up to how he might capture her likeness. Blackavise hoped to be on hand when it was explained to him that she was not to be the subject of his portrayal. Aeneas gestured them indoors. Mary Florida swept before her husband, who preceded his new employee.   Pye spoke in an undertone to Blackavise whilst they were alone on the terrace before treading in their wake.

"Don't mention Master Corrydene to him.   He discharged me. Wouldn't pay me a groat."

Where had he been for the past week? wondered Blackavise.

"I'll be sure to hold my tongue, never fear, but on one condition," he assured him.

"Quick, man, what?"

Blackavise looked at the worried youth.

"Don't go telling Lacey my base origins. I have hopes of remaining *persona grata*."

The painter nodded and Blackavise beat him through the doorway with a not unfriendly blow between the shoulder blades. I am glad I am not a taker of likenesses, thought John. The pressure of responsibility would make my head spin.

As he was not bearing this burden, Blackavise was probably the happiest person in Aynescote and relished his unseasonal festivities singlehanded. Francis Pye might have enjoyed Aynescote had he been a private person visiting, but he had his sittings to unsettle him. Aeneas, entranced by the alchemies of paint and preparation, would have been a child at Christmas had he not felt from the outset that on the sketches for his portrait something was amiss with the mouth. Mary Florida remained enigmatic. But there was something pleasing for each of them. The sense of occasion was heightened by the business of readying the library, which had a good light, and finding a suitably impressive and gilded chair for Aeneas to enthrone himself upon. He seems to have confused this with his coronation, thought John; 'tis but a picture, and should be hers by right. Piers and Jesse, bowlegged as blacksmiths, came staggering in with a lump of masonry for the artist to use as a grindstone.

"I didn't need one quite that size," murmured Pye, feeling ever more over-parted. There were brushes and charcoal and secret things to be ground.

"You must have looked an unusual pedlar on the road, with all that impedimenta," remarked Blackavise.

"I have a hand-cart. I must be the most readily identified traveller in the county."

"That's no bad thing, in these days."

No more it was. The King's authority was in abeyance, yet the death throes of the Royalist forces threw up strange dramas even yet. The man at this very moment beneath Blackavise's floorboards had fled the chasing men who had sniffed him out. Where could he run? The thought had been exercising Blackavise. The bolt-holes were stopped. Old strongholds, one by one, had been reduced. Now the icy hand of hard winter melted, it seemed even Corfe, even Belvoir, all remaining Royalist castles were fallen. Any man forced to run must become a Frenchman and live beyond the seas. Blackavise himself might not have lived so long, had his wound not sent him home, and thence, to this neck of the woods where trouble had not reached. That was chance. Now in the springtime relief and interlude at Aynescote, the last thing he wanted was man with a useless ankle planted in Black House's hidey-hole, waiting to run away. Francis Pye has tugged his handcart along the lanes, he thought, maybe he hath smelt a new broadsheet. Let's hear what he's heard.

"What cheer, Francis? If any."

"There's a strong word old Astley's surrendered. Up under Stow."

Up on the cold Cotswolds.

"The Welsh levies, of course, fled."

"Is that a surprise?"   asked Blackavise sourly, contemplating the fate of Astley, the brave and venerable Royalist commander. Of course it was inevitable, but it hurt.

"So that's why it's turned quiet down here, the hounds were called off the fox."

Blackavise's fox, the spymaster, had gone to ground most inconveniently, in his cellar.

"They'll have given up hereabouts, then?" supposed Blackavise, hoping for the spymaster's sake they had, and for his own outcome. He knew Black House to be compromised so long as the spymaster hid under its flagstones, whilst Aynescote represented a playground of innocents amusing themselves with grown adults' toys.

"Who knows?" shrugged Pye, and Blackavise felt 'who knows' made an uneasy bedfellow. He made a mental adjustment every morning after he left the old lady's sick room for Aynescote as if for a different land, for instance the Americas. Flynn Gerard might give him a sandpapering when he put in his inevitable appearance, but these days Gerard seemed to feel a ten-minute harangue sufficed. Maybe someone had told him not to repeat himself in company. Once he had discerned what he termed The Event had not taken place and the old lady was still breathing, a glass of claret wine sent him back to the Tuns, where he seemed to have found a sympathetic crony, deaf probably, thought Blackavise unkindly.

When he arrived back down at Aynescote, he found himself having to ramp up the artist's confidence. Pye cornered him, took him aside and lowered his voice.

"John, I am in difficulties with the picture."

Blackavise's expression encouraged him to continue.

"Alas, why am I faced with the husband? When his wife is as fine a rose as any I've seen," sighed Francis Pye, "why aren't I closeted with her? I could do her likeness in the dark." He lowered his voice, "John, I'm in a real pickle trying to catch his character."

"You should have told him you never let the sitter see the canvas till 'tis done; that gives time, er, for re-painting."

"I did, I protested. But, he pays, so he looks. He insists."

Blackavise made sure he was closeted with the rose during the sittings. He wasn't going to draw attention to this advantageous side-effect. All he had to do was to arrive once the sitting was under way, and there he would be, alone with Mary Florida.

"Don't forget, you are to portray me in a melancholy

guise," Aeneas had stipulated at the first sitting.

This was little help, as the expression behind which he habitually lived was an up-turned smiling bow, the smile of a man in a cloud.

"He smiles too much," complained Francis Pye, "we painters know a smile is but fleeting; one cannot pin it down."

Blackavise had stopped listening. He was more interested in Mary Florida. Here they were free to entertain each other for two hours a day, and as yet all he knew of her was that she had a tantalising gauze between herself and the world. Here she was asking after his invalid, and he was telling her about the name-day she'd celebrated for him, year in and year out.

"When I came of age, that must have been the last year Aynescote was occupied, she threw a celebration and all were invited up. We put torches along the path up the wood."

He conjured up his moment of long ago, the arriving merrymakers, the confusion of the party with its toasts, its goodwill, and his godmother jolly in a big gown. The passing of time muddled it all up, save that picture of her laughing and queening it and proud of him.

"I saw the Aynescote people back, parted at the gate and returned alone, the first time I'd been alone all day: strange how one moment sticks. The flares in the holders were dying down by then, but a wind must have sprung up, so they burnt bright for a last show. So twenty times, at twenty torches, each shadow I cast raced and fled. Like life, I thought."

"O don't," said she, "that's sad."

"Ah," he spread his hands, "forgive me. But such were the bright days my godmother would want remembered. Those were the real days, she would say."

"You are goodhearted to sit and stay by her. She would otherwise feel so lonely."

"I'm used to invalids," he said simply, "my wife was a long time not well, then a-dying."

Oh, he has no wife. She could not bring herself to analyse her relief. Freed, she looked at him undefended, asking "You've family?"

And he saw the blue-green eyes unveil, he saw heart, feeling; did not read the relief.

"I have the one son Simon, and his wife, Mistress Killjoy."

And she laughed at his deadpan manner, and he laughed his good laugh in return.

By the fourth day of the sittings, he felt Mary Florida's presence everywhere, as though she were perched on his shoulder, like a feathery, personal songbird. He would have said a nightingale, but these he believed to be little brown songsters lost in the thickets, whereas she was a set of lovely feathers and he couldn't think of a bird that would compare. But he felt the rustle of the plumage and the presence, light and free. He was sitting with her the following day talking about the design for a parterre garden, topiary being old hat with Aeneas, and he had borrowed charcoal sticks and a leaf of paper off Francis Pye, to work it out. They had marked out the symmetry, and were upon the pattern either side of the central walk, with one path leading out of the framework with an arrow indicating 'to Banqueting House'.

"I haven't matched the curve," she admitted, rubbing and smudging where she was indicating box edging. "If you fancy an eyecatcher, we could place a statue at the far end?"

Dorcas scratched upon the door and gave John a sharp awakening, for Dorcas had a visitor to announce. Nothing new, in this open house, but the name rang a loud gong.

"Master Radlett," said Dorcas.

Radlett was one of the names on lawyer Pettijohn's list of godchildren.

Don't be a fool, Johnny, there is no cause for alarm, 'tis a common enough name. Nay, that's stretching it. What's in a name? There must be plenty of people of that name. One or two? Dozens? Here he comes.

Mary Florida was gracefully rising, the small brown swords of her eyebrows enquiringly poised. Today she was an apricot fruit in ripely belled skirts, full sleeves. Her little waist teased him as she turned away to greet an apple-cheeked gentleman in travelling clothes, whose manner was that of deferential uncertainty.

"Am I intruding? This is Black House, is it not?"

Blackavise felt overly disturbed, as if he had been a papist up a chimney and been rolled forth, naked. He had a long moment of listening to Mary Florida's soft voice explaining that this was in fact Aynescote, but he was not to be cast down, for Black House was nearby up the hill, and here, most opportunely, is Master Blackavise himself, who will be able to lead you straight thither.

Blackavise felt suddenly foolish sitting there playing with charcoal sticks, and he stood up looking stern, half expecting the inoffensive, decent looking gentleman to go red in the face on meeting him. Would he tell Mary Florida that her guest was not the sort of man she should suffer under her roof? That she was harbouring the bastard, a no-good, and probably with his eye on the old lady's effects?

"My dear sir," fluted Radlett peaceably, "I had no idea of you. I had no notion Mistress Blackavise had kin. How would I know? It has been something of a shock to receive a letter requesting I come. Is there a bequest? Has she had seemly burial?"

Mary Florida turned away, biting her lip.

"I am not kin," said John bluntly. "I am but godson same as thee. She took me in as a child and thus it is I bear her name."

"Oh," said the decorous gentleman.

"Happily," continued Blackavise in an ominous tone, "she lives."

"Oh. I must apologise – I ... I'm overjoyed, naturally."

"You weren't to know," growled Blackavise, thinking, 'You are not overjoyed'.

He didn't want to have to admit that the old lady was sinking slowly, and Radlett would be proved to be right before too long. Mary Florida read his reaction.

"We've had no dealings, of course," offered the newcomer, nodding and earnestly smiling. "How interesting, sir, to discover I am not the only godchild."

Dark humour began to reassert itself. He is in for a few more surprises, thought Blackavise. Should he hold a Godsons' Feast? Or kit them out in those masks from old King Jamie's time, and make them guess each other's identity? Mary Florida glimpsed his quicksilver smile before his strong features resumed their customary expression. It had dawned on him that because Radlett hadn't known there were other godsons, that gentleman was in no position to tell Mary Florida that Blackavise was the base-born bastard of the pack.

So next morning it was open house up the hill. Blackavise, jealous of his private success down at Aynescote, passed up his visit there as a mere duty call, and sacrificed the remains of his springtime Christmas on the cold altar of reality. He introduced Master Radlett to Flynn Gerard and stood back to enjoy the effect each had on the other. Hackles rose and soft soap smoothed, while each swallowed Blackavise's claret. He wanted them to go away, he was fretting for the peace and quiet of Aynescote and the playground there from woes. Was this Radlett really going to stay at the Three Tuns with Flynn? He blinked, and prayed he had not imagined it.

"The event," Gerard hissed through clenched teeth as if that would prevent Blackavise from hearing him, "cannot be long postponed."

Blackavise glared at him.

During the passage of a testing week at Aynescote, Aeneas Lacey was unwilling to accept that Pye's attempt to capture his likeness was not going well.

"A first effort," was how he phrased his misgivings to the uneasy portrait painter, "these things must be accepted. I suggest you consider putting me in a better light."

For Pye these truths had quite dimmed the well-lit chamber, for all that the sunshine continued to slant across the library's long floorboards. Grasping his sheaf of long brushes and palette of rainbow blotches, he wilted. Lacey rashly rose from the throne of his chair to inspect his image. When he faced Pye's version of his likeness he reared back, fidgety with dissatisfaction, turned on his heel and left the scene of artistic crisis. His portraitist flinched. Blackavise followed Lacey's tapping heels until out of earshot of the painter. He was intrigued as to the next development.

"I ought to draw him out," uttered Lacey in a strong undertone to Blackavise, now his only audience, "you know, discuss his difficulties."

"I'd leave him be," urged Blackavise, "in our wide experience, we come across these artistic sensibilities."

He hadn't, but he was trying to suggest that Lacey might. Five minutes later in the anteroom, Francis Pye was whispering his frustrations to Blackavise, his only ally.

"What the devil! I don't find him easy. Left to myself I can deliver something tolerable, but he keeps interfering."

The frustrated patron now returned, followed by a serving man bearing a clinking jug and glasses.

"We'll take a break before we start anew," declared Lacey. After the unusual experience of drinking someone else's claret, Blackavise let Aeneas steer him by the elbow to stroll out of doors into his embryonic garden. The usual surge of spring thistles, nettles and new undergrowth depressed Lacey even further. Whacking at the density either side of the path with a delicate cane, releasing showers of early midges, he led his guest up the swell in the ground where he planned his banqueting house. On the far side lay the perimeter wall. Looking back at the tall house, they could make out two coloured patches on the terrace, the apricot highlight which was Mary Florida and the moleskin brown worn by Francis Pye, this tone receding as neutral colours will. Blackavise, gazing, felt unaccountably upstaged. Lacey was looking the other way.

"I must have this mound built up," he was saying. "The purpose of having my banqueting house here is so that my guests will enjoy looking out over the boundary wall. Watch the world pass by. You know the sort of thing. They will relish the vantage place I shall create. The trouble is we lack the height."

What a flibbertigibbet Lacey was; first he wanted to be a patron of the arts, now he wants to build an unlikely pleasure dome in this seedy wilderness. Blackavise was amazed at the extent of the man's ambition. Whoever did he imagine would travel so far to sit in a fancy little building and admire the ruts of an empty lane? The only passers-by would be godsons on their way to plague him at Black House.

"The world doesn't often come this way. Aynescote isn't Oxford city," he suggested. Lacey wasn't listening. The unsatisfactory portrait was irking him.

"I told the wretch, 'I want you to flood me with light. Illuminate my features'. He's delivered nothing of the sort. Nor is my face like me."

"Light's elusive; your artist'll add the highlights when the sun allows," Blackavise intervened for the painter's sake, "the weather's been a touch dull for the sittings."

"Maybe, I allow. But as I told him, he wasn't making the background withdraw from me, either. Nor has he touched my expression. I have mentioned that from the start. But even if he improves there, I seem to sit stranded on a flat background, for all the drape of material and the broken column he indicates, as if he had me pinned to the wall."

What he desires is what that Dutchman calls Advancing, Withdrawing and Shortening, thought John. He heard himself make soothing noises, alien though they were to him. "'Tis a challenge to him, to hit thee off."

"You've seen the very best pictures, I can tell," Lacey said, starting to use his long cane as a measuring stick, going over the ground where he wanted his picnic house to stand. He went down on one knee and counted each length until he covered the anticipated area, like a man stalking game. With each forward lope, the amber knob at the top of the cane gave forth its blink of gold.

"When I was moving round the country a-soldiering, I had the chance to see some pictures by masters. There's that portraitist from the Hague, Honthorst is his name, he offers a scene illuminated by a hidden light source. A candle's glow placed behind a hand, that sort of effect."

"D'you think I could get him?"

"I think he's locked away in his Dutch fastness." Painting thy betters, Lacey, the Queen of Bohemia and her sons the Princes, sitters who have real authority. Therefore their royal status needs no frippery, but lit by subtle candlelight that the Dutch master arranges.

Beyond the reach of his present companion Aeneas, who now rose to his feet, shrugging. He had tired of measuring.

"My luck's out. I make this ten yards by four, or was it nine by four? Enough of this. Come, Blackavise, let me walk you round the back."

This was better. The hillock had shown not only the house to them from their viewpoint, but behind it the quadrangles of stabling, coach sheds and outbuildings, themselves castles of stone in this county. Blackavise felt he would be more at home poking about horse stalls and boxes than imagining the reckless outlay of his host. When they descended Aeneas's unsatisfactory Alp they passed through an arch into a neglected kitchen garden where two old men were swatting sickles through an overgrown cabbage patch of twenty summers earlier. Cabbage stenches stunned the nostrils. Lacey strode busily through, masking himself with his handkerchief. Blackavise did not ask where the young men were. Armies had swallowed twenty-year-olds like Moloch. He good-morrowed, and as he trod the path, snails cracked like nutshells under his boot toes. Ten years' work might rescue Aynescote.   It seemed like the foolishness of a lost sailor who starves and suffers and thinks he has claimed a godless land from savages, merely because he has set foot on their shore and planted a flag upon it. If Aeneas Lacey with his ideas and fancies thought he might tame Aynescote, it was delusion; even Hercules would have thought twice. Blackavise smiled. There was too much to do. But at least this range of stabling stood firm, its courtyard marred only by a broken waterspout and a pump whose drips grew tears of moss. Ginger had got thus far and no further, for here were the harness horses he'd described, with their big, noble foreheads and strawy lovelocks looking out at him hoping for sugar chips.

"Next time," promised Blackavise, stroking a suede nose and the great big smacking-kiss lips. Here was Hetty, snug in a spare box. She affected not to see him, off-hand, busy at the manger. She was extremely feminine at moments like this. He chirruped to her, and turned to find another greybeard, in another sacking apron, looking sideways at him. This was undoubtedly the fellow who had dealt with Ginger, for he had the bandy legs of his kind.

"And who be 'ee, sir?" demanded the man, tempering the unfriendliness with 'sir' tacked upon the end to acknowledge that he recognised, in Blackavise, a gentleman.

Lacey popped out of the harness-room and spared Blackavise the trouble of an answer. "Get the key, Amos," he demanded, "I've something to show you now, Blackavise."

What had he got locked up in there? The Queen of Carthage, to justify his name? Helen of Troy? Twelve more portrait painters, all failed? Ginger had only heard horsey scrapings. Here came Amos with his face all screwed up in reluctance, producing a big key and turning it in the lock to a strong, studded gate. As such gates will, the hinges had dropped with the weight and the old man had to shoulder it. Inside was another stone-built yard with box doors. Blackavise saw a trough, a set of buckets, a scoop hung up outside a feed-shed door. And then he saw the horse.

"On my oath, Lacey! That's a beauty." He was a great, big chestnut, dwarfing Hetty. What a neck, what an eye. Indeed, what presence. "However did you come by him?"

"O, my elder uncle was a judge of blood and bone. This was his pride and joy, Thunderer." Lacey had lowered his tone as one sharing secrets. "Twice in the course of the conflict my uncle had his stables cleared, when Maurice swept up, and twice my uncle saved Thunderer. The second time he actually rushed the horse into the kitchen and stood him behind a large sheet hung up airing. The cook was in a great state of alarm. Ah, imagine it!"

John conjured it up.

"The times will quieten, now," Lacey asserted, "I intend within the year to have the mares up to him. His stock will be famous."

"You are a master of surprises."

"Would you not keep this surprise from the common gaze?"

"I vow I would. There's been half a regiment out, up and down here, upon their other business. My word, you've temptation here. He'd tempt anyone used to laying hands on the usual ribby old carthorse, and not for putting to in a baggage wagon. Flemish bred?"

"Ah, you've an eye for horseflesh."

"That's a Fleming neck."

"And his temperament's sound, Amos can handle him."

"So that's why you lighted on Aynescote, out of the way, to hide him in?"

"O yes; when matters mend, I shall remove back to civilisation."

And Blackavise, patting the muscled neck, felt let down that the grandiose schemes would be left half-done, or were figments that melted off with the morning mist. But he admired that horse. And felt nicely singled out to be sworn quiet about him and shown him secretly, like this.

"I'd doff my hat to your Thunderer, had I not left it in the house," he told Lacey. "Who was that Roman emperor who made his horse a Consul? Had he Thunderer, I'd scarce blame him." Lacey beamed approbation like a man who likes to be understood.

Chapter VI

Blackavise went home and opened his Pandora's box by raising the kitchen flagstone. Out crawled the spymaster impeded by the awkwardness of a strapped-up ankle. For want of a name Blackavise had taken to calling him Smith.

"Your football's deflated," he offered, bending over for a look. "Can you put weight on it, or are you still on the hop?"

"'Tis fairly sound now," proclaimed Smith testing it, disclosing Bessie's strapping, "only weak."

"The bandaging'll brace it up."

"If the coast's clear, I'm urgent for France."

"Our lanes are quiet for now, but I hesitate to say whether the hounds who came after you be kennelled, or no."

"I've got some papers; I'm travelling to see a sick

relative, once I'm clear of this place."

"You'll never pass for a countryman, with a face that pale."

"I'm a clerk."

"Mm. You must know all about travelling incognito. Here's an idea which you might try as cover: there is an artist, a limner, busy in these parts, at a house here, a house there, and of course carrying the tools of his trade."

The spymaster shrugged, his eyes showing no interest. He failed to bite on that idea.

"Ah well. You'll have a hundred ways," said Blackavise, feeling an amateur in the presence of a professional spy. "God keep you safe to France, in whatsoever guise."

The narrow eyes threw off the mists. "God hath kept me thus far, even in thy keg-cellar. I'll judge my leave-taking. If I chance to get me gone, take thy empty keg-cellar as my grateful farewell."

Could it be that simple? asked Blackavise of himself, could this last service to his Royalist cause be safely concluded? Possible consequences, had he let himself dwell, would have given shudders. An empty cellar suddenly struck him as the equivalent of having turned lead into gold. He clapped the little man good-heartedly on the shoulder and failed to register that the rodent eyes were neatly blinking on new information.

*

It was two days before the carrier's man fitted in an extra passenger. So relieved was John Blackavise that he felt weak at the knee. That was that. He'd had the strength of character to spare Aynescote his footmark. They'd think, 'Where is he?' rather than, 'Here, again?'. Or so he hoped. Then he'd crept down early, past Aynescote, past the spring-tide flow in the ford, rushing and chortling as it bathed Hetty's hooves. Blackavise reached the Three Tuns, dismounted, hitched the mare so she could eat the tussocks, and sauntered up to the tavern hussy where she was hanging out shirts on the clothesline.

"Two friends of mine are putting up here," he began, shamelessly returning her glad eye, "I want some sport with them. This shiny little coin is thine, if you would let me take a peep in upon them. They'll have taken the private parlour, I daresay?"

"They may have," she teased.

The clouds were high, the sky was periwinkle blue, and her eyes, over the ballooning thunderclouds of clean shirts, were Eve's.

"You mean the misery and the old gentleman?" He

nodded firmly.

"Are you sure it's proper? We've all heard of Peeping Tom."

Lacking an apple, he flipped the coin and caught it against his sleeve, his hand covering it. "Heads or tails?"

"Thass not fair, you said that was mine. Heads _and_ tails."

"I need but a minute's squint at your lodgers."

"I might say yes."

He disclosed the coin. "Heads: you win." He laughed and handed the upturned head of the unlucky King.

"O there, then." She gave him an accommodating wink. "Seasy, follow me and have your fun. The taproom's by their dining-room, there's a good draught at the latch-lace hole where you can put your eye."

Blackavise turned for the tavern back door.

"Shocking late breaking their fast. They're still in there now," she added, "so I can't get on and clear it. Can't see what laughing matter you'll get out o' those two – been here days, aye, and surely it feels like a month."

The door through from the taproom was latched by one of those bootlace strings of leather that break in two once a twelvemonth causing levering-up with a penknife and cursing from those caught temporarily on the wrong side. Blackavise pulled at the intact thong and applied a bright eye. Why do I do these things? he asked himself, for, through the latch hole all he could see was the back view of a nodding, affable old gentleman, and the three-quarter profile of Flynn Gerard sawing at a large round loaf and handing the slice on the point of the knife. His adversary actually appeared to be smiling. By my eyes, thought Blackavise, I did not know he could. What's that he's saying?

"… of course, the duty visits are trying, but what else can a man do? Having to brave Blackavise, that Cerberus; and she too far gone to know him from us."

"Oh, the bastard," chimed in the other, occasioning that bastard nearly to put his eye out upon the latch-end due to outraged sense of insult. So much for dear pink-cheeked old gentlemen! He'd never trust one again. He'd no right to sit there chomping bread and ham as if neither they nor the butter would melt in his mouth, and dish out derogatory remarks about innocent eavesdroppers. And, Cerberus! It was past bearing. That Gerard was a legitimised bastard, and a miserable, knock-kneed son-of-a-whore. Wheeling away in outrage he nearly knocked the girl over where she had come up behind him. He'd have liked his coin back, but in the circumstances the pain he experienced was his own fault for eavesdropping. So he strode off, piqued.

"Tell them you've more godsons arriving shortly and they have taken your best room," Blackavise flung over his shoulder, but it was too mild a Parthian shot. Everything had rubbed him up the wrong way – not the rudery especially, army life had knocked off any remaining corners long ago. No, it was the simple infuriation of finding those two, utter opposites and in their different aspects, disastrous human beings, getting along famously. That hurt Blackavise, and he chewed on it, retreating. Not one to bite on the hall doormat, introspectively, Blackavise therefore went in at the harbour mouth of Aynescote straightways on the way back. Even he, however, found himself bottled up when face to face with the person he most wished to unburden himself to, because Mary Florida asked him to play shuttlecock. It is difficult to fulminate when playing a light-hearted game which requires a modicum of concentration. Whacking at the rising feathered cork at the precise moment to give her an easy shot diverted him. Her eye was accurate and she returned neatly, but she could not run in those skirts without a breaking wave of petticoat and resultant dragging effect. She might be young and lissom but she missed her shot, swatting the air.

"Oh, I have had a morning of it," she panted, frog-coloured bodice rising and falling; the butterfly wings of her lace collar settled on the upward curve. "Master Pye hath made a great mistake by persuading Aeneas to attempt a profile study, and Aeneas hath not recognised himself in the result, so now they are locked in there to take a new shot at it; that hath not been restful, for a start. Then there was a very large mouse in my closet this morning; worse, mayhap a young rat. And I discovered from the carrier's man that some Parliament soldiers have come out of quarters chasing after that spymaster, and whilst finding he was not under the false floor in Tom Heaven's country house beyond Underhill, they relieved him of his saddle horses. When Aeneas hears that! He will be sitting up all night with Thunderer."

Fellow feeling of one who has also spent a bad morning welled up in John. She was tapping the shuttlecock up and down on her bat, the picture of wifely concern.

"Your bird's tired of hopping," said he, "come, persuade me out of doors so we breathe some air. Let us tell spymasters, horse stealers, mice, all to go hang. Let us taste the freedom of the day. What say you, to running away from all this?"

"Running away? That's what you soldiers don't admit to doing." She spread her hands in disbelief, making light of whatever provoked him to say those words, assuming they were merely his joke.

"Curiously enough, when I said it, it struck me as the best idea I'd had in the last five years."

The darker tone of his reply caused Mary Florida to feel foolish. If domestic struggles were her problems, how trivial they must seem in this man's world of death and life. She could only guess at what might have gone awry in his fighting, but it was hardly these events that were disturbing her. Mice in the closet, portrait takers and the moods of Aeneas were less than nothing in the world of men like Blackavise. Let's step away, leave doom thoughts behind.

"You mentioned the freedom of the day. Instead of running away, let us breathe the free fresh air outside in the garden where I have a favourite corner."

Blackavise formed the fancy that her glance tied him to a turquoise comet's tail. Shafts of transient amber and gold shone through the porch lights as she led him into the spring air. But she was not Orpheus, and she didn't look round at him. Where was she leading him? First, through an archway where new season's roses were overdue for the pruning shears, then into a sunken herb garden, sheltered by the warmth of the sun. Blackavise admired the sight of a broken fountain with a gumboiled cherub, armless and overfed. Below his frost-cracked basin a besom of rosemary had fallen across the flags. Weeds had gained the upper hand over the first spears of mint, which had undermined the tile-bordered square of their old enclosure and were at loose underfoot. Mary Florida swept her hand over the surface of a stone bench, subsided upon it, and looked to John for enlightenment about his previous utterance.

"Now, why can retreating ever be a best idea of a fighting soldier?"

Years had passed since he had been given such an opening to tell his story, and now he accepted the opening she offered. Mary Florida watched him throw his head back and toss his shoulder-length mane. His expression was rueful, but determined.

"Ah," he let forth, like a steaming kettle, turned away and strode across the space between the fallen rosemary and the lady, until the kettle boiled and he stood facing her, striking his fist upon the palm of his other hand. The mint he had stepped upon sent up its fresh inhalation and she breathed it in for revival; I am doing well, she thought, he must not see how much he hath affected me.

"Shall you growl further, or would it help to try speech?" she was dizzy at the prospect he actually would confide in her.

He cleared his thoughts. "Lady, you may laugh at

me. Whatever ails me is in my fool head. I don't wish to burden you. Might you spare me five minutes?" He unsheathed his sword to reveal himself unarmed and willingly lowering his weapon to her. The bare blade shone on the carpet of weeds next to the boy in the fountain.

"Why have all, save in Aynescote here, been angered or upset at the sight of me? They've been affronted, abusive, and had me struck on the poll and crammed in a ditch to drown."

"That last," she allowed, "even I can see, expresses strong opinion."

"And I know not who set forth to do it."

"I've never come across anyone so unwelcome," she declared, fiddling with the shuttlecock. "May I ask why?"

"Why!" he steamed anew, "I can understand personal misliking. I know I come too strong for some. Confound it, the souls here don't know me from Adam!"

She was subtle enough not to smile at a soldier who necessarily had half the population as his nominal foe, too eager for him to reveal himself to her. She ventured into his deep waters, toe and toe; looked at him, so he saw her rainbow, the iris, favouring the blue and green.

"Is it to do with your godmother? These other

godsons did not reckon upon you. As 'tis clear you are her favourite, this must be a great irritant for greedy men, not least where money is concerned. They are in no mood to love you."

He came and perched on the end of her bench, elbow on his knee, chin on his fingers. Mary Florida had the fancy that his strength would turn the solid stone seat into a seesaw and his end would toss her skywards.

"It never occurred to me that a bunch of other godsons existed."

"Nor they you, so it would appear."

They considered the sick old lady, locked mumbling with her secrets. Blackavise decided on the truth. He had not meant to admit it. He began with difficulty. It was going to take him some time and her patience.

"They have the advantage, that's certain. Mind you, I can't swear they all know,"

"That's nothing but riddles; art thou a disgraced rogue, a thief?"

She smiled at him, tapping her captive shuttlecock up and down on the bat.

"Only under army orders," said he, and he laughed, struck by the ridiculous, tossing his mane, "by the Lord, I've been a terrible fellow. No, 'tis not that. Old Corrydene I knew for a godson; he disliked my name and poor heredity. Flynn Gerard simply dislikes me.

Radlett, the old avuncular, he's too bland, that's as much as I have against him. Oh, and he smirks upon Gerard, a sign his brains are weak. Did one of them pay ruffians to waylay me? And if so, which one? I wake o'nights, tossing the odds."

"Is there a fortune, then?" she asked.

"I can't tell. I have no information; perhaps it will make eyes glisten in due course. The lawyer, Pettijohn, he'll know for certain. I've seen his list of godsons, but for the moment 'tis his business. Not mine."

"Dowries, portions, heirs and fortunes, ah, all cast long shadows. There's more than fourpence at stake to bring them here."

"Why should I be the beneficiary? I'm not the eldest."

"But 'tis not that!" she cried, "is it? This isn't a case of blood succession. It is simply that she prefers you."

"Oh," he said, catching a compliment. He rejected simpering. "I suppose you could be right. I had not thought of it with plain sense. So we godsons stand equal, save that she had a favourite. Remember there's no evidence that she did."

"They are wagering upon a certainty that you are the favourite to inherit."

He let himself nod, yet recalled the old saw 'never bet on a certainty'. Why had he kept his sights on all he knew of primogeniture, the succession by right of the first-born? He, to whom no such thing applied. It was irony.

"Why the smile?"

"O lady, I hesitate to say."

"Why? Art thou, then, the second of twins, and have left the elder at home?"

"Nay, but," here he took a run at it, launched himself on declaring the difficult truth to Mary Florida, "I am no father's acknowledged son. Here I stand, due entirely to the kind heart and favour of Mistress Blackavise, who befriended my disgraced mother at that dissolute old court of King Jamie's Danish Queen. I answered to John Nameless until my mother died on a bed of many sorrows, whereupon Mistress Blackavise took me up, took me home, and gave me her name." He bit his lip. "My fellow godsons do not consider the bastard that I am renders me a worthy of the inheritance they feel more appropriate to themselves, as god-fearing recipients." He looked steadily at Mary Florida to see if she still breathed after his story. She had remained calm, as far as he could tell. Even the chestnut curls on her forehead were no more ruffled than usual, thus emboldening Blackavise, who found now he could not rein in his charge against the enemy forces of the righteous Godsons. He could not stop himself.

Mary Florida was intrigued. Now he had paused she spoke. "That settles it; there is a fortune, or they would not look upon you with such righteous disfavour. You stand in their way. Thou art her favourite, and there is inheritance and they feel it should not be wasted on you. Who are the other actors in your play?"

"Old Corrydene hath professed no love for my godmother, due to some supposed disgrace, I know not what; also he holds against me that I am base born, obviously. They all seem to have wind of something. And they have kept their distance from her because of some sinful behaviour or other. In all my time living here as a boy, or since, I've never set eyes on one of them."

"Whatever could the poor lady have done?" Mary Florida wondered.

"Necromancy? A papist? A card-sharp?"

"Besides those," she said.

"I can't imagine."

"Then let us throw that aside for the moment. Now, the fortune; what are the grounds for your thinking there must be one?"

"She's rare. Her independence is famed. To start with she never married, nor were there men of the family to tell her what to do. Her treasure was always safe in her hands. When I was a boy she told me the story, of how her father put faith and investment in an adventurer's risky voyage, whilst his dead-stick advisers told him his wits had failed. She would tell me, 'Depend on yourself', but the reason she could, was because that ship did come in."

"She then, was her father's only child?"

"Indeed, so whatever fortune her father had made, he left it to her, great or less."

"And in her turn, she will leave it in her will."

She said that word he found himself unable to enunciate. Caught aback he shrugged, spread his hands. "How many a lady lives as free of interference, as she? Unless a widow, there's the trick; three husbands, be Bess and build Hardwick House."

She thought of her own circumstances and was unable to speak in reply. But the shuttlecock fell, and broke his train of thought, if not hers. He reached and rummaged for it up to his elbow in a thicket of lavender gone all woody, but smelling of its better days when he brushed the bits from his sleeve. He tossed the shuttlecock back to her.

She found her voice, "I should like to play the game better, if it did not seem one batted a bird. Are you not nervous of the godsons?"

"Godsons don't fright me, no. I am resentful of their wish to gather round the good old lady whilst she still breathes, rubbing their hands. But of course you can have no idea of warfare, beside which my present enemy is but a horsefly, an irritant. In the last conflict I have swatted more than gnats." Then he wished he had not spoken in so blunt a tone to this lady shielded away from the world and its frights. She was sitting there as if in the nursery, round-eyed at the world of men and strife. All the same she encouraged the soldier on.

"Shall you tell me more?"

He complied. "Occasionally officers call for volunteers to charge across the shattered stones of a well-defended great citadel, with but little chance of surviving. Young men threw their lives away when the defenders fired spread shot or poured molten metal upon them. Ah, such bravery brought little but death or fleeting repute. I once was a member of such a Forlorn Hope and proved one could survive. These godsons do not compare. They even failed to drown me." He had been harping on. Try another topic, John said to himself. Let us return to *terra firma*. Had Aeneas survived the onslaughts of the painter? "How's the time going for today's sitting? Is it safe to return?"

"We have a Forlorn Hope before us," ventured Mary Florida, "I do fear all is lost. Our hope is faint, that our portrait painter puts my husband on his canvas well, so that Aeneas awards him a victory. We could hire some

120

trumpeters and blow a fanfare, don't you think? Otherwise our attack upon the dinner awaiting us will be less enjoyable."

John approved her turn from the military to the domestic. He was afraid that he had dwelt too much upon the army. He appreciated her concerns that peace might not break out even in Aynescote. She needed to concentrate on the immediate household crisis, and it was her turn to be vehement. He understood fears that Aeneas had hired a painter who could not paint.

"Aeneas will make him try yet again, unless he is satisfied," Mary Florida admitted.

"I have put an eye to well-taken likenesses on occasion; I fear your husband may prove a challenge to the talents of Master Pye. Overpainting may not suffice."

"I pray the good Lord sends them something of a success today, or it will not only be the profile study but also the portraitist who is flung out." Mary Florida's rueful expression would not save the day upon which her husband was expecting a masterpiece.

"I would have had him paint your picture, when he came," Blackavise told her, "now I am not so sure."

"Oh," allowed Mary Florida.

"Better 'tis Aeneas. He can play the man."

That is one jest you cannot laugh at, she reflected,

and rose and dusted off lichen and sundries from her skirts.

"We had best retreat indoors, if we are to commiserate. Shall we brave the artist and my husband?"

"And there was I hoping it was my misfortunes that occupied thee," said John, "but let me say that airing the godsons, and beating at them with sticks, hath made me feel the better, at least. Had it not been for showing them daylight, I'd have stifled alone with them."

He paused, strong, broad, well-proportioned in the decent clothes he wore. The whiteness of his neck linen was a contrast to his outdoor complexion, she thought.

He smiled at her: a positive force. As yet he thought of her as an abstract, The Beauty. And liking her presence; capturing the Beauty. Creeping behind that came something new and silent in his mind as if on cats ' paws. He wanted her to be animated. Not the peacock eyes through the gauze. Why do women wear veils? He wondered if she knew.

*

The portrait painter's day, which had begun painfully, ended predictably. Francis Pye was shown the studded oak door at Aynescote, and not invited to linger in the porch to admire the Flemish glass. He came straightways up the hill to throw himself on Blackavise. I might have known it, thought that man, I am doomed to every stranger in the county treading a path to my door.

"At least thou art no Godson, 'tis all I can say for you," he told the hangdog apparition, "Ginger, fetch those bags up. If you're minded to try any of your urchin tricks, I'll have him paint thee."

Ginger showed his buck teeth cheerily and set about unbuckling the gear.

"I was prepared to offer to paint thee, Blackavise," complained the artist, "but now I see I'm held up as a threat to that boy of yours."

"Indeed you are. I have to subdue him somehow. You'd best set foot indoors. Be civil to Bessie here, and she'll set you a place at table."

"How doth the sick lady, goodwife?" enquired Francis Pye so civilly that Bessie warmed toward him. Blackavise, watching the gallows-thin young man attend to her reply, saw he was not aping manners but spoke with concern. Why the Almighty had not united feeling with talent, he could not imagine. He supposed it was the same in most marriages.

"I don't take kindly to this Master Gerard of thine, Blackavise," Pye offered in a tone of dissatisfaction next day, "Hold still. Now this is one of my better achievements, or it might be if you don't hop up and down."

"It is not an achievement. You are but standing me sideways against a leaf of paper, and running that stick of charcoal round my shadow. And Master Gerard is not mine. Understand? Not mine. Not even his little finger."

"'Tis an achievement. 'Tis your likeness in just the one line. You may now look."

"Well of course 'tis my likeness. 'Tis a mere copy of the cast I threw."

"I knew you'd agree with me. And 'tis a simple trick, I can't think why more people do not know it. 'Tis the only catch of likeness I know I can rely on."

"Thou art a charlatan, Pye."

"Probably; but a man must live, and what else could I make shift at?" he sighed, but with satisfaction, and brandished the outline drawing at its subject, who bent his attention upon it.

"That's possibly me," he conceded. "Why on earth could you not do one of these for Lacey, string him along a little? So you could work up to a portrait, please him at the outset?"

"He hasn't your ability to be pleased if he isn't flattered."

"So this effort of yours of me is an insult, and I too dense to realise?"

"Nay, 'tis factually accurate, as you have to admit. But Lacey ever wanted a firmer chin, and a more melancholic eye; the more he complained, the harder I found it. His chin is not firm, nor his eye melancholic."

"You're an observer."

"That's my talent. The difficulty is in setting it down."

"By whatever means, you've outlined me. I'll buy it, if thy fee be no more than a groat." The charcoal line outlined the flourish of hair upstanding from his brow, his straight nose, firm mouth, strong chin. The charcoal tailed away into Pye's approximation of neck linen. John was surprised to recognise something of himself.

"'Tis for my bed and board," Francis offered, "I could but offer small change."

"Then call it thy lodging. I'll throw my small change at you."

"This is better than Aynescote," responded Pye to this, and made a mock bow to Blackavise. "Done."

"My wits must be softer than I thought, to take thee in."

"Pity about Lacey's wife, don't you think? I would have liked a try at her likeness."

"I couldn't work out why Lacey didn't want her

captured. She is his ornament. As such she should have her portrait hung in a gilded frame on his wall."

"But not portrayed by me. Alas, I have not got my hire these two attempts now."

"Are you for another destination?   Another commission?"

"I would linger in these parts a day or two," said Pye, suddenly interested in the polish of his boot toes, "if you'd have me here."

"I'll not throw thee forth for a day or two, or whatever," Blackavise reassured him, guessing the young man had no commissions left and preferred not to admit it. "I've a weakness for company now Black House has grown so sad, and I can't have the Laceys tiring of my company from over-use. Stay, do. Upstairs there's a folio or two we might look over together, which my godmother hath put by. I haven't looked, but something might interest thee."

"Aren't you for Aynescote today?"

He might have been, Gerard being gone, but there would be no sittings to give him *carte blanche* to have Mary Florida to himself. "I have the physician upstairs whilst you have been fiddling with shadows. Is that not he coming down? I wish to hear his opinion."

Master Goodman came pattering downstairs, preceded by one of the tabby cats. In his drab clothes he was a moulting blackbird, but bright eyed. "My word, sir, she is blessed with a fighting spirit and a strong heart. Firstly, I thought she would but last the se'nnight. Yet here she is, steady." He put down his leathern bag and hopped to the fireplace, where he stood with his hands behind his back, reflecting on his patient. Blackavise, his charcoal picture forgotten, cast the drawing from him and took two leaps forward: "D'you mean she's reviving?"

"Oh dear me, no," cried Goodman, distressed at having given false hope, "she cannot last, 'tis but temporary."

"By the good Lord," sighed Blackavise, "I keep hoping like a fool."

"I hear the scavengers have started gathering," whispered the doctor, "the pair roosting at the Tuns, for instance."

"And there's Corrydene," Blackavise pointed out, "high on his dung heap."

"Come, come," reasoned Goodman, "he's one of my best patients, never in health, never in spirits. I keep a leech jar to hand especially for him."

"Don't go advocating such for me, that's all."

"I'd hesitate, sir, you appear back to strength, all the better for your sojourn here at Black House. A comfort, I believe, to Mistress Blackavise, she was fretful, distressed, until you came. She is now in better peace of mind."

"Do you really think so?" asked John, touched.

"I do. Now I must get me gone, trusting I fare better leaving than I did coming up. What a to-do, to reach thee!"

"How so?" asked Blackavise, settling his linen cuffs.

Goodman, flapping into his cloak, paused and gave a beady gleam of surprise. "Did you not get the tidings? The roads are all clogged up round town and 'tis but my bag of potions let me through. The soldiery are crawling in and out again. Spymaster's taken at last."

"No! How?"

"They questioned wayfarers, I believe, found one looked too pale. The crew he was keeping company with saw all was up, and disowned him."

Francis Pye, quiet among his sketches and folders, dropped a quill and penknife. A jolt of fear sent back frosty winter.

"Well, in that case, if you've troubled to journey here despite the soldiery poking about, let me ride back with thee?"

"Nay, Blackavise, they've smelt me once, they'll not interfere, 'tis some accomplice they've wind of. They were beating out a barn of straw when last I glimpsed them, chasing after their great rat. They'd taken farmer

Simpson's fancy riding horse his lady set store by, what a wailing."

"Damnation. And it has been so quiet lately. I'll for Aynescote and warn them. Lacey hath a fine horse to keep safe, he'll not want Parliament's men a-raking through his coals."

"No he won't," echoed Francis Pye, the play-actor.

John clattered to the door with the doctor, calling Ginger to fetch Hetty. "Now don't argue, I'll see thee to Aynescote gate. You've come up alone, and I'll prospect with thee as far as you wish."

The ewe-necked nag and the chestnut mare with her neat hooves set off with their larger and smaller masters, and as they came within sight of Aynescote's roofs in the changing light of opal clouds, a beggar with a limp came toiling up the slope and waylaid them. Cramming a crutch under one arm and balancing on his better leg, the beggar took a scrap of paper from his sleeve to hand it firmly to John Blackavise. The man stood there ingratiatingly, his palm up, in the universal gesture. Blackavise fumbled for a ha'penny, tossed it, while the creature found an extra leg to step and catch the coin before he legged it down the hill.

The title nailed John's angered eye to the paper in his hand. THE BASTARD it announced, in capital letters. He tore the scrap apart, dabs of broken wax falling to the grass. Four words sprang at him in sloping loops, with his name underlined: 'Get thee gone, Blackavise'. He read this in the saddle astride Hetty, while the little doctor looked askance. Then he tap-tapped the paper on his tautly muscled thigh.

"What do you do, sir doctor, when someone tells you go hang?" asked John Blackavise quietly.

"I prescribe them something drastic," answered he, "and see they take it."

"I took you for a good fellow! I think you have it admirably." All I have to do, thought John, is identify the patient.

Chapter VII

"Amos! Have a look out for Thunderer," Blackavise hailed the stableman across the cobbled yard, "he's too handsome a bit of horseflesh to be swept up by common troopers. Had you not heard? There's a search on for a wanted man. I know his nose isn't precisely on show over his box door, but if anyone got in his yard and saw him there would be merry hell."

"Master Lacey doan' like snoopers," Amos glared at Blackavise, who felt irritated to be lumped together with all and sundry Amos did not like, Parliament troopers not least. He turned on his heel and the flagstones rang as he strode forth. Had Amos been receptive, he would have suggested that the shut-up yard with the big horse in it would be overlooked quite easily if Amos stacked a steaming heap of dung against the studded door and shoved a fork in it, to indicate there was no way through in use. He'd best find Lacey to alert him. He thrust open the little gate which led back into the cabbage patch garden, the easiest way to get to the terrace and the house. These courtyards were a maze. This was not the gate he was looking for, but instead he'd stumbled upon a cobbled path, three steps down. Surprised to have arrived in the sunken herb garden, in all its disarray, he discovered Mary Florida, not in the least overgrown, arrayed at the centre of a spreading fancy rose and silver gown.

"I thought I'd come the wrong way," he greeted, hatting, "but mayhap I came the right way. If I don't intrude?" He tucked his deep-cuffed gloves into his belt and enquired further with his direct glance, wondering why she was so pale today. But even so, that gown's a colour for her. Lacey must find a painter who can catch her in that shade to do justice to her beauty.

"Whoever thought of calling a handful of stiffened bits of taffety tied together with ribbon, a sleeve?" he upbraided her, "are there not draughts?"

"You will next suggest standing me in a field, to scare off the crows."

"No, not I, unless that's a metaphor for black Puritan dress. How do you, lady? Why for out here? I fear you will not be warm enough with those draughts."

"There's a peep of sun coming, and I have my shawl.

132

Where have you been? Aeneas hath been starved of entertainment, so he has been reduced to unpacking more of the cases we brought, with Piers and Jesse. I am fled the roars and the shoutings."

"Oh, I have been but getting my likeness took, 'tis all the rage, this week."

"Oh no, Pye didn't come to you?"

"He did; I'm not hard done by, he's harmless." The play-actor would have been heartened to hear him. "The comedy is that he hath produced a likeness I think I recognise. Amazing, the unfairness of it, as I am not paying him to do it."

She smiled, serene as a painting herself. Why did he want more? Mayhap she did not shriek or throw things to express herself; and he allowed himself to be soothed by Mary Florida's calm because he had been tormented by that letter. 'Get thee gone, Blackavise'. The bastard's feelings were raw again. The sun slid from behind the mobile clouds, catching silver highlights upon the braid on her sleeves, while the rose-coloured skirts swelled in a little breeze and subsided at the curve of her secret thigh. Blackavise sighed, stimulated. He ought to get to the house straightaway and alert Aeneas that Amos could do with Jesse out there to disguise the entrance to Thunderer's yard. Aeneas should keep an eye on his household for a day or two whilst the chase pelted round the county. Aeneas had shunned the manly, harsh few years of the King's war, and was as unprepared as a babe for its consequences and aftermath. It would have done him good, thought Blackavise, to have a spymaster under his flagstones at Aynescote for a night or two. That way men younger than Aeneas grew up. He thanked God no spymaster hid under Mary Florida's floor to implicate her, but he was still shocked that Smith had survived in his Black House fastness only to be taken days later; that brought risks home.

"I received this," he said, and bravado had him, to pull the folded half sheet of paper from his sleeve and show it to her. "It seems we campaigners have to be afraid of goblins."

"It can't be anything serious, not from goblins," she said, glancing up at him before unfolding the paper and reading its message aloud.

'The Bastard' written there struck her with a shock, as it already had struck him. "Get thee gone," she read aloud, alarmed, her tone changing. "This is ugly. You must take heed. Who could have penned it? We talked of the other godsons, but which one is driven to injure thee? Even to trying to second the blow?"

"I do not think they intend to give me a round of cheers, no."

"How many are there? There's the old misery at Overhill, the cross man and the old dear who presented himself here by accident looking for Black House."

"One attempt, I tell myself, was explicable. Two attempts counting this warning makes me want an explanation, and a trip to the local Justice of the Peace, with the perpetrator. Or I suppose I would, in peacetime. After what I've seen on the field of conflict it seems too petty a matter to make todo over."

"Stop reasoning about the wider world. 'Tis aimed at thee. You dare not brush it aside. You stand between an enemy's ambition to inherit your Godparent's fortune. That's the sum of it."

"So if one of them desires it, which one?"

"I don't believe it can be this Gerard, the crosspatch. He sounds too unguarded, because an ill-wisher would cloak it better." She sat up so her skirts drew back, showing the neat brown mice of buckled shoes. "Are there more godsons besides you? Is three the total of the species?"

Blackavise recalled Pettijohn's list. "I saw the names at the lawyer's. I was first, Flynn last upon it; yes Corrydene the misery, Radlett. And Lyons, and someone Prigg, no – Pragg."

"And where are those two?"

John grimaced. "I've no notion."

"Are they all men, these godsons?"

"They have been, thus far."

"She must have wanted sons."

He experienced a pang of feeling towards his godmother. "Yes. And why did those she chose sever from her? Damnation, It was over me being a disgrace, it was my base origins."

"A poor reason."

"Thank you, lady," he said, and smiled the charmed smile, which gave her pain anew. Pain proves I live and breathe, registered Mary Florida inwardly, willing courage to withstand it; worse, wanting more. She studied his stern expression from beneath half lowered eyelashes as he spoke.

"I had kept fool hope going. But the physician told me this morning that she's sinking and will die. I thought she'd rally. I clung to that. She'd been so strong," he admitted.

"Poor lady."

"I'm a fool; hope is false."

Skirts twitched, the mice retreated. Mary Florida became earnest that he would pay attention to her. It was as if the frivolous colours she was wearing darkened with the sombre tone when she spoke.

"The harm is likely to drop upon thee before thy godmother gives up the ghost. Who else spoke to the

136

doctor? Does any godchild know how very ill she is?"

"They've only heard what I've told them. Over-cheerful, now I think it over."

"Maybe they plan to get thee hence while she still hath the strength to put her signature to a new will?"

"They might not need to go to such lengths," he brooded, "it may fall that she hath left a sequence of possible inheritors: first me, then Pragg, or Corrydene, or whomsoever. Any one of them could do me down in favour of the next on the list, who then walks off with treasure." Speculating further, his mind added up her acreage including Black House itself; there were tenancies, her jewellery, the Italian sideboard, acquired as a consequence of her shrewd father's trading interests here and over sea.

"You are so near the truth," she stressed, "you must take heed, you must take care. What's to stop these godsons arranging matters amongst themselves? First they had you thrown in that ditch, now they've sent you another warning. This is gathering upon you."

"So we need to know who inherits after me." But he had included her in his private life by uttering familiar 'we'. "Forgive me. I should never have spoken to you, lady, in such a way regarding what is my own *imbroglio*; I have been too long in the company of rough cavalrymen. This problem is solely mine to unknot."

"Don't be embroiled on your own," he thought she said. He would have taken her hand to thank her, had she not shaken her head no, not to do so.

That night he took six guineas off Aeneas at cardplay, and then beat him at chess, for Aeneas did not concentrate. The silence necessary for the death of kings and bishops was too still, somehow; a hooded silence, such as broods checkmate, or events. Aeneas, smiling still, was not pleased to be beaten. Perhaps he stood in need of newer company than Blackavise, who saw his host treated him so familiarly as to sit down before the chequered board with his lovelock still in a curl paper. At his elbow were the chess pieces, and. beside him a flagon, glasses and suckets on a silver dish, variously expressing the different notes of their reflective surfaces. The ruby goblets of wine carried bright candle pinpoints, whereas the cushions of little suckets were duller stained-glass pink in their filigree dish. In the tail of John's eye he was aware of Mary Florida sewing, her skirts crinkling as if petals from a blown rose. She formed the central pool of colour in the room. Twilight cast a wash of inky watercolour behind the mullions.

Aeneas, face dimmed above the wings of his neck linen and the little white twist of curl paper, was for calling for another candle and for persuading Blackavise to set up the pieces anew and make their one game into best of three.

"I had the beating of cousin Tom," complained Aeneas, refilling his glass.

Only because he let you beat him, thought Mary Florida, stabbing her embroidery.

Blackavise, expression hidden by the shadows, thought cousin Tom must have been a very poor player. He was in the act of scraping back his chair to announce he was for home, when the servant Piers popped his head round the door and they all turned round in one direction, as if to applaud a shot of old King Harry's at real tennis.

"There's a lot o' men moving up the wood, sir," said Piers, in the tone of a lesser monk announcing Doomsday to the Abbot whilst implying it was none of his responsibility.

Aeneas, unseasoned by the hundred crises of Blackavise's campaigning, shot to his feet and looked urgently out of the window. Almost simultaneously a loud banging on the big oak door was heard.

"Stay here," Blackavise said to Mary Florida.

Aeneas knocked over a glass on the edge of the table to punctuate the sudden silence with the splatter and ticking of drips.

"They've no right to come in," he said in a strained

voice, "have they? I won't have them in."

"Best let them have a look," John said quietly, "you've naught to hide here." My hat, he thought, I'd wear his wild eye if this was the door of Black House and I yet had spymaster Smith under my floor. At least I know there's no wanted man at home now to incriminate me.

"I won't have pilferers in."

The banging recommenced. Blackavise saw there was real danger of having the door stove in. "I'll see to this, by your leave," quoth he, and he strode out to speak to the captain he expected to find in charge.

Jesse and Piers obeyed him, the habit of command extended to this petty civilian interchange, and they drew the bolt, stood back, and Blackavise himself flung open the portal. Outside, the usual crowd of buff-coats, hung about with ammunition bandoliers and priming flasks and what-not, bristled at him; to his authoritarian cry of "What's all this? What's afoot?" the beardless boys at the front yielded and their officer, a decent well-set-up man of five-and-thirty, stepped up.

"Sorry to trouble your household, sir; but we needs must take a look at house and outbuildings."

"On what course, prithee," barked Blackavise, unintimidated, hoping to startle information out of the man.

"There'll be no trouble, I give my word; we chase a traitor."

Poor Smith, had he talked? If so, who had he implicated, now running away, striped with fear? Blackavise could not stop them, lacking his stout boys of what seemed a long time ago to set about their Parliamentarian ears and drub them. He decided it would be better for Aynescote to allow a search, seeing as Aeneas Lacey had nothing to hide. The officer looked in full control and would surely see there would be no looting.

"Carry on, then," said Blackavise sternly, "but I will accompany you, by your leave."

Where was Aeneas? He glanced over his shoulder, expecting the master of the household to come up with him and that they would go round together. Perhaps he had gone back to protect Mary Florida? The searchers were detailed, half to search the house, half to grope round the buildings with a lantern. Blackavise, thinking there would be more searching within doors, and worried for the safety of Aynescote's lady, accompanied the captain in charge back into the room where he had left her. She was alone. Where the devil was Aeneas? It was too late to go and shovel coin into the garden plot under the cabbages; what had he done with himself? Whilst Mary Florida flinched, the half-dozen buff coats ran through the room like a tide. Blackavise told Jesse and Piers to look to their mistress, assuring himself she was unmolested, was about to set toe to follow the soldiers 'progress, when everyone was pinned still by the crack of a pistol shot.

That's serious, that's trouble. There were shouts, there was a noise of rushing feet beyond the windowpanes and the lantern passed like a firefly, further off. The six men who had been searching the house turned and stampeded through the door they had entered by, and as Blackavise ran with them, then there was another shot, with a different discharge.

In the black darkness now obtaining, the maze of courtyards, the brew house, the laundry, the stables, echoed with footfalls and confusion. Blackavise put his eye cautiously round the corner of the courtyard wall. The first buff coats had got ahead of the party from the house and now collided with the rest, who thus surprised, drew their weapons, and for a moment the racket of engaged blades worthy of the sound of kettle-mending rang out, sharpened by the acoustic of the walls. Oversized shadows stalked the stonework and heaved and pitched as the lantern man got buffeted, the furious officer intervened, and the melee died. A shamefaced pair sheathed their swords with scraping sounds; someone rushed up, quoth it was he who had fired off one shot, and urgently swore it was at the quarry they sought. They regrouped, and chased away, leaving Blackavise behind them in the shadow.

In the house Mary Florida heard those shots, and the fluff at the back of her neck crawled with terror. She received a presentiment that grasped her; simple, odd, and implacable. Compelled to leave the parlour's false security, she sped across the library's hollow boards, and at the door to the outer world took both hands to the big key and let herself out onto the terrace. The key dropped, the door banged, and she stood panting with fear against the house wall. For her life she could not have named what assailed her. She pressed her skirts close to her flanks, still as a statue, ears straining to hear the soldiers chasing up the hill, into the trees, away. Then she ran like a greyhound with her skirts held tightly in her hands, down three shallow steps to the flagstones and into the sunken garden. It was now so dark that the spears of new scented growth in the thicket of weeds and tangles tore at her ankles. Twice she blundered into their trips and clutches, then fell on one knee overstepping the brush of rosemary across the path. She raised herself like a runner on fingertips, took two strides forwards, and fell over a great, warm obstruction. Her hands were on a smooth coat of hair which clothed a dead horse. Gasping, Mary Florida recoiled, gorge rising. The moon, insensitive, obliged from the clouds, and she knew it had to be Thunderer. A stilled, mighty heap, his rounded hindquarters, the length of his curving spine, withers, neck so sleek and substantial, the mane like his long hair was inanimate, pathetic. Her tears rolled, she reached forward half blinded crying, to pat his poor head. Then she saw worse. She bent, felt, and rose with gloves of blood. Her scream, bright as a bolt of lightning, rent the night. For the first time she knew an animal's fear and crisis. Sleeves and ribbons, even petticoats, were surface tissue, for beneath them all, at the most primitive level, a pounding heart revealed who and what she was.

John Blackavise, the household behind him, came pelting out. When he saw her, he stopped in his tracks. For a moment it slapped him into stillness, as if he had been cast into stone. Had she suddenly appeared naked before him, she could not have made a greater impression. She was feral, she was magnetic. Fear and shock had elevated Mary Florida to her vivid and essential nature. Every veil had been stripped away, the dreaminess, the gauzes of politeness and courtesy. Nothing remained save the flimsy protection of her silk skirts.

John took in the ghastly circumstances. He trod firmly up to her and took her shivering arm above the blood; he motioned that he would lead her away. He said in her ear, "My dear."

"No," she said, "no," repeating herself. Whiter than moonlight, rooted to the cold paving, she could not move but stood quivering, coiled, elemental, holding the world at bay. He thought she even smelled different, as if she had become a rare, wild animal.

"He shot Thunderer," she whispered, "he blew out his brains."

John not understanding tried to deal with practicalities. "Amos, bring a tarpaulin, cover the poor beast," he began to say, and then he, as had Mary Florida, took one more step, and discovered what had happened next. The man who shot Thunderer had alerted the searching soldiers, and one had clear sight of him running away. Only yards from Thunderer Aeneas Lacey had suffered the same fate as the horse.

Blackavise, much later, took Hetty back up the wood again to check all was well at Black House and his charges there. His godmother was restless in what passed for sleep. He bent his knee and touched her hand. The soldiers had passed by, looked in the barn and rattled round the outbuildings, said Bessie; they'd frightened off Master Pye, seemingly – he'd disappeared.

"I've no time for that now," Blackavise told her,

grim faced, "I must get me back to Aynescote. Have Ginger stay with you. Put the bar up behind me when you lock me out." That would have to suffice. He would have to stay overnight in Aynescote, he could not abandon Mary Florida in such circumstances. His poor godmother must soldier on this midnight without his protection. God send that The Event did not come for her without his being there to comfort her at its pearly gate. Could he, remotely, comfort Mary Florida? He would not fool himself. But he was her only human neighbour who could breathe and be there, and he felt he must perform the responsibilities until her relatives, if any, came. It was a long night, and he sat up on the upstairs landing upon the supremely uncomfortable arrangement of two chairs he had selected for himself. That way he was able to send the stunned servants, talking behind their hands, fearful for their futures, to bed eventually, after this night which had led to the corpse of their master being laid out upon the long dining table.

By then the first bird was calling from the woods. The thought assailed him that he would not see Mary Florida in her coloured clothes again, but in widow's sable black. What an imbecile Lacey had been not to let the noble stallion loose and take his chance in the woods, and catch him later? Why, why, had he himself not taken Amos by the scruff and made him pile dung against that yard doorway? Why did Aeneas have to be so jumpy, so panic-stricken? He, John Blackavise, a cavalryman to his bootstraps, who had looked after his horses before his men, felt he had failed by not treating Thunderer as any horse would have been treated under his command. These Parliamentary soldiers hadn't matched his own for thoroughness. He uncrossed a stiff leg and kicked the second chair clear of his feet, trying not to make a clatter. Behind the panelled door with the pediment, was an antechamber, with Dorcas on a pallet bed; beyond that again, shipwrecked on uncharted seas, was Mary Florida, in what state he would not like to name. He'd had the corpse carried in, covered over, and laid out temporarily in the empty dining room. Dorcas might know some beldame to lay out the body in the morning. The poor horse lay still in the sunken garden with the tarpaulin hiding the wreck of his head. How brainless to shoot him, how cruel; and the sound of that shot had forced the soldier to fire at the man's shadow in the gloom, and decided Lacey's fate. It could only have been malign chance that he hit him. Blackavise knew all about the inaccuracies of pistol shots. Sleepless, he dwelt on the ordeal ahead of the widow and if he could support her in what had to be done. He listed the rector, the coffin-maker, and all those cousins of the dead man. Would they have to be fetched back? He did not relish weepings and wailings, but such things must be. The image of dead Thunderer filled his thoughts. In his soldiering he had to dispatch wounded horses, but he doubted he could have put a pistol to Thunderer in his pride and strength. What sort of man had Aeneas been? Shallow and frivolous; yet, had his wife found qualities in him to give her reason to love him?

All the images of the night were wiped out by the one blistering sight of Mary Florida in the sullied rose and silver, an unprotected leopardess most shockingly spotted with crimson blood. She'd been caught in a trap, had escaped, and still breathed. In one startled glance Blackavise had seen what she had concealed from the gawpers of the world. Heightened awareness of this desirable woman, upon whom the sudden blows of blood and death had called, added to his alertness. Even so he did not analyse the events, for something powerful had been visited upon him. In the dark night flashes of lightning had passed through his mind to light up the confusions of the unforeseen. Tact required him to withdraw his presence from her grieving. Let her shed her tears, wail if she would, leave her to the womenfolk of the household. The evening had begun with the invasion of soldiery upon peaceful Aynescote; gunshots killed first the prize horse in pools of gore, then, as if visited by Nemesis, Aeneas who had slaughtered Thunderer lay dead himself in a puddle of blood. This was no moment for attempting to chuck the new widow under the chin. He oversaw the funeral arrangements, before absenting himself to Black House.

Mary Florida had no family, Aeneas's cousins were not so quick to brave the journey this time and the two who did come to the funeral were not lingerers. He was almost reconciled to old Radlett and Gerard a-visiting daily at Black House, because their irritating presence took his mind away from his desire for Mary Florida. Had a week passed? Or a fortnight? He could no longer trust himself to count the days. Even so he knew it was lovely April, at last.

Mary Florida in torments as she grappled with suppressed relief following the murder of her husband, had herself escorted up the wood by Piers and Jesse. She trotted, neatly side-saddle upon her dapple-grey mare, towards Black House and its master.

Bessie, pop-eyed, pink cheeked above her broad apron, put her disbelieving face round the doorway to Blackavise's parlour. "A lady's coming, sir, wearing a fine hat. She's come round the corner of our courtyard on a grey riding horse, this very minute."

Thank God, he thought, hands outstretched in

welcome, and so she first beheld him in the courtyard of Black House, as he walked forward to lift her down from the dapple grey. She alighted on the brown eggs of the cobbles, read his welcome, and drowned in his eyes.

Blackavise, ignoring the knowing looks between Piers and Jesse, celebrated Mary Florida's arrival by escorting her indoors. He stood aside, quick-eyed, strong as a blacksmith in his coat and white linen and gestured that she precede him into the parlour. The open casement cast sunshine upon the bright colours of his godmother's wayward embroidery on the chairs. A pair of caryatid torsos either side of the carved mantle shelf impassively hoisted their weight of oak. She turned from the handsome Italian sideboard and its display of Delft dishes upon which a quartet of blue horsemen on prancers cavorted, all too aware of the man beside her in these his personal surroundings. Beyond speech, tongue-tied, she wished him to speak, to give her a lead. The door resonated behind them and the latch settled. They were alone with the caryatids and the Delft horsemen. There she stood in the colours of midnight, each full black sleeve caught with a pearl to show white silk beneath; a black ribbon was tied upon her arm. He thought he'd miss the colours, her favoured apricot, frog and rose. But she was no crow. Her chestnut hair was neatly coiled behind, tresses curled against the natural peach of her cheek and offset the mourning darkness. The peach had paled, though.

"I had no idea I would see you this morning," he cried, un-self-aware, delighted, "I am so glad you found you could come up. Will you not take a seat?" Without fuss he plumped up a cushion by the window and watched her subside upon it. "Let me call up a glass of wine." Acting upon the thought, he crossed to the door and called for his best claret, which Bessie had concealed from the godsons. At last he had a guest deserving of his godmother's superior cellar. Mary Florida began to rally among the usual formalities of a first visit.

"I complimented you on the frog colour, so permit me to do so upon this dark cloud you are wearing."

"I had to mourn for my father last year," she told him, "I never thought I should so soon bring the black out from the chest in which it hid. I have come to thank you, for all your kindness."

He paced the room, uncertain how to behave. In that instant the nightmare pictures of hot and furious conflict surrounding the Royalist lost cause, the firearms aiming to kill him, his bloodied comrades, their hopeless bravery, reduced as if he had picked up the wrong end of a perspective glass. All nightmares fled the sunny parlour. In heavenly contrast the lady of his wishful thoughts glanced up from the window seat six feet from him.

"You were kind enough to send me a letter," he murmured, inclining his head and bowing toward the widow.

"That was but half my thanks," she told him, "I wish to tell you face to face."

He was determined not to appear too eager. Nonetheless, he might touch on Mary Florida's present circumstances, given that she trotted her dapple grey up the woodland path to Black House especially to thank him.

"Sorrows come," he said quietly, "and pain. I would not have had you taste them."

She had turned away from him to look out of the window. Had he been clumsy? Would she tell him about her sorrows? Could she? Was she nervous of being alone with him? All of these? Evidently she was not willing to give the confidence he wished for. Instead she spoke of another slant of reality.

"This house hath a living presence, unlike Aynescote which was empty for years, left as a shell. It has no imprint of living. There is the sense here of the many years your godmother hath been enthroned as a queen."

"What? My godparent queening it in a borrowed

crown, and robes of her own embroidery?" The idea
amused him heartily, not least as this was a safe topic to
pursue.

"Well then, what do you think of our good queen's
garden?" he joined her at the casement, pushing the
arrowhead catch, opening it, "I'm afraid our topiary
walk is gone to fuzz and sproutings."

"You lack a man with shears, that's all. I would be
happy to lend you one of my gardeners."

"I accept," he said ruefully, standing back, careful
not to crowd her, "our house lacks men in the garden
wielding clippers. The steward went off to the war and
Bessie's husband with him, neither came home. Our
Ginger's still a eunuch, or so his mother doth fondly
hope. The place might have become a nunnery. So we
have had the regiment of women, until I arrived to ruin
it. The topiary's paid the penalty. No gardeners."

At this unusually gentle tone, she turned, and put up
big eyes to net him.

"I have no idea of what I have to do."

Ah. Of course she has no interest in hedge clippers.
His wits bounced in all directions. Now John, don't go
off half-cock. What's she afraid of? A life without her
husband? To end up as a lonely widow, without
Aeneas's misdirected energy and empty schemes of
grandeur? Or had she discovered the fortune to be a

phantom, that Aeneas had spent it all? Was it all these, and more? He must not get this wrong. He must encompass what she said and what she had not said. Their two presences filled the room, as if pent-up communication rebounded off the walls, hurtling to and fro. All of which hatched and shadowed the live portrait, which was of the Beauty so close to him, unframed but breathing. Claim whatever you want of me, he urged silently, but let me know, that I may perform it. He was beset by her; in the little pause Mary Florida was very aware of the strong gentleman with the flashing eyes.

"You say you're afraid of what you have to do?" he began, forswearing caution, "Why? Gather up little by little. I don't intend to be impolite, or too precipitate, so do not take it so. The history of this house reflects my godmother's long life living here; take a look out of doors, you'll see what I mean. There's the horse of clipped box you see from this window, that my Godmother cannot get right regarding the tail. She hath been at it for years, and no doubt that horse will see her out, me and all the godsons. The horse will swish yet." He seated himself at the other end of the window seat, carefully leaving the width of a casement and a half between her knee and his. "She hath known a life most rare. No father and no spouse to give her instructions.

This is an unusual freedom. She might have been a widow, with that freedom. When you have the means, independence follows. This is heresy, so whisper it not that I've told you; but know it all the same."

Mary Florida wanted him beyond words. The conventions expected of a grieving widow hemmed her in. She was torn by the crisis in the sunken garden where she might have let herself take the support of John Blackavise's strong arm. But the instinctive embrace – any man would have offered it – would have been impersonal at the disaster, and he'd have performed it and let go. Now politenesses and convention held her and, widow as she was, though certainly free as he had suggested, she was chained as never before.

"I spoke that speech a twelvemonth too soon," he thought, "too forthright, it is my downfall." But he would lighten it by touching on the latest gossip. "Francis Pye hath fled me," he tried, "I spoiled his sense of failure, I recognised my likeness. He can't have been reconciled to improvement."

The lighter voice was easier for Mary Florida. She took up his tone. "Are you sure 'twas improvement? Or is it that you are thicker skinned than other sitters?"

"He did but run a charcoal round my shadow. I could recognise it."

"Why did he vanish?"

"No notion. But I remember telling him, with his folders and materials, he was vouched for on the road; he is as proclaimed as is a snail by his shell."

"I wonder if he is aware of that?"

"Whatever do you suggest?"

"Only a thought," Mary Florida shrugged, "because he was no catcher of likenesses."

"That's incompetence, not King Charles's peeper at keyholes."

"But he's gone from house to house, of course he has, and only at the last two do we know he's been truly painting. Or attempting to paint. He's travelled about, freely, just as you point out." She shrugged.

"Yea and nay, for I know well I relied on all manner of tuppenny spies, watercress dames, hobbledehoy boys, whoever I could use. I'd have taken knowledge from the rooks in the hedge, if they'd count the enemy's ordnance and troops for me. Little spies, anyone I could recruit to do it. The deeper matters had deeper disguises. Almighty God, was Pye doing this? Was he living a double life, his subterfuge inept portrait taking?"

"Would you think him capable of double dealing?"

"That's unanswerable," he declared.

There, she was natural again. Praise be. But how could she bear to live in the soulless house of Aynescote

after the events of the past few days? The house had
been invaded by soldiers, Aeneas had shot the stallion,
and as if in retribution had himself been felled. How
could she want to remain? Yet there'd be a pause, a
breathing space. It would be unseemly to be at the
packing cases straight off. She must sit still and be seen
to grieve, sad Niobe holding a damp kerchief to her eye.
Was she grieving? She was pale. He couldn't know.
But her extremes of fright and shock had splashed a new
set of stars on the night, which he, a navigator, had to
learn without a book. Try and be delicate, Johnny. Say
no more. Ask her to come again. Tomorrow. Every
day. Keep her mind from thoughts of packing cases.

So Black House changed places with Aynescote.
The open house of Aeneas Lacey lapsed, as had the
solicitude of its first visitors after the tragedy. Those
innocently gawping at the new man, the new show,
shrank back upon the tidings of what had happened.
Most felt so short an acquaintance had absolved them
from more than a note to the widow. Had Aynescote's
brief candle been the light to a mirage? The years of
neglect would revert to the dull old days, the memory of
each neighbouring gentry's single visit settling over its
chimney pots again.

Meanwhile, don't let's turn our thoughts that way,
nor our footfall, in case that ill-luck touches us. But

Black House was braver, had been a happy home far
longer, and against its southerly walls the gillyflowers
were ready. Its mistress had no wish to leave. There
she lay, shrunken, inanimate, as if she could neither die
nor stay. But she was peaceful, and the sun chased dust
motes along its rays in her chamber. I no more would
want to die and leave than she does, thought John; she
who held court here and stood at the font to the odd
clutch of Gerard, Radlett, Corrydene and me. But damn
it, the frustration of coming here too late to ask her the
simple question: "Why these particular mewlers and
pukers? And why did everyone but me run away?"

He gagged on the mystery, yet again. He didn't care
if she hadn't left him fourpence in the will, although he
accepted that she must have done, or was assumed to
have done so, hence the threats. But who did know, for
certain? The lawyer wouldn't tell secrets. Did Gerard
and Radlett know each other's thoughts? Was old
Corrydene isolated without consulting these two? Mary
Florida had jogged his memory by mentioning the other
names. When all this had died down, he'd better make
enquiries about Pragg and Lyons. Everything seemed
unreal while he made his imprint on the counterpane and
enclosed the old lady's knotted fingers in his hand. She
had ruled the roost these many good many years; the
jolly big woman, striding about, elbows working; the

picture of energy. He thought about the plump girl who was teased and mocked, who grew to hold her place in society. He forgot the old lady as Mary Florida occupied his inner eye, scented, breathing, desirable. You do not say 'Be mine' to the widow a fortnight after the funeral. You do not. Am I mad? Perhaps merely deranged since that dreadful night rent asunder her veil of concealment. How had she lived, with Aeneas? How had she kept the burning brand of herself, with fires, damped down? What had she been, when alone with him? What might she be, with him? Torments claimed him, and yet barbs of that nature were sweet. Had he been poetical he might have recognised seventeen had come back to get at him, like a comet's long journey away and back brandishing its silver tail, but he wasn't doing that, not then. He was imagining smoothing her peach and ivory hide.

Chapter VIII

While John Blackavise's hopes were wrapped up in Black House, Francis Pye was flushed out of the priest's hole up at Winnows, the house of a secretly papist family of a century back. That nest had been cleared out then, and a sad to-do followed, with the family laid low, and no cuckoo in the cavity for many a year, until the nephews who inherited ran a safe house for Royalist agents. A string of night travellers knew the knock to give at the little gate, able to find rest and relief on the way they trod between Heaven and Hades. It was mere ill-luck that the searching soldiers knocked where the cavity sounded. Only an inch or two gave that hollow note, and others had missed it altogether. But there might have been a tip-off. This time the searchers went inch-by-inch. And by then Smith was dead. Pye escaped by the further exit. They took his folders and the leathern bag with his equipment, but he had sloughed them off, as does the snake his skin. He ran by luck round the Winnows back wall and came upon the officer's horse standing with his near fore shoe off, waiting for a trooper to take him to be shod. Pye put leg astride and whacked him and kicked him and got more speed out of the three-shoed animal than the ribby old jade had thought he had left in him. And they chased him. He had a head start, but his hoof prints were easy to follow. He had no choice of direction, as he had to avoid the row of troop horses hitched under the overhang of Winnows's stable roof. Therefore Pye found no option other than to bolt back the way he wished to avoid, but as he put heels vigorously to ribs, the wind whistled in his ears and he told himself, 'What fox hath not had to double back when earths get stopped, but goes snug to ground in the end?'.

Horse breathing hard, man breathing hard, they came flat out over the ford at the Three Tuns, spraying ducks with mud and splash. At the crossroads Pye wrenched the horse's head round, desperate to avoid implicating Black House where he'd been given shelter, turned left, tried a byway, lost his pursuers in the wood. Thus it was he went flogging and urging round the perimeter wall of Aynescote itself, at which point the poor beast went dead lame beneath him. Reduced from a dash to a hobble in a matter of yards, Pye flung himself loose-limbed as a puppet to the ground. He bodily pushed the horse into the further coppice woodland, shoved and heaved, hands to hindquarters, risking a kick. Got the beast under the canopy of new leaf, and himself, a landmark yet, stranded on the edge of the track with the sound of hooves drumming and a hoarse cry faint behind him, but coming fast.

Self-preservation got him to Aynescote's wall where years of neglect gave a stepladder of broken stones where he leapt up and over into the curled bronze pennies of beechleaf drift. In a stagger he was out of the hollow where they had collected. No time to look back under the beech trees, but he heard them still coming. He was hidden by the lettuce-green canopy of spring, running doubled up, breath roaring. Then he had sped to the end of the trees where the wall was low, and if he did not get himself concealed, he'd be seen. Not I, he told himself. I've not been bred to die stranded, like a flounder. The only alternative is the house. Why hadn't this approach led to the maze of courtyards t'other side? Here he was like a flagpole with the flag up, announcing his presence to all the Parliament men. He was outside the line of mullioned windows where the Laceys and their company dined – journeymen painters, below the salt. He had run out of time. Here came the scrunch of hooves on Aynescote's front gravel. He could hear an order being given. They'd be round here, upon him. He urgently banged on the window.

Mary Florida within recognised fear when she saw it. She read extremity on Francis Pye's gargoyle-face, gasping for breath, limp hair flapping, ribs heaving. She opened the window, and so eager was he to avail himself of it that she nearly added a black eye to his distractions with the edge of the casement.

"For my life, hide me."

She looked round as if for mouseholes. An immense table without benefit of hangings; the dozen chairs standing back at the linen-fold, the six stools the same, a pair of court cupboards, the painted cut-out figure of the lady fulfilling its destiny as a wallflower. It was like seeking concealment when forest leaves shed in winter. Pye had no idea why Mary Florida was clothed in the black of ravens, but lacked either information or time to make any sort of tactful enquiry. There no time for questions, the hourglass was dropping its last grains. Outside, there were demands, protests, and the loud tread of boot heels. Mary Florida blenched. Pye threw himself at the right-hand door and she rushed after him.

"No, no! 'Tis a blind alley!"

That way led to her little parlour with her tambour frame and daybed with its barley-sugar twists. Now they had bolted into the same hole and were cornered.

"You were never a painter. You were nothing but a deceiver! Now the buff coats will take you for a spy." Courage wrestled with disaster. She gestured at him. "Cast you down on the floor, make yourself small," Mary Florida pummelled her fists on his shoulder, forcing him under the daybed. How could such a beanpole get small? Even as he doubled himself up like the folds of best pastry, chin to knees under the cane work, she could hear the tramp of boots. The daybed was placed on the diagonal across the corner of the parlour. She reached for the tambour-frame, threw open the lid of the sewing-box by her elbow, and was twitching her skirts to waterfall over the hiding man as the latch sprang. A deferential officer came through in a rush, followed at his back by a clutch of buff-coats all hot and steaming from their galloping and then their running noisily through her house of Aynescote. Behind them she glimpsed poor Dorcas, dismayed, mouth open. Her mistress attempted a reproving cold eye to quell their advance. It halted the tow-haired bullock leading the charge

"Madam, I apologise: my orders are to catch a miscreant, and we've run him close. So close, that we intend to do you a favour and make sure your house and grounds do not hide the man."

Why wasn't he the captain from the night Aeneas met his disaster? That man would have been sorry for me, he wouldn't have insisted he looked close. But Dorcas, like a terrier at the back of the room, was worrying at him for Mary Florida's sake. The broad-shouldered young man must have heard something of what happened here, for she saw him glance at her mourning clothes.

"You leave her be," squawked Dorcas loyally, and her mistress tried to look as helpless and pathetic as possible. Repercussions from the botched work at Aynescote a fortnight back had been sufficient to stop this fellow from any roughness. For a moment he stood and looked at her, and she, big eyed, looked back, her pulse striking louder than the church clock.

"I am so sorry, madam," said the officer, discomfited by his duty," I must ask you to rise so my men can check the room. Then I will leave you in peace."

O God, send me a good strong lie.

The Almighty heard her plea. Mary Florida had no need to pretend she was pale. There she sat with her feet up, skirts a black thundercloud falling to the floor. She did not rise.

"Sir," said she, "I have been widowed but a fortnight, and I am constrained as you see. It is not sorrow alone that keeps me prone, but the hopes that I am with child, for my physician fears I may miscarry."

Now shift me, thought Mary Florida palpitating. Don't you dare. Not after what happened to Aeneas. This officer may be a husband and father.

"Your pardon, lady."

She never heard what else he said, except the rushing of relief in her ears.

When Blackavise got hold of the rumour (via Ginger, a passing pedlar and three of the soldiers who had been at the house), he was unhorsed from the decorous palfrey he had allowed his thoughts to ride these last few days; that horse of thoughts shied and dug its feet in, allowing Blackavise's spirit to hurtle through the air and crash to the ground. It trod him and kicked him as painfully as if there were an actual beast. Nothing, but nothing, was so excluding as discovering the lady of his urgent dreams was with child by another. The very act, the mattress dance, the idea of her smiling beneath a man wearing a curl paper. Husband, snorted John Blackavise, of course he enjoyed her. Twice nightly, were I he. Why didn't I think? Aah, he cried to himself in a great knot, and quit his godmother's sickroom because he had begun to march up and down like the army again and had unquietened her. Already she had moaned and shifted. Calling for Bessie, he fled down the stairs. What a horse of false colours hope was. But he was expected at Aynescote. He could not go. Was it her fault? No, no. The hair shirt of clopping down to Aynescote on Hetty held no appeal. But he was not the sort of man who cancelled with a headache. If men set on him and left him for dead, he arrived nonetheless, feet first, carried in. What had she done to him? Tormented with a mind's-eye of Mary Florida swelling with her tiny waist grown like a poppyhead, all in her black-rose clothes, he got him as far as her stable gateway and reeled off Hetty still daft with the news. As he set foot to paving, he noticed the fast-kept gate to the yard which had housed Thunderer was an eyebeam ajar. The sun had painted an unusual perpendicular stripe there, down the woodwork; had it been a dull noontide, Blackavise would not have noticed. The stripe broadened, and Francis Pye wandered out to him, bright as day.

"Where've you been?" began Blackavise, but his slow wits overtook his speech, "my God, you haven't implicated her?"

"Nay, for all we had a close shave."

She mustn't have frights! Why had this idiot chosen her house for sanctuary? He must get him gone, if need be with the Blackavise hand on his collar.

"How is she?"

"O, a mite pale. But the searchers didn't touch her.

She saved my skin most neatly, has she told you?"

"No," said John forbiddingly, "I've yet to see her."

"Look, I must get me away this time. I don't want any more scuttling. I'm for France. Which means, first the coast, then the tide. And, I lack the means to pay my passage."

"I'll pay," glared Blackavise, "you deceived me."

"Damn it, man, I meant to."

This was fair comment. That he was scratchy this morning was not Pye's fault, and it was irrational to blame the lawful, dead husband. Pye had said that Mary Florida looked pale. O God, prayed Blackavise, let the child not kill her. He knew then he could not bear to see her, and instead focused his eyes on the string-locks and hangdog look of the spy and failed portraitist.

"You are a convincing fader into the background, boy. I never thought it of you. But can you fade, now? They'll not give up searching for you, will they."

Francis Pye shrugged, causing the dishmop of hair to dance on his shoulders.

"I must get me to France," he said, "I badly want to live to see my grey hairs."

Blackavise nodded, resting his hand and his weight against the cool stone wall. The slant of the sun lit his left shoulder-blade. With half of his straight back warm, the other half shadowed and colder, he took hold of his life. Even if he was warmed by the comforting waters of Black House, out in the wide world the tide was ebbing fast, flowing chill from the disasters of King Charles, whose fortunes Blackavise had sworn to follow. In addition he was agitated by the thought of Mary Florida, whom he could not face.

"I'll go with thee, Francis," he declared, "they'll be out looking for a singleton. We'll make convincing play actors at it. Come up to Black House at dark. Tell Mistress Lacey what we are going to do, and why I don't come in now. Tell her I need time to think out a plan for our journey. And get her to lend you a horse."

He decided he would have to spend two nights protecting Pye on his escape to the coast. He had passed a night away from Black House after Aeneas made Mary Florida a widow, and his godmother had not taken that absence as the sign to die, had she? So when Francis Pye hurried through the doorway of Black House under the shawl of twilight, Blackavise scuttled him upstairs that they might ferret about in the jumbled rooms for some sort of disguise.

"I laid out some clothes for our Ginger to attend me in. Pity you are not twelve and a page in the making; the boy was desperate to wear that chequered mask over there," he told Pye, the beanpole, "he's the age for parading himself like a monkey rather than sober-suits at my elbow."

"I look like a vagrant," sighed Pye, "just a hedge-creeper like to get my collar felt. Let's see what you've got. I'd prefer to look like a decent citizen about his lawful business."

"That would, in your case, make a change," allowed Blackavise, throwing up the top of a domed chest and ransacking within. It held dusty lengths of cloth. "This is no good, we've no time to have a suit made up for you; ah, now whatever?" Beneath, like a squirrel's buried nuts, he uncovered silvered gaskins, gauntlets, and a head-dress in which some ostrich must have felt one hell of a fellow.

"These are no use! Are they yet more old trappings from the masquerades?"

"That's all I need," Pye pulled a rueful face, "you would set me up in cardboard armour and put me on the road as a mountebank in a raree show."

"If I come up with a bearskin, I'd chance it," Blackavise assured him, "make a living from thee upon the road, should you prove a bear who could dance." Play-actor himself; amazed how normal his outward show now seemed, when beneath his mended ribs his heart ached in a void. He turned to a pile of boxes in a closet, investigated and they tumbled straight out on to his foot spewing more relics. Blackavise vowed to spend his spare time sifting through them when he came back. What was it about these half-masks? This one here was frozen in manic glee, the other, blank disguise with eye-slots and a knot of coloured ribbon tied jauntily at the side. Perhaps he was still a Ginger at heart. But this wasn't getting the business done. He wanted a good servant's livery for Pye, or a gentleman's unobtrusive broadcloth. Black House was a nest of women and thus unhelpful in this crisis. Next he disclosed a whole cupboard bulked out by stiff skirts and petticoats, some with the horseshoe pads still tied round the hips at lapsed angles, as if the petticoats were drunkards. Behind them a folder had been long forgotten; it fell, with a bang and a puff of self-sneezing dust. The habit of handling such things made Pye the artist bend and pick it up.

He fiddled the ribbon tie apart; Blackavise peered over his shoulder, looked, disbelieving said, "Goddam," and fetched up the candle. The amazement and a snort of laughter were involuntary. He was not one to feel bashful at the sight of rude representations of the female form, not after the army and his adult life. But these told a story. A series of little drawings had been scratched with a quill in brown ink. First a row of seemly maidens, prancing in ostrich feather headdresses and floor-sweeping skirts, and holding wands; in front of them a more important female, some sort of goddess to whom they were attendants. Next drawing, no goddess, but one attendant, singled out, a bulky girl, with an exaggerated brown-ink bosom like a pair of puddings. Three different pictures of her followed, each more cheerfully abandoned than the first one. In the final one, she lay on her back with her legs spread. It was undoubtedly his godmother. He baulked, but there she was, displaying herself to a man, presumably the artist.

"Good God," said Blackavise, his Royalist intrigues forgotten. Pye might have evaporated into the candle's aura. The past makes us what we are, thought Blackavise keenly; the past far more real and immediate than his pressing personal involvements.

"She kept these! Kept them."

He could see the evidence in that big box, the costumes she'd put away confirming the drawings. She'd kept them too. Who could have drawn such pictures? Who? Why was she proud enough to place these drawings so carefully and safely away? What experience had the artist of her open thighs and what, in this final sketch, in sepia cross-hatching, looked like gleeful coupling? Something like respect grew upon him for the lady who had rescued him; so she had been a one-woman harvest festival, a giver of fruits and sunshine, if one might so phrase it, to the man with the bottle of ink and the quick-scratch quill.

"Old Queen Anne had a taste for those masques, with everyone heaving with drink, spewing, or worse," he heard himself muse aloud; but he didn't tell Pye, who was now peering over his shoulder and chuckling, that he thought he knew the subject. That, if anything so remained, was private.

"You ought to keep those," Pye was saying.

"They're to your taste?" asked John, quirking an eyebrow.

"They're well delineated. I admire such skill."

"Of course you would, wouldn't you."

"What a subject!" cried the artist.

"Now you're going to tell me, you could have achieved a likeness, given a subject like that."

"I doubt it," said Pye disarmingly, "I would have been leaving too hastily in case she captured me."

Perhaps that was it. Perhaps the real artist had fled, leaving the un-wed Dido, red-eyed, with memories and the sketch sheet. Blackavise thought of the other Dido, down the road. The lawyer's first mention of her had been nearer the mark than he knew. He wrenched his thoughts round, but Pye had caught him wool-gathering.

"Come on now, can you think of naught but lascivious pictures?"

The two sorts, Blackavise wrestled and threw from him. "I don't know what we are going to do with you," he said to his companion, "most of this is female gear. And my clothes won't fit you, you are such a whippet."

"The other matter's this: every fishing village where I kept someone friendly, with a keel to push out on boat trips, is in enemy hands."

Now Pye tells me, thought Blackavise.

The alliance formed by Gerard and Radlett missed their bear to bait next morning when they arrived at Black House from the Three Tuns. Meanwhile Ginger had received a note from Mary Florida too late to hand to John Blackavise. Why didn't he tell her he was for off, wondered Ginger, doggedly reading the superscription at the pace of his moving lips.

Smelling an opportunity to put on what he thought of as his livery jacket, he said to Bessie, "I got to reply. An' if I write, I'd have to wait till I did it, then take it. Quicker just to go."

Bessie, busy folding the clean laundry, wasn't listening, nodded, and he dashed before she asked why. He hared off down the hill, into Aynescote gate, delivered, came strolling out of that same gate only to be apprehended by a strange couple riding muddy nags, who looked sniffily down at him.

"Art thou Blackavise's boy?"

"I am," quoth Ginger, throwing out his chest into the jacket, and failing to add this nonetheless was an enquiry that caught him away from home.

"Then prithee announce us."

So he did as he was bid, deferentially, demonstrating to Mary Florida the respect his master, Blackavise, would wish. He considered her to be dashing about very spry of a sudden, after all that care of herself and the foal she was carrying. Sharp pangs assailed him because he had missed the dramatic and bloody night when the soldiers chased in and out of Aynescote. In contrast these two new visitors here looked dull old Master and Mistress Respectable.

"But this is not Black House," quoth Mary Florida, "this is twice it hath been mistook. I must look to getting 'Aynescote' written up."

"I intrude, Madam," the newcomer apologised in emollient tones.

She, feeling all rubbed up the wrong way, thanks to Ginger's initial message and the return of her unopened letter to her hand, saw an innocent couple ingratiatingly bowing, he all eyes and teeth, she one of those go-by-the-ground little women like house mice, in a crumpled sandy coloured riding cloak. They saw the mourning. He saw she was handsome.

"If I may present myself? Julius Lyons, your servant; my wife," he paused, "we are for Blackavise door. This boy here misled me."

If looks could kill, thought Ginger, and stood nearer Mary Florida, who felt guilty of being in a bad humour, and to compensate had glasses brought, and wine to pour therein, to repair her self-esteem. The second sip went down the wrong way when she realised she'd seen the visitor's name on the list of likely beneficiaries. Master Lyons followed his eyes and teeth by advancing on her, uncertain if her fit of coughing allowed polite behaviour of those newly introduced to pat a lady on the back, so he hovered, tutting.

"Master Blackavise is not here," faltered Mary Florida when able, setting the glass on the tray Ginger was assiduously handing.

Lyons, disappointed at missing the chance to feel his hand on her shoulder, settled for second best by taking his glass back from his wife, ignoring the sour glance which she gave him. At Mary Florida's information he stilled the glass with his lips extended to it, an inch from the rim, as if caught kissing. Mary Florida was reminded of family meetings when people who know each other too well are forced to embrace. On another level, a chant of names ran through her head, linked by those Christenings at the chilly font years ago. Gerard and Radlett, Corrydene, someone and Lyons were John Blackavise's fellows, of whom she'd told him to beware. It is not always wrong to think ill of people.

"But you will find Masters Gerard and Radlett, who before you mistook Aynescote for Black House, daily thither," said Mary Florida indifferently, signalling to Ginger for her glass back too. The couple in front of her kept their inner shutters down, the lady with her glass-bead eyes steady, he at last consummating his glass and lowering it in one tilt.

"Mistress Blackavise continues steady," Mary Florida informed them disingenuously. She was letting these new godchildren know all was not closet and secret up at Black House, that she, a widowed gentlewoman of standing, was informed as to the affairs at the neighbour's. Obscurely, she wished to declare herself part of the world of Black House. Why? Merely because, if they thought she knew things, they would have to take her into account if they had hole-and-cornerings in mind. Not so obscurely, at the front of her mind, she wanted to say to the defected John Blackavise: How could you run off without a word? Did you not include me by sharing that list? Whomsoever wishes you harm may stand before me, even these two, or are occupying a bed at the Tuns. Where are you? Not here dealing with them. Why have you chosen to rush off to save Francis Pye?

Ginger, overparted, took it upon himself to offer her another pouring of her own wine.

"Put it down, boy," she instructed, disappointing the travellers after their one glass, for her late husband had been proud of his good nose and kept a prime cellar to demonstrate it. She refused to use bumpers of sack to blot out Aeneas, for all the nightmare mind's-eye blink of her last sight of him. She knew herself to be clearheaded and sober, but dared not dwell on the picture of bloodied Aeneas nor upon poor innocent Thunderer. Oh why had John left her on her own without giving her so much as a word? Did he think he was the only one bearing frights? Had she not faced disasters in her life? Mary Florida flinched, assailed by another fright from another time. Pye might have been the murdered secretary Rizzio and she could have played that other Mary, Queen of the Scots. Even as those assassins had struck down Rizzio, Pye could have met death inside her own house at her skirts. Why ever had John been so hasty and gone off holding Pye's hand? It had been the spy's risk; he chose his calling. The pair of them wouldn't save the King now. At this moment she felt the need to persuade the uninvited visitors in the Aynescote parlour to gird up and get on their way, for they were outstaying. The newcomers showed all the signs of sticking. Mary Florida's disenchantment with the coven of godchildren rose in a panic.

178

"And are you for staying long?" she essayed, wishing to find out what the absent Blackavise would want to know, "the Three Tuns houses the other gentlemen, Gerard and Radlett, I believe; you will, of course, not wish to lodge at Black House, as matters stand." She had done John a favour, whether he deserved it or not, thought Mary Florida; he won't want to find their boots sharing his guest bed in Black House. Perhaps her fair chamber, bright with its refurbishments, its flowerbed of cushions, gillyflowers flavouring the air from a blue and white Dutch pot, had not turned so gloom coloured as she. But the black clothes furnished her excuse, and she raised a lily hand to her brow, murmuring they must forgive her. This brought on a welter of bowing and hatting, and she stood back, ready to let Ginger play his part and usher them out, gesturing quite prettily in the old-fashioned coat which made him look handless. His knuckles would emerge, presumably, from the cuffs when he grew into them. Mary Florida sank down into her black cloud of mourning, unthinking, but still existing. Too much overactive emotion had beaten about her ears this fortnight. Here was Ginger back again, with another interruption. She had seen enough of him this day.

"Now listen, rascal, I don't employ thee."

"But Mistress, listen,"

He wasn't being pert; his bent knee and urgent undertone told her she must focus her attention on whatever his message might be. Mary Florida sat up amid the cushions.

"Them callers stuck in your porch while Jesse fetched up their horses, she said to him, put out like, 'why isn't Blackavise here?'. Theo Radlett said, an' he shushed her, told her 'we'll talk to Radlett'. 'Yes', she says, 'and how is he going to work it?', an' then *he* says, kinda quiet like, 'make an end of it this time'."

Make an end of what? feared Mary Florida, an end of John? Her round eyes met the boy's.

"Now steady," she said, "we don't know."

"He's been knocked on the head already," Ginger spread his handless cuffs. "'Twas I that found him, remember. Madam, some no-good thrust him headfirst into that ditch to make sure. He's got a thick skull, Madam, or he wouldn't have come round in time."

"I remember." What to do? What if John had drowned in that ditch, leaving one of the other names on the godsons' list to inherit? The question is which one? Which of them had caused the note to be sent, the one telling the bastard to get him hence? That was a threat, or even a last warning that there would be a repeat attempt. Drive him away, and he wouldn't need murdering, no mortal sin committed that way. But he hadn't gone.   Saved by chance, because he was off chasing wild geese in the hope of speeding Pye off to France. Where do people take boat for France, men with Royalist, endangered hides?   While winding and unwinding the black ribbon on her sleeve as if it were a curl paper, Mary Florida asked herself where safety can ever be found. Every port and coast for France were in the clutches of the Parliamentarian foe. Ginger, fixated as if a gosling emerging from his shell, gawped earnestly at Mary Florida as he knelt on the shiny beeswaxed floorboards trying to make out her hot thoughts.

"I don't know where he's bound," she cried, putting her hands to her head.

"I do," swore Ginger, like a bridegroom.

Chapter IX

Mary Florida set out after him. She took Piers and Jesse with her, but felt fearful, as well she might. As a child her security had come from her father's presence, all her life she had to jog decorously along under another's command, snug as a nun with the Mother Superior. She had been lucky in Ginger's information, because their destination wasn't that of a common inn like a Rose and Crown or a White Hart, but of a house, with an unusual name. It was called the Pharos.

"The what?" she had said, "That's a lighthouse."

"I think it is a house, Madam, he was joking to Master Pye and saying they ought to set a lantern on the roof."

"Where is it, then? What did you catch of what he said?"

"Said it was in the country he knows, he said, that's

Sussex, ain't it? He said, 'I know someone who'd help us', and Master Pye asked 'Why?' an' he says, 'he's a pillion passenger I picked up once, injured, on a retreat'."

He'd rescued someone, then – but wasn't Sussex full of iron foundries which forged the ordnance that blew poor Royalists to kingdom come? She had long considered John Blackavise, no doubt out of perversity, to be the sole King's man ever found there. But wait, he had said he lived over the other side, out of the deeps of the Wealden forest, where the road through the downs rose before reaching the sea.

"Silvercreek," exclaimed Ginger.

He'd heard John pronounce it. Indeed, he had been attending as if he were an embryo Pye gathering information for a pat on the head and promotion. The boy nodded to Mary Florida, his chest swelling, for he had helpfully put his big ears to what Blackavise had been saying. 'This is the time to trust one's friends. They say, if one wishes to be deceitful, tell the truth. So I am after deceiving these enemies of yours, Francis, by taking you with me. This is no time to try and blandish a sea-captain who is unknown to us, who might sell us for more than I can pay him. So let's for Silvercreek where my loyal friend lives, on the inlet, where his house stands up tall like the Pharos to keep his feet dry from the tides'. So, not all Sussex men were of Cromwell's persuasion. Mary Florida tried to guess how many others shared John's manly individuality; she failed to analyse that this was the very quality dismaying her now he had left to rescue Pye. At the next moment Mary Florida lost all grip on sense. She wanted to warn Blackavise. She would set out protected only by her incompetent serving men, with pistols they had fired but twice, to search for Silvercreek, for all that trouble dwelt on the open road. John had told her that not far away his son Simon and his daughter-in-law were in occupation of his home, from which he had deserted to Black House. He'd touched on the landscape, and his memories of the humpbacked downs, described how the inlets beyond cut into the coast like cavities into cheese, where the bill pushed out into the choppy sea. She remembered telling him, "I have never seen the sea," and he'd laughed and said the dirty old London river was no substitute for real salty air that smelt of tar and herring.

I will set out, vowed Mary Florida, dismissing Dorcas before stuffing a few necessities into a saddlebag. Should I look at the folios in the library downstairs to look up John Speed's map to guide us southward? She had to clear her muddled idea of Sussex as fields bordered by offshore sea-monsters and cockleshell galleons. Could she survive the journey? She was not the only one alarmed by her plans. Dorcas, with her eye to the crack of the door, was convinced that her mistress was unhinged, what with one thing and another. Mary Florida prayed she could rely on the ebbing of the conflict. Bruised souls must be restoring what they could of their old calm life. Would she ever find this strange Pharos, or know which fingerpost and turning to take at crossroads? There might well be deserters. The old tides of masterless men probably overlapped shoals of the disaffected, and there were already beggars and vagrants. All of whom hopped up and down in Mary Florida's heated imagination, to menace or to rob her, even to take her turn at being dropped into a ditch for dead. But she had fired herself up. It was bad enough that the godchildren were planning an end to Blackavise. To add to this, that man had rushed away upon a fool's errand to help the wretched Pye.

All the while she considered this with a saddlebag in one hand and a comb she was in the act of packing in the other. Mary Florida had heard a persuasive voice, singing a siren song. It warbled, 'Be brave, and he will be ashamed that he went off and left without a word, but managed to borrow the grey saddle horse for the runaway painter nonetheless'. So she wanted to be dauntless in his eyes. She wanted to ride up to this strange tall house in Silvercreek and announce that she had news for him and had come to warn him in time to save his head and skin. But first she had to arrive there.

Piers and Jesse said "Yessm," and went off to saddle up, making faces to each other like a pair of turnips.

She managed to look matter-of-fact and haughty, assuming her position in charge now she was their new mistress. She swore Ginger to secrecy and sent him back to be the temporary man of Black House, this status justifying exclusion from her journey. She charged him to keep an eye on the godchildren. John told her that she could set a course, sail her own flagship as a widow, a free agent. No-one, not father, brother, guardian nor husband existed who could tell her not to go. This journey had been an abstract concept, of course so far, even as a book is to the reader. Even so, she was hardly setting off to chart the Indies, and Piers and Jesse were beside her. Please heaven the roads be quiet, thought Mary Florida fervently, if innocently, as the three riders trotted out of Aynescote gate.

The riders put their horses' hoofbeats to the highway south. It was a beautiful spring morning, not appropriate to misgivings. The conflict had died down as if its stormy seas had been tamed by doldrums and calm weather. The riders tracking the spy to the coast experienced a sense of travelling in the green basket of wayside weavings of hedgerows and banks of white blossom. The late spring was marked with scents and waftings, doubly welcome after the long winter months. Mary Florida felt that her head might have popped from the hole in a dark tree in which she had roosted over winter.

She couldn't know the route John Blackavise and Pye had taken, only their destination. Every milestone and signpost led them southward. Either there were no deserters left, or the sight of her big serving men deterred them; no beggar importuned them, no greasy gypsy crept from the undergrowth. They heard not a word of pedlar's French, the hedge creepers' language. In truth it was a lovely day to be out wayfaring, buoyed up by the jingle and movement of trotting along. Aeneas had been wont to complain that if ever he were forced abroad the rain would fall upon him and upon all England, so as far as he could discern through driving downpours. He had been convinced that every dreary little settlement was carpeted in mud and peopled by defectives who ought to have been dissuaded by a rigorous Table of Kindred and Affinity from marrying their relations. However, the sunny day had cast good spirits over the highway. Here were decent beldames, there squeaking little boys and a puppy dog, as if they knew that life was worth living. Perhaps it was all too cheerful, thought Mary Florida, for she caught a glimpse of a red-faced young man hopping with difficulty on a new-looking crutch and peg leg. At sunset, she was relieved to be installed in a decent inn full of head-cracking beams, in a room overlooking the town square. Drained after hours riding side-saddle, the inevitable sensation beset her as if she were still trotting, even though she had dismounted. Dawdling round the Aynescote riding tracks with an occasional canter was poor preparation for riding all day. A jolly serving girl brought a platter with a slice of pie and a pewter mug of sack, after which Mary Florida locked herself in the chamber by turning a key fit for the Tower of London. She fell exhausted into a clean feather bed, where she slept until the chorus of shouting birds awakened her. She was visited by the notion that John Blackavise appeared before her in the shape of a well-set-up wraith who looked at her with an urgent eye. "Why are you behaving like this?" he demanded to know, "I would never ask you to follow me across half of southern England."

When she opened the shutters, daylight restored reality. When they set out, the road the old Romans once had trod led the three riders along until they glimpsed a different world through the gap in the downs. Reflected light and the mewing of seagulls tantalised them until they caught sight of the gleam of the sea. Closely cropped sheep grazing gave way to saltings, parted by a sliding, slippery ditch. Was this all there was to the Silvercreek? It was a gunmetal rather than a silvery flow because a bank of clouds had swallowed the declining sun. Mary Florida saw there were a couple of run-down cottages and a hard on the margin of the creek. On the side were a few upturned keels like little brown roofs; netting was spread, and there was the pungent smell of fish gutting. It was at this point the riders sighted the landmark. They forgot the long, rutted road behind them and looked at each other in triumph. They surely had sighted the Pharos, a tall narrow edifice which was disclosing one storey at a time as they drew nearer. Eventually they drew close enough to see the building was set up on a plinth so it might survive the proximity of the creek, high tides and storm waters, and that it was sundered from the little creek by a private quay where two small boats bobbed. So here it was, a most unusual nautical castle, timber framed and infilled with the grey-faced flint of Sussex. On the landward side bleached waves of sand swelled into hillocks tied together by the roots and straggles of samphire and tamarisk, blown the one way of the prevailing wind. The orange disc of sundown was

189

descending beneath an underbelly of clouds and threw a ray as it sank, illuminating three seagulls wheeling among the fading colours of the day.

Mary Florida felt distinctly uneasy and out of place as she inhaled the salty air. Questions that needed answers had filled her mind throughout the ride to the coast. Had John Blackavise arrived and had he packed off Pye to safety across the Channel? Or were they waiting upon wind and tide? Would he be displeased to see her? But better far, that he were alive, breathing and cross, than unwarned and unprepared for the second attack which Ginger had overheard the ill-wishers planning. She could not forget that they intended to "finish him off this time." The intention to thrust him headfirst into that watery ditch to drown might have misfired, but had resulted in his impromptu arrival at Aynescote and how he entered her awareness. Thus had she come with 'forewarned is forearmed'. That is why I am here.

Mary Florida dismounted, very cramped from riding a long way side-saddle, twitched up her hood and advanced upon the iron-studded oak door. She had learned to outface Aeneas's housekeeper when first a bride, learning that a show of assurance would protect her. Now she must draw on that. Diffidence would not do. Now to signal Piers to step up to knock upon the bastion of the studded oak door. He obeyed, the stronghold fell as the servant within obediently fetched his two gentlemen, a pudgy youngish man, with one hand on the hilt of the sword at his belt, and an unarmed and nearly identical older version. Father and son adjusted their expressions on beholding an unexpected and travel-stained young lady in a cloak and hood on their doorstep. They then offered too quick a welcome, as she could not fail to notice, even as she introduced herself to them.

"I apologise for arriving unannounced, but I am seeking a Master Blackavise who intended to pass this way."

A quick exchange of glances took place, the pair allowed her in, and the younger man slipped out of a secret door in the panelled hall that didn't look like a door at all once closed. She heard herself take a shot at explanation.

"I must apologise for arriving without warning, but in these difficult times unforeseen business had forced me to risk the journey."

The gentleman standing before her could not have repeated a word she had said, even had he been threatened with the gallows for failing. Preoccupations held him fast. He looked attentively vacant under his bird's-nest of grey hair with its bald spot emerging like a single, large egg. He assessed Mary Florida as though for possible later examination. He was not aware of the various undercurrents of her arrival, none of which bore close scrutiny. The younger version of his father reappeared, black bird's-nest, no egg as yet, and very politely beckoned Mary Florida to follow. She stepped across the hall, her heels clinking on the flagstones. In this seafarer's house she might have been a black galleon under the sail of her billowing cloak. The younger man stood moored by the door gesturing that she precede him up stone steps leading to another chamber, where firelight and one solitary candle attempted to penetrate the growing darkness. Overhead a fine model ship hung suspended, complete with sails, pennants and rigging, and through the diamond leaded lights the view of the creek yielded to the sunset and turned a lurid, temporary vermilion.

Another door opened and John Blackavise came in alone, broad shouldered and as strong as ever, wearing a servant's leather jerkin and a grubby white shirt with a plain turn-down collar and full sleeves. As the fire and the candle flamed behind Blackavise, she failed to see his expression of incredulity, fear and surprise. As Mary Florida was struck by the living instant, so was he. He allowed the sunburst revelation that, as she stood before him in good health and looks after two days in the saddle, she could not be with child. Overwhelmed by this realisation he became tongue-tied, trapped between the joy that she had come so far to find him, for whatever reason, and fear for perils she might have encountered in travelling. He found his voice.

"What the blazes did you think you were doing?" he demanded, "You're not telling me you've come from Aynescote on your own, because I shan't believe it. Have you left a Troop of Life Guards waiting outside? Had you been a soldier, would you have stood in the front line at Naseby?" He was amazed at her audacity.

"Piers and Jesse are the two-man army of stout Englishmen who fight under my Battle Flag," Mary Florida declared, undaunted by the man's attitude, "the Life Guards were too busy this week to join me in hunting for you." She cast her eye about the room and was relieved to see no sign of Francis Pye. Perhaps he was already safely embarked on the broad sea? "Has Francis gone?" she asked, "or is he still with us?"

Her questions recalled Blackavise to the present world. "He's about to be off. There's a safe vessel due on the tide; I have agreed to take oars to row him out to board it. God willing, in half an hour, we shall be out on the water. But Mary Florida, don't let us waste our life talking about Francis. He'll soon be nothing but a memory. What the blazes brought you here? Has my godmother died?"

"Oh, forgive me," cried Mary Florida, in a panic that she might have caused him pain, "nay, I did not come for that."

"Then, what did you come for?" he demanded with his usual directness, his eyes unavoidable deep blue arrows. He had advanced, was clasping her small, gloved hands.

"More godchildren," she replied, vehemently, "named Lyons. A married pair mistook Aynescote for Black House, and as they were leaving Ginger overheard them discussing a plan of mischief aimed at you. You must never forget the depth of hostility the godchildren have towards you. They are up to no good, that's for certain. You are at the top of the lawyer's list of interested parties. That's why I have come so far to forewarn you to protect yourself on your return."

John tightened his clasp on her fingers. He was no longer the cavalryman accustomed to fight the King's battles from the saddle of a horse, but due to take charge of a rowing-boat on the bucking waters of the Channel. By the shock arrival of Mary Florida, the living breathing woman he desired, his vital preoccupation of rowing the spy to an escape vessel was stripped from him as if the cloak had been rent from his back. He would have pulled her to him, held her, but the young man of the house put his head round the door with particularly maladroit timing.

"Excuse me, Captain, time for you to be gone if you want to catch this tide." The head withdrew. Mary Florida's first sight of the ocean had been but half an hour ago. She was spiked by horrid fear of that cold and vasty deep awaiting the two King's men. With the driest of dry mouths, she prayed that whoever Blackavise had hired were seasoned seamen who had done nothing else all their lives.

For his part John remained in the tidal ebb and flow of private emotions. As if by the powers of a necromancer Mary Florida stood in front of him. Had he waved a wand? But his attention was necessarily claimed by spies, heartache, and the imperative business on hand, which he had to complete. He had squared his shoulders and inflicted the rescue of Francis Pye upon himself, and was set to see the promise through. For all that, he was still holding Mary Florida's hand within its soft glove, and he most keenly did not want to go. Such were the warring emotions in a complex moment. He made the effort to master himself.

"Time and tide famously wait for no man," he smiled at her in the half light, "not even for the King's spy. Let me reassure you this is safe harbour until I am back. Under the cloth on the sideboard is my tray of supper

195

and a drop to drink. I bequeath these to you. It's the least I can do. Drink my health. My friends will nourish you for my sake, because I once saved their soldier son when he was unhorsed. We were retreating from a bloody slaughter. I put him up behind me. He had no more wish than I did to join the dead in the graveyard."

There was a scratch on the further door, but as John crossed the room to open it, face-planes etched by the firelight, he paused before reaching for the latch.

"I'm in your debt, lady."

She sank down on the bench by the table, where the dirty candle wax was gumming itself to a brass tray, and he still had his eyes upon her as he swung the door open to admit Francis Pye in his disguise. Therefore John absorbed fully that she gasped, turning utterly, sickeningly green. He had no time to ask why, for he had to whisk Pye away to catch this particular tide. The spy stepped forward in his full disguise to impress Blackavise, which it did.

"Good god, Francis, I knew you could act a part, but I had no idea you were marked out for the stage."

Mary Florida was struck dumb at the sight of Pye in his costume, even as his only friend shooed him through the door to begin his journey across the dark and heaving waves to France. In her single startled blink they were gone. Blackavise clattered down the stairs, distracted by Mary Florida's anguish, his fears for her outdoing his customary singlemindedness. Was she with child after all? She had that sort of pasty colour of a woman with child. Let not childbirth kill her, oh not that, he prayed, as he swung his great cloak over his shoulder and shoved Pye into the gathering gloom over Silvercreek. Mary Florida was left alone to relive the nightmare memory of her late husband's pleasures in wearing women's skirts and petticoats. She drew no comfort from the glowing grate which failed to deliver its fire-pictures to her, for all that it flamed and shot noisy sparks up the chimney, because in her mind's eye she saw that door opening again and again, and the mousy gentlewoman advancing. The effect of gawkiness and self-effacement were typical of many a well-bred English spinster; anyone's unmarried sister. But it was the travesty of a man in those clothes that undid Mary Florida. Francis Pye had looked all but comely in skirts, with a glimpse of white neck, his moustache gone, and his dishmop locks thrust under a lace cap. He would have passed a casual glance, even from a nosy Roundhead captain. Mary Florida was undermined by basic disgust, not at poor Francis, but at Aeneas, who found his pleasure by aping a woman, unembarrassed by what he had under the skirt.

The minutes crawled slowly by. It seemed that John

Blackavise was away for a week. She speculated, unhelpfully, all night. Had he got himself drowned alongside Pye, who, after his unsuccessful career impersonating a portrait painter, was now portraying himself as a woman? The fear of John floating face down, dead in the sea and gone for ever, overwhelmed any thoughts of Pye maybe gasping for air amidst the flower of his sodden petticoats. Unable to fasten on John's strong manly presence in the void of his absence, she needed him to blot out the discouraging memory of her husband.   John's precipitate departure had not denied her the delivery of her warning, but she was now trapped, sleepless in this strange tower of a house overlooking Silvercreek. Circumstances had imposed her upon the hospitality of strangers, all because Ginger's alert big ear had brought the news that the Godsons were still plotting John's assassination. "Make an end to him, kinda quiet like; get it right this time." She pictured a bunch of roughs lurking behind the spring greenery guarding the entry to Black House. That was bad enough, but he might already be drowned along with Pye. Where were they? Dead in the water? The fright of seeing Francis Pye in skirts, a man-woman, beset her.

Dawn and the birds began the day early, and John returned. When she set eyes upon him he had already

198

spent two hours in bed, freshened himself, and was sitting in his servant's shirtsleeves eating a slice of bread and a cut of mutton. He looked perfectly at home in his hosts' dining parlour, under a row of model yachts in the Dutch fashion.

"Safely shipped," he greeted her, rising to move a stool to the table that she might sit with him. A keen inspection told him she was no more than pale this morning; no tinge of green.

"You caught the tide as planned, then?"

"Indeed, but I feared our pirates weren't coming. We'd put out in our rowing boat, and there we seemed to sit for ever, like a duck on the pond. Then in the dark, no moon, we heard creaking, and then came a lantern lit and a hail. Off he's gone."

"You were so long a time away."

"The wind failed with the tide; I am unused to the task of rowing, look, blisters, the oars fought back."

"Blisters for the King."

"More than he deserves. But I threw in my hand with Pye, as did you. He tells me how you most bravely hid him from those soldiers."

"It was thrust upon me. I had to hide him. What you've completed was premeditated. Cold blood's more praiseworthy."

"Hmph," he said, dismissively. He needed to talk to

her, needed answers, and he could not do so here with his two hosts ready to bound in upon them. Nor would it be ideal trotting along with the long ears of Piers and Jesse only yards behind them, leading the spare horse Pye had ridden down. It wasn't going to be the journey home he had planned. He had jettisoned the idea of a stop at his own house, a mere five-mile detour off the high road behind the downs. It had seemed only right and proper to take a look in, to be sure Simon and the fearsome Susan were in health and allow them to inspect him. But it was beyond the realms of sanity to arrive in the company of a lady in stark black, lovely with her long-tailed eyes, and she widowed only weeks back, gallivanting out with such as he. He could imagine the frosty reception. If matters were to progress between them, he would proudly brandish her beauty. But this was wishful thinking. So he decided to pass the overnight stop on the way north in the anonymous lodging of the Coldharbour Inn, out on its own under its gibbet trees where the road humped up and down. The curious thing about striving after anonymity was that the first living creature he saw there was bailiff to his Sussex neighbour, coming out of the taproom door. Blackavise acknowledged him with a nod, supposing him to be returning from market day. He was faintly irritated to be caught in his servant's clothes, reading a gleam of, "He's come down in the world," from the other's expression. But he forgot about that soon enough, urgent about Mary Florida.

Business seemed slack in the Inn, and a bit of haggling achieved rooms upstairs. There was an inch of a sitting-room made up from a blocked-up passage, and the whole nest of little chambers were a-bristle with low beams and supporting timbers as if he were trying to walk about in the capsized bones of a ship under the sea. The slope of the steep roof was to blame. But there was a little fireplace soon crackling pinecones and putting fireflies up the chimney. He was impatient. He had thrown Mary Florida into the further chamber, and now he hauled her forth.

"Come and sit down," he told her, and she sat in her riding clothes now draggle-tailed upon a long stool in front of the growing fire, the skirts throwing dark billows over its dull leather and tarnished brass tacks. He felt overbearing standing above her, and therefore came round the further end of the stool and placed himself so the leather and brass marking the space between them would have seated another besides.

"Mary Florida," he said gravely, "we are journeying together and therefore should aught befall you, I feel responsible. So I ask you to forgive me; are you with child, or no?" He had tried to sustain a level tone, but dark strains coloured in.

Mary Florida, perhaps wisely, burst into tears. By the time she had regained her voice, she felt his arms round her. No-one could have sat between them anymore. She loosed a flood tide down his shirt. With his face on her ruffled copper hair, John might have marvelled at the day she floated past him at Aynescote and trawled him in the net of a faraway glance. But she had not answered him. As he comforted her, his heart agitated because he had talked himself into believing she was with child, when he would be lost. Now she was about to tell him. As she looked up drowned eyelashes appeared as black stamens in the rain. The blue flowers looked back at him. Can I bear it, he thought; I can't.

"I am not with child; did Francis not tell you? It was the only ploy I could think up, when I hid him beneath my skirts, that day the soldiers searched. They requested me to rise so they might check beneath the daybed where I sat. I could not rise, they would have found him, so I had to give them a reason not to insist."

John Blackavise struck his hand on his head. "Dear Heaven, that!" He realised Francis had tried at least once to tell him the circumstances by which she had rescued him. He'd shut him up. Now do I say thank God, as I wish to do? Or did she love Aeneas? Here I am beyond sense about her. Don't let me throw away my chance with my fool tongue. So he sat tight, letting her ride in his embrace, and as un-amorous as he could make it, and let her cry. He held her, he clung; she'd had ordeals, and she had come to warn him. Now why had she done that? It was a shaft through clouds, but he baulked at hope, because he had hacked at himself with the idea Aeneas had impregnated her, and was still daft with relief. Relief was still striking home but had not got so far as actual hope. He had not got to that word at all.

"I was anxious. When Francis came in, you went white; I thought my fears were true," he said. "I thought, you should not have ridden."

She went pale again. "It was when Francis came in," she began, but her voice faded.

"What is it? Could you share it with me?"

Silence arrived until she could express what she found very difficult to tell him. The sight of Francis Pye the man-woman, the man in skirts, had caused a nasty mind's-eye memory to resurface.

"I could not abide what Aeneas did."

He endured forebodings.

"I'll try to tell you. It is not easy for me to list Aeneas's unnatural habits."

"What the devil did he do?"

"I had no idea of his hidden life. Why should I? It was beyond belief. I hadn't even heard of such behaviour." There were no facile words with which to describe what he found stimulating.

"What behaviour?" he demanded, fascinated and anxious.

Mary Florida wept again.

"He came to me dressed up in skirts. He wanted to shock me; he always wanted to shock me, it aroused him. There he was, in one of my favourite bodices, half-laced on his chest, I could see his dead-mouse fur; a skirt, my skirt, pulled up showing what he was, and he came at me laughing like a jackass. He would force me, and have me like that. When he had finished he would parade up and down and look in the mirror, and hold up his skirts and laugh."

John had the sense to remain silent. And to think I only feared he kept the curlpaper in, he reflected.

Chapter X

John Blackavise may have understood that his life's wish had come upon him, but he comprehended that he must not throw away the miracle by claiming the moment too hastily. She was no phantom, but a breathing woman with her head on his chest, her soft hair tumbling down his shirtfront. It was scarcely possible for him to remember that he was a gentleman and constrained to behave like one. Yet now knowing she would be his opened a new ache to join Mary Florida in the pleasure of complete abandonment before his enemies dug a hole for him in God's earth. Ever since he had first glimpsed her at Aeneas's party he had wanted her. Through the black mourning clothes he was clasping the Beauty, her breasts swelling against his chest, and he was ever more determined that the godsons should fail in their plan to murder him. Overriding

manly instincts and erotic messages, the Godsons'
threats faded beneath the siren song of amorous hope.
She had crossed three counties to warn him to look sharp
when he returned to Black House. Good God, what a
spur to be quick with her. This was the precipice of his
situation.

"Have thy tears dried?" he heard himself say,
offering the flag of his handkerchief, "I promise you one
thing, I shall take Aeneas from thee and I'll despatch
your frights for good."

Mary Florida looked up into his face and he revealed
a few of his inner emotions. Then she went to rise, trod
on her hem and found herself his willing prisoner. She
let him kiss her, wanting him to chase away Aeneas's
ghost. John, intending to beat the opposition, even
though dead and gone, began gently as if her mouth
were a butterfly. Another kiss, to tease her out, then
stronger until she kissed him back. So, now to the
pleasures, he thought, stunned and exhilarated: she's
willing.

"Shall we love each other?" he was dizzy, for he'd
just felt her little tongue.

"We already do," said Mary Florida, surprising the
hairs on the back of his neck as he heard her. Perhaps
he could hold off and wait; this was gorgeous. "You
honour me this day, to give me your love with a kiss,"

said he.

Beneath Mary Florida's defences, Aeneas had vaporised. Don't spoil the moment, John, lighten it. He had better make a joke of his servant's clothing.

"I was forced to wear Bessie's husband's jerkin to take the servant's part necessary when escorting Pye as a lady. You are embracing a blacksmith, or worse."

He seated her on the long stool with him in the firelight, asking about her journey down, and explaining the arrangements he had made for a passage across the Channel to France for Francis Pye.

"However did you come across these people in the Pharos?" she asked.

"The young man was a casualty I hauled up behind me on the off chance he'd live if carried to a surgeon. It happened in the chaos of yet another of our military retreats. As you could see, he has survived safe in his Pharos, with a grateful spirit. So I can rely on their co-operation whenever I need it. It is to their great credit they came to my aid. They were as nervous as a cat walking along a mantelpiece. Otherwise I should have been hard put to get Pye away; there are few King's men left. I told the father that the war is as good as over, so his son no longer risks death on a battlefield. The boy was glad to get him back to his lighthouse; he tells me he can't sleep away from the sound of waves. Silence disturbs his slumbers. When he is really anxious, he takes a perspective glass up to the roof and watches every far-off sail crawl by." He was holding Mary Florida's fingers, the white star points of her lace cuff covering his broad brown hand, and as he spoke, he pictured Aeneas and what he'd learned about the darker side of his too-smiling outer show. But the pinecones had faded in the little grate. Time had called the shades of evening.

"I'll have the serving wench come to put thee to bed before the owls hoot. You must be over weary."

He called down to the serving girl for some light. While she was fetching a candle, John relinquished his full heart and his cloven hooves, releasing Mary Florida from his arms near to the temptation of the Coldharbour Inn's best bed. He could hear the serving girl coming upstairs. Silently he imagined Mary Florida as Venus after as short a delay as possible.

In the whirligig of John's life next morning, the horseback journey took its place as an interlude of calm. All trotted sedately northward, Piers and Jesse taking turns to lead the spare horse which Mary Florida had lent to Pye. Blackavise and the lady were formal with each other because of the ears and eyes of the two serving men. He did not want to be caught flirting in case he frightened the horses or their grooms, let alone

Mary Florida, and turned his thoughts ahead of him towards Black House. He reflected on Bessie and Ginger's irreproachable loyalty to the King that put many to shame, and had indeed installed the spymaster beneath his kitchen flagstones. Surely the threats he had attracted from the Godsons could never pierce its old walls, nor harm him within them. Good old house! For all that Black House was a lesser building than Aynescote, that establishment's short-lived carnival was at an end. That house was draped in gloomy mourning for its murdered master.

At Aynescote gate, Blackavise indicated its carnival queen should go in alone. He was not for leading her about like a mountebank, his captured leopardess in widow's weeds. Certainly not while he was dressed as a blacksmith, not so well turned out as Piers and Jesse in their matching, sober broadcloth.

"I'll go in at the Tuns," he told Mary Florida, "rather than disgrace you in in this dirty shirt and jerkin. You trot on." He watched her go, and when she looked back he swept his wide-brimmed hat above his head. By then she was too far ahead for him to read her expression, but he read the flexing of her body as a personal cipher, a new code for him to learn. By midday he judged the Tuns would be free of its cargo of godsons. His intention had been to wave airily at Messrs Radlett and

Gerard as he trotted Hetty up the wood and they returned down it, having quitted Black House for the day. But, not so. He ducked under the low doorway of the Tuns hat in hand, and advanced to get a jug of ale from that girl of theirs, she lazily polishing a lantern glass with a radish twisted out of the corner of her apron, when he beheld Flynn Gerard sulking in a corner with a pipe and the tavern cat twining round his ankles in the way of cats when they discern a man does not like them.

"Oho, Gerard? Not abroad? You've missed the notch on your wand this day," Blackavise offered, not unkindly.

"Hmmph," said Gerard in his usual vein.

"Where's old Radlett? Not unwell?"

"He's at Black House," Gerard's enunciation was impeded by clenched teeth; the clay pipestem broke in two, as such things will, and accounted for the fact that the Tuns' yard was littered with the remains of smokers'tools amongst the oyster shells and the broken casks awaiting the cooper.

"Pah," said Gerard, and threw the bowl into the ashes of last night's fire.

"You've strong teeth, anyway," commented Blackavise, sunny yet with his secrets. Gerard gave him a slow, dark look and grudgingly offered to stand him the ale. Good grief, thought his oft-times host at Black

House, is he actually going to pay money for me to drink it? He was, though, and when the jolly girl wandered up and poured from the jug, she was given a drink too, so Blackavise did not have to attend too closely to Mary Florida's fears. No-one would poison such a walloper, as far from being a conspirator as any great big baa lamb, even to get at Blackavise. He had taken Mary Florida's cautions seriously, due to his intention to last long enough to tell her she'd been foolish and that he had a thick hide. He wondered what mischief the two latest adversaries were plotting, those Lyons. He ought to have a quiet word with Ginger. With every vulture that gathered, life at Black House became more complicated. Once he had returned to his fastness, John wondered if everyone had been mistaken. Perhaps his godparent had bequeathed her house and estate, her fourpence and whatever, to found an almshouse, or to the one name on the lawyer's list whose footprint he lacked. At which point he would have to make way for the triumph of the beneficiary and be quick about it. Where would that leave him with the Beauty if inheritance bypassed him? But it is not like that, he told himself, as he fiddled with his neck-linen and settled the broad-buckled belt round his waist. He looked at himself straight in the glass. He had yet but the one chin, no luggage bags under his eyes, and the spray of hair his scar had thrown up was quietening down into a tidy helmet of thick hair beginning to silver. He looked away quickly in case he saw worse and went clattering down the wooden stairs to weigh up the new vultures. Until now the animals went in two by two, but no longer. Gerard and Radlett, who had hitherto been bound together like twins, had sundered. John would have laid odds that the latter had discovered Gerard's prickles did not suit him; but it seemed once he had listened to Ginger, who had been the temporary Noah in the Ark while he had been away, that it had not been quite that simple.

"They've had a falling-out, sir. That Radlett, he come up with the Lyons as if he'd been using that twinkling eye and the kindly bit on them all along. That poor old crosspatch Gerard, he had to trail in behind as if to carry the bags."

"This yesterday?"

"Same day before, only yesterday more so."

So now Blackavise wanted to see for himself what had changed during his absence. Two by two, compared to a threesome tracked by a straggler, creates a very different effect. John waited in the parlour for them, his elbow back on the mantel shelf as the high ground, for unless he was revealed as not the beneficiary according to his godmother's will, he was staying put, and intended them to know it.   Radlett, all manners, presented the newcomers to him, nice as pie.   They stood in a line before him as though Radlett was a book between two brown-bindings, pressing him close to hold him upright.

"Mistress," said Blackavise briskly, acknowledging them one and two whilst watching Flynn Gerard behind them in the unmistakeable guise of Left Out.   Three mornings ensued, and they were just the same.   On the fourth morning, Flynn Gerard came up alone; and early. Blackavise was in that half world of private routine whereby a man gets from bed, throws his shirt off and breathes the fresh air of day, full of springtime cadences, at the window.   He had scraped the bristles, and once he had stuck his head into the billows of his clean white shirt and subdued it, he intended to run upstairs to check on the old lady.   He was thinking: marvellous that the loan of Mary Florida's gardeners hath transformed our wilderness.   It is neat and trim, now nearly every one of those topiary pieces has been barbered.   Then the door behind him opened unceremoniously, and turning he saw Gerard standing there large as life, with his hair combed.

"Now see here, Blackavise," began that gentleman in his usual tone.

"What's-to-do, man?" enquired Blackavise, waiting

to pounce. He wondered if Gerard had a horse pistol concealed, ready to finish him off. But then he wouldn't have wasted time doing his hair.

"I want to talk to you without eavesdroppers." Gerard was advancing as if Blackavise's chamber was in no way singular to its owner, and By-Your-Leave uncoined metal.

"Do I wish to talk to you?" suggested Blackavise to insert a doubt of it before matters ran on.

"All right, all right. I'm not in the mood for dodging the issue. That's what I'm here for. You'll thank me."

This seemed fairly remote as Blackavise read it, but he was intrigued, and stood larger than Flynn Gerard, and so was disposed to find the reason for the visit.

"You're up and out betimes," he said conversationally.

"Something's afoot," declared Gerard.

Certainly there is, thought Blackavise, remembering that taste of ditchwater in which he had been cast to drown. Very certainly.

"What's come your way, then?"

"Well," hissed Gerard, bending toward John with a look of a conspirator, "'tis you they're after, you'd best have a care. The Lyons man, him."

This was fascinating, but opaque.

"What do you know, exactly?"

"Two things. Mind if I sit down?"

Gerard sat down on the edge of the tester bed and beckoned confidentially to its recent occupant.

"I overheard them talking yesterday. Theo Radlett said he hadn't known Lyons hitherto, but I think he has. They were in the nook at the Tuns by the chimney corner and my room's over it. I could hear the voices up the chimney. And it seems plain they've known each other for ages. No courtesies, straight in: 'Now Theo: what went wrong?' says Lyons. 'Not wrong exactly,' said Theo, 'merely a trifle slowly. I thought we'd discussed all that.' So, 'I'm not pleased,' says Lyons, and you know Theo, all butter wouldn't melt, he is, he said 'I do hold one reservation, having viewed matters *in situ*, as it were'."

Gerard assumed his own character again and gave John a lizard glare.

"I didn't make head nor tail of it till this bit, and then I really put my ear to the chimney wall. Radlett named, you, yes you, Blackavise. He said, 'I won't be easy in mind until we have made sure it is the bastard who benefits. See to it, would you?'."

"He didn't say 'Blackavise'?"

"Well no, but he meant you, didn't he," said Gerard, innocent of offence.

Curiously enough John did not take more than a

weary exception to the description; he was growing used to it.

"There's more," quoth Gerard.

He paused, infuriatingly, as if for effect at the long-banned theatre.

John had to prompt: "And?"

"I felt slighted by Theo and those two, of course I did. But as Mother tells me, that is life, I must not be so hot."

"You have a mother?" asked John Blackavise; somehow he could never have thought it of Gerard, who might have arrived under the proverbial gooseberry bush, complete with prickles.

"She's a wonderful woman."

"Good lord," said Blackavise aloud, "bravo."

"Don't interrupt. Where was I? Ah. Yes." Gerard began to bounce up and down, as if rising to the trot of the mattress aided his narrative flow. "I heard no more, but this morning, ha, this very morning at cock-crow, the Tuns had the news from the milk girl, who got it from some swain she hath in town, that Pettijohn the lawyer, had his place broken into and his office ransacked. So there."

"You mean, he is our godmother's lawyer, and they'll have taken a peep at her will."

"Wouldn't they."

"Yes, I'd say; if they could find it."

"I think they have."

"Gerard, I wonder if you are not right."

"So you think it too? I had the thought grip me," Gerard grimaced, "near squeezed the breath out of me, if I admit it, all last night."

"I don't say me nay to fellow feeling," said Blackavise, forthright, "but are we not strange bedfellows?"

Gerard bounded off the quilt as if to make this a literal assumption. God save us, I'm not for that, was Blackavise's sardonic reflex. But the level gaze with which he favoured Gerard only asked him 'Why?'. Gerard, fussed, read the query, and spent a moment beating imaginary eiderdown fluff off the seat of his breeches.

"It is your fault, sir, that you are an acerbic man, but I perceive I began over censorious. I see your regard for our Godmother is genuine."

"My hat, Gerard, that's handsome," said Blackavise, concealing even should it kill him, the urge to laugh. "Well, if we are to soldier on as better friends, I shall miss the old Gerard, but accept the new." And recall the old one, should I fear me I am got soft; 'tis said, one misses an irritant. He suspected, however, that the new Gerard would be just the same as the old one, if no

217

longer aiming his personal battle-axe solely at Blackavise.

"Don't forget our godmother may have left thee all her fortune, Gerard."

"Why would she? Mother and I never looked to her, and of course I assumed you were no different."

He was now looking out of the casement to protect tender underparts of conscience from the sharp stings of having to sum up Blackavise, then a thought came.

"Look out that Theo and those two don't ape affection. They'll be up there, holding her hand at the bedside in relays, see if they don't."

"O no they won't," said John grimly.

"Well said," and Gerard gave him an under-used mouth twitch near to a grin, which he wasted on the morning air and the pair of workmen he noticed below, in sacking aprons. He saw they held shears, and were clippety clipping. "Were they supposed to be doing that?" he asked over his shoulder, "Look, they've docked that horse."

*

'Sweetheart', penned Blackavise, later. Unused to such terminology, he hesitated before decorating the sentiment with three flourishes, 'would it be possible for me to escort thee into town this day, to see a man-of-business? This journey together would give me great pleasure. '

As he signed his name Ginger came in with a fresh shirt.

"You're opportune, boy. I need a message run down to Mistress Lacey at Aynescote. and I expect her answer. If she says Yea, run back up the wood; if Nay, you can run back, but slower."

*

But for the sable mourning she wore, she would have looked as fresh as any day in May. Over her side-saddle down the horse's flank her skirts fell in a black cascade. Behind her waited the Gog and Magog of Jesse and Piers, letting their mounts lean down to pull the tussocks by Aynescote gate.

"They are discreet," was her murmured greeting, as John bowed over her gloved hand, smiling at her.

"I shall tire of that," he said, "marry me."

"I will not," she said, rather uppity, "I won't be widowed twice in a month. Also you gave me that lecture telling me that I am now a free gentlewoman and can laugh in the face of the world, which I am happy to do."

She felt dizzy with the relief of breathing freely and knowing she could tell him later that she had been susceptible to his attractions even before the night Aeneas was killed. But she remonstrated, "it is too soon," and he knew it to be true, the Church required an interval after a sudden death. He must get someone circumspect to ask the Rector how long the outward show of mourning lasts. Here was one task for which Ginger was not equipped. In the meanwhile, let them tittup the horses into town as slowly as they could manage, he in the part of neighbour and protector.

"What are we about?" Mary Florida asked, "What man of business?"

"Pettijohn, the lawyer."

"I know him a little. He came up about Aeneas's affairs."

"He's had burglars. His office papers have been thrown about like autumn leaves, I hear, and I want to know if the doers of the deed were looking for my godmother's will, which I understand he drew up. I hear, from Flynn Gerard of all people, who hath suffered a conversion on the road to Black House, if it lasts, that at least three of the godsons want to be sure whom they must do a mischief unto, before they set another set of roughs upon me."

"I like none of this."

"Well I do see that it is admirable of them, to check first."

"Pooh," said Mary Florida spiritedly, "it did not stay their hand the first time."

"True. Perhaps the pair of Lyons have been working on the fierce, fluffy rabbit of Theo Radlett, to transcend his natural nature, presumably of his hunger toward a salad lettuce. I don't know. People!"

"How do the Lyons strike you, now you've met them?"

"Theo Radlett was all over his new friends these Lyons, pouring himself like, like custard over them. Don't laugh. Remember, Radlett fell out with Gerard, first off. As though one of those infant friendships, that upon wind-blow veer and sunder and cause tears."

Mary Florida saw the cast of characters in this pageant verged on tragedy rather than comedy. She adjusted her expression. "I'm not really laughing."

"Let's be factual. What did I see? There I stood, besieged in my parlour, which is my godmother's and not mine, if it ever will be, so I cannot have anyone thrown forth. Also I had Gerard as skeleton-at-the-feast, taking from me my natural role, the one I wanted. Instead I had to stand there and admire Mistress Lyons let Radlett pinch her cheek. She let out a genteel cry of pleasure. As his was the softer complexion and the more genuine pink, it was not a picture I'll dwell on. Lyons himself stood by, lowering the fast-ebbing tide of our Godparent's claret, and I waited for someone to go away."

"That, so far, is exactly like any family gathering."

"Matters changed. I'd assumed Flynn Gerard might be wounded, but he was not lifeless. He was up at Black House first thing, and he tells me that he hath heard our Ginger corroborated."

"How?"

"He had his ear pressed to the Three Tuns chimney, and eavesdropped."

"Which led to why we're visiting Pettijohn?"

"If he has been broken into, I want to know what he thinks. What's missing. Who he considers did it."

"Is the old man you so disliked, what's-his-name, that Francis was trying to paint – is he conspiring with them?"

"Corrydene? I wish I knew. He certainly did not care for my parentage, but that's his privilege, as matters stand."

"Do you trust Gerard's words?"

"Yes I do. After all, Ginger had it first. And Gerard is at least constant. He does not like anyone, much."

"He could have that writ up on his tombstone, it would pin him down exactly."

He suddenly wanted, centuries hence, to immortalise Mary Florida for posterity: 'Beloved wife of' (let it be me), and he'd have writ 'a luminous beauty'. Whatever caused him to think of epitaphs? Gird up, John, he reasoned with himself. Concentrate on the lawyer.

The lawyer's dignified portal, approached over the little grey eggs of its cobblestones, had the surprised air of having a panel stove in, and the clerk, in shirtsleeves, was standing there warding off gawping boys. He admitted Blackavise and the lady, recognising clients.

They found Pettijohn in a great state, standing in the midst of his ransacked chamber. Blackavise was struck by the contrast to the easy, lived-in order of his previous visit. Sets of books had then been elbowing each other, as books do when one is withdrawn and they lapse; an account-book or something had been left open on the stool one would mount to reach the top shelf, and it all had an everyday air, as if the weighty glooms of its owner had been floated by the evident personal pleasures he had in his work and those who consulted him.

Blackavise must have paid attention to all this before, but now he saw the lord of misrule had played his tricks, not least on the sleepy atmosphere. Now the ruffled calm was echoed in the unquiet man.

"The times are out of tune, Master Blackavise,"

lamented Pettijohn, "why should I be exempt? Look at all this. I'm distracted. The realm tears up and down, widows, orphans; why am I disturbed, that I am broken into? 'Tis my turn, I suppose." His heavy irony was belied by the distress on his face. Mary Florida did not know what they could say to comfort him. It was the state of chaos which was the blow. It would take but an hour, less, to sweep up these foolscap sheets, make a clearing of the floorboards, set the books back, but it was a sorry sight to see books face down on the floor, broken-spined. Good gracious. These spines had been slit. The interlopers had been thorough. Someone must have cleared the shelf with a brisk side-sweep to see if private papers had been hid behind. It was the habit of order the lawyer had lost, an affront to his tidy mind. Here came Mistress Pettijohn, dumps writ upon every one of her convex surfaces. Her cap was limp, her dimples fell, as did even the proud bosom itself. To see a substantial matron thus sagging, was dreadful. Mary Florida stepped across the little roofscapes of the upturned books, hitching up her skirts; she put her hand on that of Mistress Pettijohn.

"Tell me you're not hurt?" she asked.

"No; but it is God's mercy we are not! They did not mount the stairs, you see. When I think! Oh, Oh, and our daughters upstairs with us."

"My dear, they were not after Anna Bella or Kate." Her husband shook his head.

"Or me, you imply," snorted his lady with a return to fighting spirit toward him.

"Thank heaven for that," soothed Mary Florida.

Mistress Pettijohn became cross with herself, recollecting the greater trial the younger lady in her mourning had so recently undergone, and here was she carrying on.

"Forgive me, dear," she said, "will you not come aside with me, and I will bid Jane bring us a pot of chocolate? I had best not let things run away with me."

John let Mistress Pettijohn bear Mary Florida off towards the pot of revival, saw the lawyer's lady give a hoik to the cap and dimples as she went. Damnation take these meddlers, he thought fiercely, they take hold of bystanders' lives, innocent, decent people; intruders who had frightened Anna Bella and Kate. I'm not done with yet, he vowed to himself. It is for my affairs that trouble crossed their door. They'll regret it. Let's not lie down and die. Certainly not literally.

"I'll not pretend I haven't a notion," he said to Pettijohn. "I fear 'tis some connection with my godmother. Is not her will lodged here? There are those who can't wait to look. Do you think 'tis that? Would that, if I may ask it, be the object of the search?" As if to plead his own good intentions, he bent, retrieved and handed a spread-eagled ledger to its owner.

The sad pears of Frank Pettijohn's face registered grim satisfaction.

"I still hold that item," he assured John, "I keep upstairs, a handful of documents I ascertain best kept from the common gaze. Your godmother hath long kept her legal papers here. That something was afoot, I believed justified my removing all those scrolls and parchments that touch her affairs into a stout locked box in my strongroom upstairs." He looked at John with a small gleam in the depths of his elephant's eye.

"Bravo," said that man, gleaming back.

"I said, all her parchments; you need not fear one was overlooked. They are safe, Master Blackavise."

"That's what I am glad to hear."

"The poor lady is yet breathing, and someone grows impatient, I suppose."

"Someone is tired of throwing dice to see who gets the hatful; if hatful there be."

They were steadily picking up and heaping a several-storey house of the law books thrown on the floor, and now started on the next pile.

"We cannot know for certain what they wanted, only that I had visitors I did not invite."

"True," said Blackavise; but he knew all right. He

reflected that as Pettijohn had taken precautions, the lawyer knew as well. Then he thought, 'So my adversaries are still in the dark as to what the will hath writ in it. ' He needed to tell Mary Florida, and felt her absence as if she were on the far side of the moon, although she only sat drinking chocolate in the lawyer's family parlour. He wanted to hoist an Admiral's flags to signal her: 'I should be safe to walk in broad day a whiles. They haven't read the will as yet, haven't proved it is me inherits'.

At last Mary Florida reappeared, rustling in night-black skirts, whereupon John offered his arm and indicated it was time to leave. Outside, once down the three steps and treading the cobble eggs of the street again, he squeezed the lady's arm.

"How did you account for your interest in the lawyer's burglars?" he enquired.

"I told him I wished to find out if my papers were amongst those taken; you are my neighbour, and were so kind as to escort me. Master Pettijohn is my lawyer as well as yours, I lodge my papers there just as your godmother does. Learning his office had been broken into, I needed to know if mine were lost," she shrugged, diffidently, "did you mind that I said you were escorting me?"

"That I escort you? Why not?"

Once he was her husband neither he nor Mary Florida would need to explain why he accompanied her.

"Some explanation seemed called for," she said, spreading her hands.

I hope I am a good cause, Blackavise thought. Aloud, he sighed, "I'm angry at what happened here. Pettijohn, wife and maidens put to frights. I must resolve it. Matters drag on so long. Yet how can I resolve it, until the worst of days, when we all have to know the contents of that will?"

He was feeling outrage that Mary Florida at his elbow should be lapped by the ripples of the stone thrown into his small pond. All he wanted was to be a quiet frog and sit on his lily pad. Stepping out of the backwaters of Aynescote and Black House was good for them, he decided, to discover market day and the roaring of beasts and men, to smell cattle, feel the disputatious times. His lily pad was away in that little pond at Black House, and if troubles lay in wait for him, maybe they were nothing but mayflies. Here was the real world, a great lake with ruffles and eddies on the water and real life, in the shape of an indignant pig, which had burst forth from its pen and was being chased by its custodians. The press of people parted as if by command of Colonel Cromwell, the farmers laughing. He had a reason to keep Mary Florida close so no hog or cutpurse came too near. Three silly boys roared after the pig, their shouts encouraging the fleetness of its trotters to escape from them.

"They'd best throw a net over it on the next circuit," John said, enjoying the hubbub, half hoping the creature would upset a market trestle, or a termagant market wife. The stir had upset the bullock in the nearest pen, who added his song to the nasal tones of unhappy sheep. The church clock spoke from its tower above, and a gale of beery laughter from the other side of the square indicated that the pig had surrendered. John leant on the pillar which supported the upper storey overhanging the Market Cross tavern, with Mary Florida on his other arm.

"Are you sated with chocolate, or should you like a bite of the landlord's pie? We might well try now, before we're swamped by all those farmers." He discovered the landlord girding for action, who gave them a little private cell, ordered a fowl to be fricasseed, and showed them to their seats. While the cook dealt with the bird, he'd give Mary Florida a minute to herself, he'd smell the world the once, now he was here and the assassins hadn't discovered he was due for a fortune. He could, perhaps, buy his lady a trinket. Pah, what a nonsense these godchildren had created! It was all a black bubble that this circuit of heaving, mooing life on busy market day had punctured. Here was broad day, thank god, and warm sunshine, and the stalls were basking in its rays as he strolled. A pie-man; a granfer with rows of little wooden butter-pats and moulds hung up; a pedlar had a tray with pretty ribbons, which rainbow display danced in the spring breeze, drawing John's eye.

"Those pink rosettes," said John, fumbling for change, "catch!" he called to the man, as he thought she won't be in mourning for ever. Behind him a cobbler had come out of his shop and was arguing with a scrawny youth with skinner's nasty fingernails. They had matters keen upon them, as real as ever were John's. Everyone was out and about giving his fourpenny-worth opinion, that was what the times bred. Are we all lost sheep? he asked himself, listening to two godly greybeards haggling epistles and some verse-for-verse meaning or other. Well, he for one was all for silly simple men thrashing it out for themselves. That's all it boils down to: these separatists, anabaptists, priestbiters; we're all at loggerheads. The cobbler seemed a good King's man, like Blackavise. He was condemning John Lilburne, the low-church fanatic who annoyed Colonel Cromwell. So why did Blackavise behave like the passing big dog who unites two curs who fought over their bone?

"There is one point in favour of that Lilburne fellow," he offered, unasked: "he hateth old Crop-Ears Prynne."

But they didn't turn on him; the skinner gave a leer and spat on the paving at the name of the fanatical pamphleteer, and the shoemaker cackled. Blackavise felt it was a good day, and went to see if his luck would hold with a flavoursome repast with Mary Florida. He was hungry. At this point of decent human optimism he met Master Corrydene crossing under the overhang of the market house. There was no reason Blackavise could think of why the miserable old person might not emerge from his fastness, but it gave him a jolt. They both put helm up and tacked to avoid collision course; here came that boy of his, carrying a parcel, and he tacked too, like a parent vessel's dinghy. Blackavise derived satisfaction from hatting in a dignified manner, at which his fellow Godson gave him a dirty look and the boy let his slack mouth drop wider, ready for the next passing blowfly. What's Corrydene doing here? John wondered, settling his hat. Then what if that boy was not as simple-minded as he looked and up to light-fingering through other peoples' documents? Frightening Annabella, and Kate.

*

Blackavise spent a sunny afternoon with Mary Florida in the gardens of Black House. There were no phantoms at his shoulder, the shrubbery hid no threats. He was on the point of raising the stakes of amorous involvement, when she interrupted his plans by asking where Pragg, the last of the godsons was.

"I suppose he must join the other vultures in the motley crew of godsons when the will has to be read?"

"Pragg? He'll be dead, or taken ship for the New World, I hope," answered Blackavise, but he wasn't concentrating. The godsons could go hang. It was more to his taste to breathe in the scents of this unthreatening garden. He was standing with his lady amidst the daisies on the green grass, next to the topiary horse.

"He hasn't much tail left to whisk the flies, has he," she regretted, "Abel said he was mortified. He can't stick it back now. It took no more than one good snip."

"I once got me a Roundhead haircut by roughly the same method. One good snip, and then the fool had to match it, all the way round. It grew back in time, though."

"So will your horse. Could you plant another sprig to attempt this tail another way? Have it grow up from the ground, twine it in at the place the tail should start?"

"Would it cure the fault of swishing upward, to

which the old tail was prone? We could but try. Success would please my godmother. Years, hath she battled to grow that tail." ·He wanted to snatch the moment, staple it firmly, tie it with sea-farers' knots, bear-hug it close, as he prepared to open his conquest of Mary Florida. He steered her to the other side of the horse, behind the green bastion of clipped hedge. He felt the warmth of the sun and anticipated the warmth of Mary Florida. Behind them reared the old house, whose walls supported lichen and skeins of early climbing roses.

"I want to make this place my home, if I possibly can," he expounded, moving half a step nearer to his would-be lover and clasping her about the waist. "My house in Sussex is not what this place means to me."

"Why do you say so?"

It was time to give her his story.

"My house was a sad house. My late wife was a long time unwell. She seemed to think Mistress Killjoy would be a suitable match for Simon. I voiced reservations the once, then, bethought me, it is not I that will have to kiss her. Simon must have courage I hadn't credited him with."

"Oh, how unlike my own father. His insistence was, it was my duty to wed his favoured, blue-eyed boy and no argument did he brook."

"Did you voice reservations?"

"It was my duty to the family, father said. I tried tears."

She had a stern parent, then. John would have softened.

"I was fortunate, Father insisted, that he'd got Aeneas for me. I spent a week locked in my chamber."

"Had you not a lover to rescue you?"

"Dozens, but not a one that would brave Father. Also I had nothing against Aeneas, save that he was a milksop."

John brightened inwardly, outwardly pulled a face.

"I might have done better by aping a milksop. My soldiering, where's it led me? Save I took up the cause, what was it all for? True, after all the crashing of gunfire I did not end up amongst the corpses, nor am I maimed for life. I tell myself, 'tis the King that's reduced, not I: yet he's the King still, and I so far am Blackavise."

"You talk of the dead, and lives endured with limbs missing," she spread her hands, "such are outcomes from obedience to orders."

"I don't know if I can claim even that," he said laughing, "I left the field unconscious, on a hurdle, no white flag flying save that binding my brains. When I came to, I was on my way home and discovered there I had surrendered to my daughter-in-law. I accepted the

234

King's circumstances, I have to, but I baulked at my own."

"Then I hope the good old lady hath decided to deliver thee."

"I don't care to dwell on that, while she's yet breathing."

"The world's still breathing and going about its business."

"True," he allowed, "an awful thought came to me, I think that the world, which means the market-day stage, is getting to resemble Simon and Mrs Killjoy."

"How so?"

"The times are shifting. Even I can see it from behind my blinkers. The mourning clothes you wear did not set you apart as I expected today. The spectrum's faded, we saw many were wearing blacks and greys, save that there was one riotous soul clinging to a bit of tawny. Market day other times, there'd be a bright note or two, farmer's wife in a blue tucker, wenches in the colours. But today I felt my own cloak struck a highlight. And people have taken to wearing those severe hats, taller; we aren't all Puritans, not hereabouts, yet we seem set on the fashion of new times."

"The undecidedness of it all," said she, "I'd been hid away, I hadn't seen it till now. I had never wanted to know how the wind blows."

God help him, he didn't want to know either. Here he was, by his topiary ramparts, not feeling at all Puritanical. His chief care was merely that Ginger should not spy him embracing the widow, whom he had walled in against the clipped hedge. Pansies hemmed her skirts, thereby reducing the mourning effect, their cheerful faces upturned in purple, white, and gold. Mary Florida's magpie sleeves were slashed showing the white contrast, fastened with little pearls. Where had he heard pearls were tears? She'd never look a Puritan, because of the bright hair. Perhaps he should not bend over her so publicly in case the gardeners, in their sacking aprons, were poised to form a rude chorus, or Bessie, pop-eyed, might sight him from a window. Let him lead her within doors. In a moment the rags of that water-colour cloud would overlap the disc of the sun, and he would make that the excuse.

"There's a shower above in that cloud," said he, concealing his next idea, "come indoors. May's inconstant."

It was safe at this hour. The new-found allies had returned to the Tuns, and Gerard, who had come so early, had rushed off so as to miss them. Only mornings were open house. Privacy's the thing. Desire spoke to him in a siren song. But the voice was Mary Florida's, smoothing the path he had in mind rather helpfully.

"May I see the pretty things? Ginger said you have masque costumes."

Chapter XI

It wasn't a bedchamber to which he led her, but it did involve climbing the creaky stairs to the attic over the sickroom. He would show her the masque costumes of yesteryear. The very act of ascending gave Blackavise a shiver of entering the forbidden, of tiptoeing Mary Florida towards temptation. His, certainly. Would it be hers as well? And now here he was hasting to play with carnival toys, as if they were a metaphor for the secrets Mary Florida held beneath her lace and stays. The widow's garments only made the temptation sharper, because it was outward show to tell the world that she was forbidden territory, as is a nun in the cloister. So the tissue and whisper of her underskirts as she mounted the stairs behind John teased him. He heard her following him, but he was too wrought up to look round at her. Now they were under the roof gables, lit by dormers. The timbers stretched the length of the house in a demonstration of a painter's perspective; it occurred to John that thus had Jonah admired the ribs of his whale.

"Ginger wanted a livery to attend me," he gestured at the masks on their hooks, "dressed as a nose and a set of ribbons. So far I have vetoed the embellishments."

"The masks are a strange treasure trove. Like sprites. They'd wink, if one came up here by moonlight."

He opened a closet at random, brought out a moulting costume of peacock blue and flourished it.

"What do you think to this? Look, we have feathers should you want to try flight. Look at this headdress. You'd be a large bird; at least ten feet tall. Beware fowlers."

"I see 'tis shedding a trail on the ground your fowlers could follow." Mary Florida was playing his game, possibly unaware of his motives.

He was wondering the while if washday would keep Bessie and her girls pegged down in the laundry. It should do. He was in luck.

"Didn't you say there is a crescent moon?"

Had he? What had he said about it? Oh yes, they had mentioned moons and sparred a little, on the day they'd met.

"Diana's crescent emblem. I declare I'd not play

Acteon."

Acteon, torn to death for the glimpse he had of the goddess presumably pink and damp, bathing. She'd turned him into a stag and hunted him to his death. Looking wasn't enough before oblivion came, thought John fiercely. Could he now persuade and capture Mary Florida and have her? Was she too aware that he would attempt her?

"I've seen that moon we keep. I hardly remember which of these baskets holds it, now let us see."

Here were chests of memories the old lady had squirrelled away in the days of heady abandon and misbehaviour. The painter and he had a deal of entertainment rummaging about, though after Aeneas's enthusiasm for dressing in ladies' clothes, he must not say a word of this to Mary Florida. In a roar of laughter, stuffing Pye into stays before throwing petticoats over his head, John had told the new-made lady to suck in, or his stays would burst. But there had been no merriment out in the cold world when that gentlewoman and her servant Blackavise, in Bessie's husband's cast-offs, trotted forth. Straight-faced, they had minced their horses past a knot of Parliamentary men at the Five-ways Bridge. They had not been merry out on the water, either, straining to see the boat coming to pluck the spy from the nets and barbs and catchings of his covert life.

The smelly fishing smack had been a limbo, wallowing on the tide. Now he was returned to Black House, and it was as if he had paid gold to an honest necromancer with a magic wand, for here floated Mary Florida in the black cloud of now somewhat dusty skirts. He threw a dome-topped chest open.

"Here's the moon, and, what have we here? A nest of little moons. Look, these are headdresses."

"Lovely," she extended a finger to stroke the dust from the pretty old toys.

"This silvering's flaking, like dreams," he said spontaneously, surprising himself by his burst of poetical thought.

Half fascinated by the tumbled roomful of moulting treasures, half fascinated by proximity to Mary Florida, he murmured near to her ear, "Ah, these keepsakes, I don't believe my godmother hath ever thrown out so much as a brass hatpin. Clearly, when she retired here she never laid out upon anything new again."

"Mementoes are the treasures which prove life happened," Mary Florida assured him, reflecting upon the poor, dazed old lady downstairs. She wondered if the last pictures in her mind's eye would be of all these masks and costumes made new again, dressed and animated, a whirligig around the sunbeams of her youth. She was dusting silver gauntlets off ready to try on, when the corner of a folder took her eye, shoved behind the dome-topped chest. When she pulled it out, a long cobweb swagged out behind it, and she squeaked when the spider ran. Blackavise was putting it out of the window before he saw she'd opened the folder, and when he came back she was turning the sheets.

Oh good grief, more bawdy drawings. Same hand, same quick-scratched couplings, here a satyr with a huge member, there three lewd girls, the first, laughing, the representation he took to be of his godmother. He shied off like a bucking horse. How did he pass this off? He could have done so with any other living person, not with she. Mary Florida turned the sheet a right angle and looked up at him.

"Look," she said perfectly straight, "look. It is signed Matthias Pragg."

It was, too, in a curlicue-infested lozenge down at the bottom corner of the paper, beneath the cloven feet of the Pan-creature. Blackavise's embarrassment vaporised.

"Pragg!" he cried, "the last name on the list! Thy eyes are gimlets."

"'Tis he!" She dropped the folder, dust rose and she clapped her hands like a child, giving Blackavise a gleaming sideways glance.

"Thy godmother hath a strange taste in mementoes.

242

There's no doubt she led an overactive life. She is far from the elderly saint I had been picturing."

"Francis and I had already found another equally alarming batch."

"Like these?"

"These are worse. And if I'm not much mistaken, that big plump creature in the drawings is meant to be my godmother."

"Surely not!"

"Look at the artist coupling with her, in those representations. The interesting thing is that she kept every one of the drawings. She must indeed have sat here in Black House cherishing the multitude of her memories." He cleared his throat. These drawings and the costumes and disguises were probably his legacy in the will. But he kept this ironic thought to himself.

"She wrote that name, Pragg, on her list."

"She did. The past makes us what we are. I find myself wondering why she bothered with the rest of us. Though I dare say the reason must be that, demonstrably, she'd lost him."

"They were friends enough, the once," Mary Florida ventured the hint of a smile upon him.

"The several times," he said, ruefully," I'm still taken aback, one blow from yon ostrich plume, and I'd be prone."

"Was he married, or inconstant?"

"I wonder. After Master Pragg, she was reduced to her godsons for consolation," he sighed at the loneliness of being cast aside, for whatever reason.

"Is this a dreadful shock for thee?"

"I think it was wonderful," he told her steadily, and connected into her azure eye, knowing in his heart the urge of a man who had married a pale, unresponsive and latterly complaining wife, for a wanton. But she felt a stab of anguish as she examined his strength and stature: he will take me and possess me, and I fear knowing him, for all that I want him. She backed away from him till she met a low obstacle which caught her behind the knee and tripped her. She found she had subsided into the shallow bowl of a great silvered shell, and was neatly trapped, as if in one of those dreams where one cannot rise and run away. Why hadn't she looked behind her? This length of old tinsel must have been thrown over it, and now she was entangled by that too.

"Please give me your hand," she had to ask. She was captive in the attitude of someone who has failed to rise from a curtsey, one knee under; the graceful scallop shell shone and faded beneath her. Its underside rocked on the floor as she tried to rise. Her heel was fast in a bit of the tarnished material, and he saw he must untangle her or keep her trapped. So he did both, first by lifting her to her feet, but setting her upright in that silver basin, kicking a cushion under to hold it steady, that he might come at the captive.

"Whatever happens do not be Diana," and he kissed her on the mouth. He had already likened her to a fruit, a sunny apricot, a ripe green melon, while she wore her colours; day would follow the dark of this temporary mourning show. He must override convention, and was already holding her in a tight embrace that she might feel his body. Progressing, he unpeeled the lacy moth of her chaste collar, loosening the upper strings of her bodice that he might reveal her throat, neck and a shoulder before moving south for newfound anatomy. Stimulated by his discoveries, he kissed her again, murmuring to her, reaching behind her back for the lacing strings until she sighed and let him free a tumble of swelling breasts that he might suck her there and then. Mary Florida, all shame ebbed away, yielded to pleasure. Abandoning their scallop boat they slid to the beach of dusty floorboards, leaving the great shell behind them. He dropped on one knee and pulled her down so that she came on top of him, and then in the tussle of getting close he turned her over. Her skirts were still down, but she would feel him, satyr that he was. She was stroking his face and his hair. Had he sold his soul and died for this? Would it be a heavenly

245

dream? He wanted her in the here and now, haughty Mary Florida cool in her temperate zone, veiled of eye. Oh but she was in his arms, alive on his floorboards. Did he really please her? There's more, Mary Florida, there's more.

Then they heard footsteps on the stairs. An ebb tide forced upon them, he was dismayed at being seen grovelling on the floor with a newly made widow. She sat up with parted lips, blushing, trying to subdue the surge of bosom. By the time the door opened, although she had succeeded, she'd no time to dust off her skirt, and black reveals contact with unswept floorboards.

"Go away, Gerard," said Blackavise calmly, "Why art thou here? Thy hour is mornings."

That gentleman took in that his fellow godson had been struggling with a lady of quality whose averted face and deshabille told him what went on, as clearly as the message had informed King Belshazzar.

"I have been sitting down below, this last hour," said Gerard in a narrative tone, "in order to tell you I have had my traps brought up."

"What! Why?"

"I have moved up here, of course," Gerard gave the pair of lovers a patient explanation of what seemed obvious to him, "I have come up from the Tuns. After our last conversation what else did you expect, prithee?"

I hope that is rhetorical, thought Blackavise, for I doubt you want me to tell you, not as I feel this minute. My God, at last I have the anticipation of a week, or however long it takes, to have Mary Florida sweet in my arms and, pray God, eventually, in my bed, and you arrive here. If ever I needed privacy in Black House, it is now. I could kill you, Gerard, he thought, giving that man a poisonous look. Difficult to remain lofty, when you are caught trying to tumble your darling and are not sanctioned to do so by clergy. Gerard wasn't for departing, amazingly; having caused his upset, he hadn't so much as turned for the stairs to let the lady do what she could in the way of retrieving the situation, her hair and lace collar.

"I came up, because I thought I heard strange sounds up here. When I got me here I glanced in at our godmother's door, of course. There are persons here, below in the parlour, after you, Blackavise."

That was what had fetched him up here, then. Blackavise lessened the glare with which he was still favouring Gerard and attempted to look as if mere idle curiosity would fetch him down to interview them. But he shot a glance at Mary Florida, and absurdly they both thought: it can't be that man Pragg, can it? John asked himself why on earth the missing man should choose to answer Pettijohn's summons now, he hadn't done before. What difference could having seen his name writ on the pictures make? He'd turned foolish, if he thought so. But Mary Florida bit her lip, fearing it could be trouble. John's memory leapt back to the day men jumped out upon him and left him face down in ditchwater. One day soon, his godmother would quit this life, and the whole place would be his. Recklessly in the moment he abandoned 'if' about the inheritance, and he understood the other godsons had too, for all their dark looks toward him. The Lyons and Theo Radlett, even Flynn Gerard here, had not set themselves up to challenge his, Blackavise's, occupancy of Black House. They tacitly agreed he was the favourite. So be it, he had said privately to himself, I loved my godmother all my years. But someone don't love me. So I have held my Black castle fast, and stood siege, and dispensed her claret when she would have wanted me to. Yet all the time I am watching, watching, in the tail of my eye for trouble. Has it come to get me now, I wonder? Has Gerard given me the forewarning? Has Corrydene come? Who is it downstairs? It would be too long odds that I read the name Matthias Pragg upon the marge of a page, and find that conjures him up in a thunderclap.

Please let there be no more ill-wishers downstairs. Please no, prayed Mary Florida doubly discomfited, by embarrassment and unknown persons below in the parlour. She smoothed down her moth's wing collar so it covered her shoulders, while fiddling to tie the strings in a bow. Gerard had the belated grace to look out of the window.

"Go downstairs, Flynn," said Blackavise, now able to be conversational, "I'm coming."

Gerard clumped off noisily, pigeon-toed. John found himself overtaken by the intimacies of lovers putting themselves to rights, as he brushed dust from her black bell skirts.

"I want a desert isle, with no Gerard, no interruptions and no strangers," he declared.

Mary Florida looked around in vain for any reflective surface in which she might check her appearance for wreckage, dust or giveaway moons caught in her hair. "Do I pass muster?"

"I prefer you undone."

"O don't be so cheerful! Who can it be, downstairs?"

"Only one way to discover," he told her, "Gerard hasn't met old Corrydene, I wonder if 'tis he? But no, he'd never besmirch his shoe leather by entering Black House, especially with me in it."

"Who else could it be? That Gerard doesn't know?"

"There's Pettijohn, who wrote to fetch him but hasn't met him. The doctor? No, he'd have announced

249

himself."

"Come on and we'll soon find out."

"You're game?"

"Of course. I'd die not knowing, now."

She began walking towards the stairs, holding her skirts up to avoid a second tidemark of dust. Outside the parlour door Ginger was shrugging into his official coat of duty.

"I got caught out in shirtsleeves, I've been humping the laundry hampers," he excused himself, bass and squeak together.

Blackavise threw him a repressive glare and trod him to one side, poised to throw the door to his erstwhile haven: "Who are they, boy?"

"Declined to say, sir."

So he assembled Mary Florida formally, with her little hand resting on his, giving her a glance to which she nodded, ready and perfectly stately, so he threw the portal. He found it brave and good of her to front them like this, and they advanced into the still life of the parlour. There Gerard and the wooden figure of the little black boy holding up the platter of oranges stood frozen at the window next to one another. Blackavise felt Mary Florida's hand tighten, and in the tail of his eye her pearl ring jumped a trifle; her fingers were cool on his hand. Via this connecting link he felt her breathe.

Then he and she stood still, she with her eyes cast down, and her cobweb lace and sable mourning proclaiming her a lady of quality. When upstairs, Blackavise had thrown his jacket over his shirt again, he'd neatened, too, so he presented his usual prime-of-life strength and vigour. His force of character did not need to play a part. Their appearance must have shocked the newcomers somewhat, for they now visibly reared aback. Oh no, thought Blackavise, 'tis all I need. It was his son Simon, and Mistress Killjoy.

Chapter XII

As Blackavise introduced her, Mary Florida decided that this polite usage had been invented to give people time to raise their own drawbridge, re-deploy their forces, or to withstand a siege. She responded as if a somnambulist to the little rite John delivered, and then, as he turned to introduce Flynn Gerard to his offspring, Mary Florida put her head and chestnut ruffles over the battlements to take stock. Simon was a fidgety young man, rather pink from embarrassment at this moment, with high shoulders and a beanpole frame the opposite of his father's physical presence, not robust, she thought. John's daughter-in-law, a fat young woman in doom black, at the same time similar and dissimilar to her own, gimleted the better-favoured Mary Florida with disfavour. Only minutes earlier she'd been in Susan's father-in-law's arms with her stays undone.

Mary Florida was still on edge from Gerard's crass interruption of the entanglement with her would-be seducer. All she could think of doing was to wear the disguise of the sphinx and hold her tongue. John, she was encouraged to see, was not hastening out reasons for her presence. He had introduced her perfectly naturally, and her state of mourning had denied Simon, or especially Susan, any opportunity to demand what she might be doing here with his father.

"I suggest you might try lodging at the Red Lion. Bessie hath tasks to fill six pairs of hands, whilst she looks to the invalid," he was declaring firmly if disingenuously. They'll not swallow that, he thought. I mustn't laugh. It is not amusing. But it was. Here was Mistress Susan with those currant eyes in her pale bun face, about to stab him for so suggesting, and now she had another adversary, for what was Gerard saying?

"I beg to mention the Three Tuns hath a good chamber newly empty."

John himself nearly choked on that, and could have clapped Gerard on the back for the effrontery of it. He hadn't wanted Gerard under Black House's roof, but by Heaven, he desired his kith and kin here even less.

"Oh no," Susan clamped down on that, "we have not come all this way to be lodged out. Have we, Simon."

"Of course not, Father."

253

Mary Florida was trembling on the edge of laughter, because he sounded so antique, and so used to the pecks of his hen. She would next be pecking John, it would be her duty – Heavens, don't laugh – what a thought.

John was thinking, Ye gods, tomorrow betimes there will be a raree show in here, with two Lyons and Radlett up from their flea-pads to add to this.

"King Charles, hath, I learn, this day a week back, given his Royal Person over to the Scots," said Flynn Gerard abruptly, as if the wish to shine in company had long lain dormant inside him and now awoke to greet the dawn. This claimed Blackavise's attention.

"You've got hold of a rumour, man," he declared, exasperated, "the Scots hath hardly taken Oxford City."

"Nay, I saw a broadsheet that states the King hath got himself out of Oxford, and ask me not how, but over to the Scots in disguise, at some place in Nottinghamshire. He wants to live and continue as King still."

"My eye, he does. The whole castle of cards is fallen down, then," reflected Blackavise aloud; matters were long gone that could be mended. He dimly appreciated that the King believed he would be King no matter what, and no matter in whose hands he breathed. Humbled. That was what he had become. As were they all, his supporters. But standing there, now, beset, it all seemed remote, away from his crowded parlour, as if he had his eye to the wrong end of the brass-banded perspective glass such as his friend had showed him at the Pharos.

"And that's another thing, Father."

Had he ever licensed Susan to call him Father, and in that tone?

"What is?"

"The time is lost when you might favourably have compounded, you have ignored it, haven't you."

He had forgot it, so what? When the settlement had to be made he could scrape it up, he supposed. He'd be damned if he'd go crawling to Parliament to compound early for his estate and save fourpence. He supposed Susan felt by that, out of perversity, he was penalising them. All right, he was perverse. But Simon had been sitting at home and taken different convictions to his father. And that, by Blackavise's reckoning, gave him the right to pay up what and when he chose and not go toadying promptly.

"I'll pay when I must," he said, "fear not, Simon, I'll not beggar you."

And of course this set Gerard off glaring again, as if Blackavise had been hinting at his coming inheritance, which he hadn't intended. Was this the matter which brought the pair of them to Black House? No, or they'd have got here in time to guide his hand to sign up to the payment before the due day, whenever it had fallen. A voice broke in upon his thoughts.

"I shall keep you no longer from your family," Mary Florida's words came in upon him like a gunshot wound. She couldn't go! She was turning in a swirl of black clothing, had distanced herself from him, never mind that he bled and felt pain. Of course, she was showing the proper instincts, but he felt inclined to make a public show of himself and shout out 'Don't go, I want you here with me'.

Mary Florida, oblivious, was asking, "May I ask your boy to call Piers and Jesse? I will not trouble you to see me forth."

She had bowed to Gerard, who noticed a sprinkle of silver flakes on her hem as the single reminder that he had not been hallucinating, upstairs.

She was bowing to the two young people of her own age. She had amazingly bowed to Blackavise as though she had just met him. Outside the parlour door Ginger came to do her bidding, and once he was charging away to do her errand she went in search of Bessie. Bessie, her arms akimbo, hair in strings, came out of the laundry room exuding damp; she looked as if Mary Florida was the last straw.

"Let me send up my girls, Bessie," suggested Mary Florida, "I expect you know your master's son and daughter-in-law are come? There's more than enough for you to do. I think they are set on lodging."

"I can't cope with anymore, madam," Bessie's large blue eyes seemed filled with steam, "'tis all the nursing."

"Oh please don't cry! Harken. I have kept my maids on with little employment. I'll send them up to you. Sit you down until your soul hath caught up with the rest of you. Now then?"

Bessie didn't argue. And Mary Florida left, after writing a scrawl for John and putting it into the hand of Ginger. "Here's a coin for you," said she, leaving nothing to chance.

*

The atmosphere had not lightened in the parlour.

"Ebb Brown's bailiff, of all people, Father, who remarks into my ear as if laughing up his sleeve at me, that he hath seen you 'dressed in old clothes'." Simon stammered, hard put to frame his words. "He said he saw you slinking into Coldharbour Inn with a, a, with what I take to be THAT lady. What are you playing at, Father? You have shown us all up."

John realised that no matter that Flynn Gerard's ear was pressed to this chimney, he must summon some rejoinder to concentrate the mind of his strait-laced interrogators. Do not rise to the bait, John, he told himself, you know you have a short fuse. Count to ten.

"Damn it, Simon," he began too soon and too loudly, "I did not slink."

"So you were there," cried Susan, "I told you, Simon, Ebb's man wasn't wrong."

One thing Blackavise would not be telling them was that he had been occupied in embarking a Royalist spy on the tide for France; what could he now say, since he'd admitted Bailiff Big Eye had been right?

"Mistress Lacey," he began in a very quiet shout, "had need of a journey upon business of her late husband's, and I was but accompanying her upon the road, times being what they are."

"And who, pray, had stolen your clothes?"

"Did Ebb Brown's man tell I was left naked? Forsooth, Susan, should I care to travel in my best?"

"But *she* did, I gather," pursued Susan.

"Do you mean to tell me that is the burden of your journey? That?" cried Blackavise, beginning on army tactics a little late, of attacking to defend himself. "You are about the making of Alps from molehills, and are a gossip to boot. I am not well pleased, Susan."

Susan sighed and he saw the buttonhole mouth purse. If she so much as hinted she'd pray for his reformation, he'd go off with a gunpowder bang. "Father," said his son crossly, "how do you think we felt, when we arrived, weary, travel stained, we had a foul mouthful off the heel of the landlord's pie in some tavern – we get in here, and that rude boy informs us his mother is busy and you are not at home."

"He said that!" cried Blackavise thinking 'did he, I shall tip him a sixpence, for I know he knew different'.

"Yes he did. And then that strange fellow, Gerard, informs us he is resident here. What did he say he was, another godson? And we sit here, Susan yet with her cloak on, whilst he abandons us, and when he reappears he announces he'd found you but still we wait."

"Then that door opened," complained Susan, "and you enter cool as cowcumber leading in that lady as if you had got the Queen of Sheba by the hand. Large as life. Exactly who is she, pray, that creature?"

I quite like the Queen of Sheba, reflected John cheering a moment, but, "That lady as it happens, and you do not term her 'creature', Susan, is neighbour at Aynescote down the hill. She hath most sadly lost her husband very recently."

"So why is she up here with thee?"

"Mayhap, Susan, she bethought her to enquire after her neighbour, my godmother."

Susan gave a look to her husband, who had been trying to look out of the window; but he knew his cue, she'd rehearsed him.

"It was bad enough hearing reports of thee hopping about the countryside with her, Father, but consider Susan's feelings when you fronted us with her here; we do not like the way we understand you have been out and about with, er, an unknown lady."

"As if our feelings have nothing to do with it," sniffed John's daughter-in-law, "gadding about."

Blackavise considered he kept his temper pretty well, when they had released him and he retreated to the citadel of his tester bed. He had done what? Been seen once, in shirtsleeves admittedly, escorting an utterly respectable widow, and that same lady had chanced to have footprint in Black House when his children came. He was an adult man, and free to do as he chose. Why did no-one want him to be happy? But they didn't know Mary Florida had already been making him happy. They were merely suspicious that she had. And that was dog-in-the-manger, clearly. I haven't had her yet, she's innocent. I won't let them put their oar in. Why, because they are got to be adult, am I not allowed to be the same, for all I got there first? Her presence had come as a shock to them, for how could they allow he had come close to capturing a butterfly? The rose of Aynescote, was she, and that she was Susan's age, was no reflection on Susan, but on his god-given luck, if it held and if he could hold her. When his godmother died, he'd have some tangible bait. If the godsons didn't make a pact to ensure he never saw that day. Life was precious, life was sweet.

"She's sent you a note up, sir," whispered Ginger, tugging at his sleeve.

The note's simple message, 'Come in the morning' bid him down to Aynescote, away from all the foes.

*

"The parlour at Black House is turned into a menagerie," he greeted her, obeying the invitation, "with me the bear, to bait."

But he was laughing, entering her house in a rush, and on sight made a dash for her. Light on his feet for the size of him, he had Mary Florida off her buckled shoes and into the air over his head, the brackets of his hands at her waist. Thank God, Aynescote had returned to being a sanctuary, because she was there. He plunged into the consequential anguish of offering his heart to her, indeed lowered Mary Florida so their hearts beat together. Could it be true, that I have placed her back on the floorboards and she is standing here, smoothing down her skirts, breathing and startled and laughing? At this, the sun put in a sudden theatrical appearance,

261

worthy of any stage, throwing a diamond lattice of light through the windowpanes upon them. The library where he had found her, for all its empty shelves, seemed waiting for the play he hoped to write upon the air. Nay, playwrights and bookworms could go hang, he was for the real world. This was better than living off old tomes.

"At Black House this morning, did they all come?" she wanted to know.

"They did, and they still are."

"Who stalks whom?"

"They all stalk me, I think."

"How have you escaped, pray?"

"Easy. No-one but I sit by the invalid. I declared I was for my tour of duty, and no-one bothered to check I stayed there. I'd gone up with that wench you sent Bessie, bless you – and after two minutes, even to my eye, Godmother didn't know if I were there or no. She sinks, poor wretch. But, I cautioned your maid to sit tight, and came creeping down the back stairs to liberate Hetty and get me here to thee."

"And do the godchildren warm to Simon and his wife?"

"Ah, at least we have a comedy. Theo Radlett purred round Susan, what a gelded old fat cat he is, Gerard began harping that if we were deluged by my relatives,

all those present should have brought up their kith and
kin. Which Lyons hath done, so he provoked daggers
there."

"What a melee."

"And I did no more than play strategic withdrawal to
the sick-chamber. I left them at it."

"You have a good character for sitting fast by
sickbeds; vouched for until they check and find you
evaporated."

"I didn't like pretending, nor did I want to leave," he
shrugged, "but the old lady really did not know.
Whereas I hope you know that I am here, breathing?"

"You are difficult to ignore."

One success, then. Better than the last parting.

" 'I shall not keep you from your family'," mimicked
John, "I am surprised you missed me."

"Ssh. I discover instant dislike, from that daughter-
in-law."

"She was the same when she met me," he raised eyes
to heaven, "I did not measure up."

"I felt as you did on first fronting the godsons when
they resented the cut of your cloth," she shrugged, self-
possessed, tightening the black ribbon in her hair. John
realised despite the raven dress she wore, the black
drapes hitherto half across the windows were no longer
proclaiming doom, so she must have sanctioned their

removal. He crossed to one of the big twin globes, turning it with a finger to examine its oceans for sea monsters.

"'Tis disconcerting. I've met better manners, from enemy captains. With them, I've oft made terms. Susan does not negotiate. She is ever right, and I am a worm; a simple creed but effective."

"And yet, you are not always bombastic."

"I try to be, with Susan," he said, "on principle." Then he paused and gave her a sharp look. "What do you mean, 'not always'?"

"Ah," she swept a glance across him, "are we all not in fear of thy shouts and fierceness? Except for Ginger, who thinks he can manage thee, and most days, for me."

"I had thoughts to subdue you, Mary Florida."

"No, you did not."

She had her hand on the bats and feathered cork on the table, and threw the shuttlecock at him, forgetting the sable clothes of decorum, glad of his good spirits.

"You told me that I was in possession of a freedom which many would envy, one I should hold to and prize, for no-one has the mastery of a widow such as I."

"I should never have told thee, I see my error. Are you about to beat me with that shuttlecock bat?"

"You can't but see the sweetness of freedom. If I can't be bought, I can't be sold."

"What makes you think I want to try?" And he chased her and crowned her with the shuttlecock. "Hold still. There, I crown thy impudence. Susan complained I led you in yesterday as if I held the Queen of Sheba by the hand. Mayhap she would prefer me, had I become a slippered pantaloon and given myself up under the white flag, to the frightful widow, a beldame in Sussex, she thinks could out-shout me."

"How old does she think you are?"

"Ah, don't," said John, wondering how old Mary Florida thought him. He shot her an alarmed glance. "Do you know what tomorrow is?" he asked her, "my name day."

*

"May the twelfth," he told Hetty, pulling her girth up a hole before mounting her to go home, and she waved her neat small ears to show she'd heard him." I know the day, yet I'd forgot, days tick on by," and he caught himself speaking aloud to his mare, fell silent, yet inwardly voluble while they trotted away up the hill, the twigs bearing green leaves saluting the brim of his hat. May had rushed up on him; the days of waiting, of wanting Mary Florida, had established a pattern, merging into a se'nnight, a fortnight; but his name-day was come, and with it, memories of all the others. The first one, ever vivid, when his godmother had him breeched, and he'd had a small sword to wave, and amazing breeches, to make him Jack-the-Lad in one go, and she'd called him that, hadn't she, 'Rascal,' she'd said next, 'I have a little horse too sprightly for me, could you lend me a hand?'. And round the back, in the Maytime sunshine, came old Will leading the horse with which she needed a hand. He had been too keen to show he knew what made horses go to think it strange his godmother had chosen so small a pony to ride herself. Later, he had wondered why the neighbours didn't call, but Aynescote then in its decay was mouldering in the backwater next to them, its blank eyes sightless from want of golden candlelight, and the world passed Black House by. Perhaps he would have liked other godchildren to sport with, but the work boys toughened him up and made a man of him and rubbed his corners off, while his godmother, unreproving, jollied her cuckoo into presentable youth. His mother, it seemed, had left him money into which he came at the proper time, and the rest was history.

He couldn't help reflecting, when Hetty clumped out of the green-starred wood and Black House filled his eyeball, as to whatever type of child Gerard, and Theo Radlett, and Master Lyons could have made. He decided: Radlett a toady, Lyons probably a sneak, Gerard, a disconcerting, look-you-in-the-eye boy who'd give you the creeps. As for old Corrydene, he couldn't have been a child, ever, he'd been fledged as an adult misery, and that was that. And someone had taken a horrified look at the lewd drawings, and withdrawn from Mistress Blackavise as if from contagion, and word had gone round: 'my dear, I think you should know'. Had she given the other boys ponies? Or had they merely taken the apostle spoons, as mewlers at the font? He'd been the only boy taken to live here. And the others hadn't been back since. If the truth were told, he thoroughly disliked them being here now. He felt it was his place, his duty, to perform the mourner's part, because he had lived in her family here, in the fabric of home. And now they were all gathered, interlopers, wishing him ill, rubbing him up the wrong way and disturbing their godmother's peace until she found the long night which all must face. All this had sat at his shoulder for a week or two, but the coming up close, and as it were, the tapping of May the twelfth upon his door, concentrated the burden of it on his shoulders. Strange, that he should feel it suddenly like this. But he did.

"She's not right," Bessie bent her worried blue goldfish-bowls up to Blackavise, "I do sense something's changed."

"Oh, not today," prayed Blackavise, panicking. He sat by the bed as if determination was a talisman he could impart to her. The sun made the daily crawl from easterly to southerly, and changed the angle of the warm patch that striped the bedchamber floor. It was marked by the two round buns of tabby cats, as if set to rise and be twice the size once proved. Bessie bit her lip. She thought, where did he learn to be so patient? He can be a great bolting horse, but not with the old lady.

"Them three have got here, sir," she informed him, "parlour's seething."

"O Lord, have they? I'd best go down," responded Blackavise, coming to life. He patted the sad hand. "I'd rather bivouac here, in truth."

But he hastened lightfoot downstairs to the parlour and there found Mistress Lyons irritating Susan, and Gerard brooding out of the window, Master Lyons and old Radlett conferring knee to knee. Simon was actually pleased to see him, and offered a platitude about the bright day.

"Different light, from Sussex," he said.

"I'd like to travel," said his father, "I've heard that in Italy, the light's like nowhere else."

"Have you not done enough trotting up and down this country, this five year?" asked Susan pointedly.

"I think I will take me up to glance at our

godmother," said Gerard hastily, evidently wounded by an acerbic tone not his own.

"Good morrow, Blackavise," cooed Radlett, the toady.

"We shall see," returned Blackavise. He wanted to shout 'Go away'; this was a delightful room when it was his alone, with the view over the garden, and the jumble of comfortable seats plumped up with his godmother's bright embroidered cushions. Now the weather had warmed up, the fireplace was cheerful not with flame and crackle, but with a sheaf of dried seedheads and the pearly circles of honesty. But today the little black boy was crowded by interlopers.

"How long do you intend to favour us with your visit?" he asked Susan, hoping for the best.

"I can't discuss that in front of company," came the ominous reply, but she got up, bulging as trencherwomen will, and herded John to the window, there the better to be private with him now that Gerard had yielded the position there.

"I've said to Simon, you should not be left here to carry on with that widow. I hate to think what people will be remarking. Your behaviour reflects on Simon and me, if you did but care to think about it."

It wouldn't, if you were not here, reflected John; to hang with affected delicacy. The sooner he could persuade them to get them hence, the happier he'd be. He did not give a toss for what Ebb Brown, let alone his man, might be thinking in Sussex. All he wanted was a little time to go by, so he could claim Mary Florida as a lady bereaved who had done her bit of mourning and could own him, Blackavise, in public. And she surely would, once he was set up in Black House and the godchildren had gone. Curiously, trapped in the room with them like this, he felt quite safe, for no-one could thrust an asp at his bosom or use a dagger to make a hole in him quite so publicly.

The parlour door opened and there stood Gerard, mute. But for all that his lank hair lay dead on his collar and his big feet as always emphasised his pigeon toes, a cutting edge entered the room, as if with a man who has suddenly spoilt his beauty with a raw cut turning scarlet when shaving. The Lyonses and Theo Radlett, Simon and John, turned as one, alerted.   Only Susan, impervious, took no note. Then she too looked up, cross because she felt excluded from aught that went forward without her sanction.   Mistress Lyons dropped her kerchief and Gerard wavered between advancing and running for cover. He visibly marked time there on the threshold, before opening his mouth for speech.

"She's died," he announced too loudly, and making them jump as well as attend to him.

'I heard him', thought John Blackavise, 'dear Heaven is it come today?'. He rushed from the room, up the twenty stairs, yet a little still voice told him, don't hurry, you don't want to know. But it was an empty room, her bedchamber, and that marked his acceptance. He knew she'd fled him, fled the bright May day, his name day. There was a hateful sense of ebb away, as if within John all the happy times had died with her. As if the infant days, the seasons with his pony, existed because both participants, boy and his godmother, lived and shared the link, all the links, in their chain of days. He felt very bad, and had his hands to his head when the others came crowding the doorway. Why wasn't I here? Holding her bony fingers. And then he had to deal with them all, and Bessie weeping.

Chapter XIII

Death had unchained him, though. Deaths make
freedom and let loose the pent-up tide of other lives.
Curiously, when the first bout of grief faded, John felt
life surge through him once more and he would be new
again. Having seen the old lady decline, he was grateful
to have grieved his loss and to have completed his
mourning before her last day arrived. Now let the
pattern settle. He'd sat tight in Black House, and none
of the godchildren had got to him. He was the bastard
still, but sticks and stones, he thought; this bastard is in
possession. By the time Pettijohn put in an appearance,
hot on the departing heels of the rector whose extempore
platitudes had been a trial to Blackavise, his whirligig
head was subsiding. Bessie was having a lie down, and
Blackavise merely wanted to get the formal
acknowledgement, so the godchildren might sigh and go

their ways and leave him King of Black Castle. Nobody had got an eye to the will sealed under its guardian cherry of wax in Pettijohn's strong box, and the day was warm and bonny, with the bees humming outdoors in the herb patch. No-one had been able to guide the old lady's hand to sign a new document, they'd come too late, and resentment had been a tribute to their understanding that Blackavise was top dog. Pettijohn the lawyer, his pears of jowl and long nose serene, strode into the parlour with his clerk behind him, carrying a leather case.

Blackavise, still a little numb that he survived and thus was floated on new waters, sat flattening embroidered carnations on the best chair. He wasn't looking round, but he sensed Flynn Gerard lurked on the window seat, that Theo Radlett stood behind his elbow, undoubtedly with that characteristic clasp of pink prawn hands before his paunch. Simon had hauled his daughter-in-law tactfully away, he was pleased to realise; which left Master Lyons fiddling with the tie to his neck bands, and his lady tapping her shoe like a deathwatch beetle somewhere to the rear.

Pettijohn cleared his throat. It was as if Black House parlour froze. Would they all be discovered a century hence, covered up with briars and cobweb?

"I will sum up," rumbled Pettijohn, "this will, made

some score of years back, is a brief document."

Was he not going to declaim the famous phrase, as dignified as the burial service itself? wondered Blackavise, crossing his legs and waiting. Ah yes, he was: here came the rolling foothills of "Last Will and Testament," forward to, not mountains, but a chasm. Godmother Blackavise had left all she had not to a godchild, not a one; but to Matthias Pragg, should he survive her. Should he not have done so, and only then, to Blackavise. No-one else merited a mention, save a bequest to Bessie. The parlour picked up inner musics from silence, as if many vibrating instruments played in conflicting keys. The cacophony held them fast and deafened. The lawyer and his young clerk sat watching, themselves involved and anxious to see the reaction.

"Who's Matthias Pragg, for God's sake?"

"Where is he?"

"What do you know of this, Blackavise?"

Blackavise, curiously, was quite calm. He heard, his wits ticked, he understood. He could grapple with himself later, if he must. The pairs of accusing eyes bent on his only made him the master of himself. He did know who Pragg was, though not where he was. But he wasn't going to tell them anything. He was going to think on his godmother, first. The terms of her will told the godsons to go hang. Those who had never thought

274

to search her out, know or comfort her, were now full grown and would pay for their indifference. As for he, himself? What had she done for John Nameless? Nothing but bless him with kindnesses, a basket of riches, not least the journey from the font to his claim to an adult life. What more could anyone expect? It was strange that he felt his obligation died with the old lady. But, but he'd wanted, he'd assumed, Black House would be his. Down to the topiary horse, to the fantastic masks upstairs, nothing was his. Not an item. He'd needs retreat to Sussex and be thrown back upon the children who had turned into earnest adults and rubbed all his hairs up the wrong way. Diminished, he beheld the future. I counted on it, he thought, fool that I am. As he bit on the loss, he resolutely said aloud, so Pettijohn as well as the godchildren heard him:

"I can't conjure up this lucky Master Pragg for you; no, not I. But it is her wish, so that's as should be."

It cost him, but he said it. He was commendably calm, really; as if outside himself another John stood back and watched the others make their show.

"That will's been made a devil of a long time," Mistress Lyons was saying in terms that would have shocked that old coot the rector. "Is there not another one, hid?"

And as if to stop the lot of them from breaking up the

house by ransacking the property of the absent Matthias Pragg, he heard lawyer Pettijohn's gloomy, authoritative tones saying that to his certain knowledge this was the will and she had made no other.

"I know this," he declaimed, "for we had occasion to discuss the matter when she last consulted my opinion and instructed me to prepare the letters which attracted you here."

That added up, thought Blackavise; you've no last chance to be re-instated, Johnny.

"And did you send to this, Pragg person? He hasn't troubled to journey, has he?" Thus, Radlett, the prawns clasping and unclasping.

"That is his privilege. To come, or not," Pettijohn responded.

Blackavise felt twin serpents now searched his vitals out. One, gnawing well; Mary Florida – he would be naught in her eyes. He could not give her Black House with full coffers newly his. He was reduced where it hurt, in what he had wanted to give her. Tribute to the Beauty. He had a notion beauty demanded something of the sort. He could not bear that lack. So, self-preserving, he turned to the other point, and he kept that quiet, too. He knew of a certain, that Corrydene (who had not chosen to come, either) was a godson. That Theo, probably as plump and pink then as now, was

Christened and named at the font. Lyons and crotchety Flynn Gerard were godchildren. Even as he. Yes, and he, John, was the youngest. Gerard would be nearest him in age, for his string-locks weren't grizzled yet, his demeanour was of firm early middle life. Lyons now, was cut more hatchetty, a hewn-at effigy with those rapier eyes, a man of fifty. And Blackavise wouldn't wager if Corrydene or Radlett would be the senior, they being physical opposites. He saw the latter as a marshmallow with white hair come early, the other as shrunken like some nasty old bird on its perch. But that didn't mean they'd be more than five and fifty. So, thought John, the mistress of Black House lived a long span. Many years ago now, Matthias Pragg had whipped out his sheets of paper and a little pot of ink and set about scratching likenesses. He wasn't a godson, that's certain. He was her contemporary. They'd been lovers, hadn't they? That was a different link, jolly, human, mirthful sin. Of course, John saw the difference. She couldn't hold him. She'd never been a married woman (had this Pragg been already married? Or smelt a fatter dowry? Or taken her as a joke? Such things have been), but she'd kept the drawings, the evidence. She'd never forgotten. She hadn't wanted to forget. It must have been love, for her.

He wished obscurely that his sad dead wife had left

him feeling half as keenly, half as warmly, of the days when he'd got Simon. Not every woman gives of herself. But he ached for what he hadn't had, and it gnawed him that he hadn't known what his godparent clearly felt for the vanished, roaring artist. She *should* leave her inheritance to that man. He was one-to-one, as lovers are and godmothers to small nameless boys, are not. John Blackavise sighed, and knew the difference, demoted. They needn't have taken the trouble to try and remove me. I wasn't the obstacle they thought.

*

Frank Pettijohn and the clerk Alan felt the collective weight of having had to withhold expectations. In the over-warm, juicy May afternoon they rode down the hill away from the bereaved. They hatted suitably gloomily at the coffin-maker going up the hill, and more cheerfully at the returning rector, he being the better able to bear things, and the air was full of biting gnats and flies.

"Let us turn in at Aynescote gate, Alan," the lawyer suggested, "'tis too warm to bear trotting."

Alan abandoned hopes of the Three Tuns ale, and meekly followed, swatting at the flies with his hat.

Mary Florida was a refreshing sight, and an equally reviving change from the crowded roomful of people feeling sweaty and disappointed in a confined space up the hill at Black House. There she stood, alone in her airy chamber with the window open and a breath of air ruffling the petals in a great bowl of potpourri. Master Pettijohn advanced like a galleon in full sail upon her, and she called that girl of hers, before he so much as spoke greeting, to bring a cool draught for these gentlemen and not to dawdle about it. By the time she had made them welcome and sat down with them, and seen the tide sink in their tankards, it came upon the lawyer that he was half-way to mentioning the business of other people to her; which was unlike him. But anyone may learn the contents of a will, once 'tis read. Mary Florida had less to preoccupy her than John, so she went straight to the vital point and chased it further than he had. She sat with her draught of wine untasted, and let her eyelashes do the talking to Frank Pettijohn. For the rest of what she showed, the masks in Black House displayed as much, and she did it without the paint and cardboard. What had the lawyer said?

"I'd best get to writing again to this beneficiary; hope this time he responds."

"Shouldn't you go as fast as Puck? Make sure of him?" She wished he had a more Puckish figure than a life spent at his desk and at the trencher had given him.

Pettijohn lifted his nose from his tankard and made a disclaimer, thinking of the heat, and the distance. "I don't relish trailing over to Silchester, but I do daresay it is incumbent upon me to do it. Tie up the ends." He wished he might delegate to Alan, here, whilst feeling duty's hand on his shoulder.

"Silchester! You have his whereabouts?" And inwardly she thought if this man Pragg is only to inherit if he lives, John may be more alive than he, and Pettijohn must go with all speed and prove the matter. For now I must drop a hint, or a keg of dynamite behind him, or he'll dawdle about and not put his leg over horse.

"I believe 'tis likely that Matthias Pragg has to be a very old man," she murmured, and Pettijohn, startled, looked at her over the rim of his tankard.

"Really? Why so?"

Now look innocent, as if it is of no import. Let him find out for himself. "Oh," she dropped her eyes to her clasped hands, "I think he must be the age of poor Mistress Blackavise, give or take a season. There's a scrap of paper up at the house in his hand, indicating he can't have been a godson, they were adults together." Too true, she thought remembering the drawings, and coloured. Blame the heat. Ah, nothing matters, as long as I have succeeded in concentrating the lawyer's mind. Where is John? Still embroiled up at Black House. I have thought it out, but he hasn't, or he'd have alerted Pettijohn straightways, who wouldn't be sitting here in two minds as to whether he should set out to discover if this Pragg be very elderly, or dead.

"Mistress Blackavise lived a longer span than the Almighty gave us," reflected Pettijohn lugubriously, and then he looked at Mary Florida and a small candle lit in the dark of his eyes as he awarded her a smile.

"Master Pettijohn," began Mary Florida, deviously, soft voiced, "I've let Aeneas's paperwork slip. I really must find an escort to Silchester, where Aeneas did business with his uncle. It would be exceeding kind, if we might take horse and journey in each other's company."

Pettijohn thought John Blackavise would turn out to escort her were he not committed to put on a show of respect at the funeral, if only to hide his disappointment, while the rest of the godsons packed their traps. He thought Blackavise had taken it on the chin, poor fellow. Did she mean what she said? Would she step out with him?

"Well, I don't know," he began chivalrously, "if you should think of stirring out, as yet, and in this weather?"

"'Tis growing urgent," she told him, shrugging, "for

I mustn't let the last of my husband's late uncle's affairs slip, must I? The sad event at Black House hath recalled me from indolence; there is Uncle's old house sold, and as yet I have not seen the final accounts."

"Ah," said he, "dear lady, then I will escort you, certainly."

He congratulated himself that he was still stout and active enough, that this creature would look to him for protection. A rather flattering prospect. She was in such looks again, and made him feel the heat of the day had quite ceased to try him. It was a good thing that the lady had to tease his wits with the sort of legal alternative he couldn't let rest. Pragg, or Blackavise? A greybeard, or the likeable man up the hill who might have outlived the mystery man. Might have, was no part of Pettijohn's legal vocabulary.

Mary Florida could have challenged him to a bout of shuttlecock on the instant, out of joy: he'd listened. Thank the Lord, that the late uncle's house by sheer good fortune was actually built and standing in Silchester. And she'd thought fast enough to tie that fact in with her sudden-jump plans. She didn't dare wait for John himself, because if he came, all the godsons would come, in a herd. As it was, he was safe in their company, for if he hadn't inherited, they had no need to harm him. None of them knew Matthias Pragg was the age of Methuselah, rather than the age they were. She must persuade the lawyer to get off with all speed – the morrow morn – while they were all at the aftermath of the interment and the baked meats of today. She'd sent Dorcas off to help clear the feast, and had thought, poor John, truly grieving, had to put on a show, whilst tasting Dead Sea ashes.

"Master Pettijohn," she was saying whilst brooding within, "I find you a tower of strength."

*

When John discovered she wasn't there, he would have taken hemlock; had his hold on her been so slight, that she was off without a word? Proving, utterly proving, that if he didn't get Black House and a fistful of guineas, he didn't entice a freeborn lady shorn of male chains. Who told her that, he galled himself, but me? I gave her the truth, and she listened. I told her she answers to none other but herself. He relived the bad moment with the men at the hole in the graveyard, watching anew the good earth take his happy days, and swallow that the old lady had loved him less than the man who'd spoilt her good name years ago. He could reconcile to that; but it hurt him now, as it had yesterday when the rector droned and the fellow godsons adjusted their expressions of tasteful sorrow. She'd put them all through this charade, gathered them all together, let him expect. Well, that had been his own folly. He could live without Black House. Could he live without Mary Florida?

Susan brought him round, fairly promptly. When he returned to the house belonging to Matthias Pragg (his little sketches upstairs ready to cheer his return, thought Blackavise with less charity than hitherto), Susan and Mistress Lyons were sitting like two black broody hens, one greater, one lesser, in the parlour. Mistress Lyons got up and went to her dear, and Susan to her father-in-law.

"Now you have all seen the play, I think you should go home," declared Blackavise.

"There's no cause to be sour," returned Susan, "for all you've made a spectacle of yourself sitting here waiting to inherit."

"I did no such thing," cried Blackavise, nettled, "unlike these others I came by chance, without a letter to fetch me, I'll have you know."

"Simon is anxious to be away; I suppose you have not much to pack up?"

He comprehended she expected to lead him away by the nose, like a performing bear of whom she had charge, and take him back to Sussex chastened, repenting the defeat of King Charles, the impertinence of coming to his godmother, and, oh yes, of being descried in the company of the Queen of Sheba. All of which he clung to.

"From what Mistress Lyons hath imparted, your godmother was not all you were led to believe," Susan told him as if bracing up a child, "so put the whole episode from you, 'tis best."

Blackavise felt resentment. And his wits twanged, and he became aware that rising through shocks and irritations, he had identified a truth.

"I shall not accompany you for the present," he heard his normal voice, and prepared to parry whatever Susan next said, oblivious, for he had let surface the truth already netted by Mary Florida. The absent Matthias Pragg must be at least a hundred, or seventy plus. Or St Peter had admitted him. Pragg had never been folded in the same sheep pen as the rest of them, had he? No. You do not bracket innocent mewlers and pukers bawling at the cold water from the font with adult fornicators who get detected and earn a bad name. John had found those drawings, thus knew this. The other godsons don't know. Only me. Well, have I outlived this Pragg? 'Tis possible. Nay, likely. I may have the house yet, and the rest of the estate. Don't shout about it. Find out. Susan was still droning on.

"We can hardly leave you here, can we?"

285

He pretended to be listening.

"The new man'll be displeased to find you still sitting here, won't he, and Simon and I do not like the sound of the way you've been disporting yourself up here, we would have you gone."

"Be quiet, Susan, I have things to do."

"What things?"

"That," he brushed one hand against the other dismissively, "is my business."

"'Tis that widow," Susan with the button-hole lips pursed added to his woes. But he wasn't wearing that, from Mrs Buttonhole, not he. Here came Simon, looking awkward.

"Listen, boy, you can get you away. I've a bit to see about."

His son stood on one leg rubbing the toe of his bucket-top boot on his other stocking, like a stork; he looked very young and earnest, and Blackavise was sorry for him.

"Two things, Simon. I am a free agent, as art thou. I shall inform you as and when I choose to come to Sussex. In the meanwhile, let me wish you well, and a quiet journey thither. Remember next time I am reported to thee, I am about my own business, and it is not a crime to be abroad in my shirtsleeves. I don't need you or anyone else to chase me up on the grounds that

some farm bailiff misliked the sight of me. Ever again."
At which he turned on his heel and left them to each
other, as they deserved, and set about clearing his head.

By the time he had parted from Flynn Gerard, Theo
Radlett and Master and Mistress Lyons (the last trio
looking him too frankly in the eye and Gerard too hotly),
he was hopping with impatience. Let them be off down
to the Tuns and pack up their traps. They hadn't
drowned him, had they? Good riddance.

"Ginger, hath thy long ears failed thee?"

"I haven't heard a word," Ginger admitted, "I don't
know where Madam's gone."

Damnation! So Blackavise rode Hetty hotfoot into
town and hitched her, blowing, under a shady tree
outside the lawyer's door. The clerk Alan, alarmed by
the vehement, insistent gentleman, let him have the
address in Silchester, and told Blackavise that it had
surprised him to see his master, Pettijohn, rouse himself
at all, let alone so early.

"'Tisn't like him," Alan spread his hands; "but he'd
got him away at an hour this morning when usually he's
still sitting in his dressing-gown."

"I see," said Blackavise, but he wasn't listening, was
wishing it wasn't Silchester, full of Puritan fanatics.
Last time he'd been there, he'd had his troopers, and
now he'd have to go without reinforcements. So he set

out and unbeknowing chased Mary Florida, as she had once chased him. But she already had told the truth to her lawyer, who had been sufficiently interested in what she chose to tell him about Matthias Pragg not to be pompous for more than five minutes.

"It would have been a shame," she'd wheedled, "if you trotted, and Piers and Jesse and I trotted, half a mile apart."

He wasn't cross, he was starting to be clear-minded. He found himself expansive, insofar as he allowed himself such an indulgence.

"I first met Mistress Blackavise when old Crabtree was her man, and that was years back, when I was a young sprig Alan's age. Her will was already made then, and I vouch that there was none other made in my time. I thought that list was godsons all."

"So did each, and she chose to gull each one."

"'Tis hard, being abandoned," Pettijohn said in his plummy voice, "mayhap, that was the message."

"She who laughs last," suggested Mary Florida unoriginally, giving a touch of her heel to the riding horse, that he might catch the lawyer's big grey's longer stride, "but why would she include the one godson who did care about her, in the punishment?"

"Depends on when this Pragg fellow died, if he has," Pettijohn replied, "if he's been bones these many years, she may have thought that will is well enough as it stands; it would go to John Blackavise anyway. That's my assumption, for all it wouldn't stand up in a court of wigs." He shook his glowing jowls. "I've seen a great deal of that sort of thing down the years. Intentions are the one part, setting them down utterly another. You'd scarce credit; but older souls forget that circumstances change. I can ask, is more thought required, but if the answer's Nay, I can't do more, that's that."

She had cause to be grateful that Aeneas had made the one will after he wed, and never looked at it again.

"I dislike jaunting abroad," Pettijohn sighed, "yet for all I could have sent Alan out in my stead for me, I've a brick in this wall, and though I'm old and stout and 'tis warm out riding, I want to see the outcome. Someone ransacked my papers, a lawyer's papers, and I tell you this, while sitting in Black House parlour yesterday, I wanted to know which of those godchildren had a hand, or I may say hands, in that."

He loomed over Mary Florida on her smaller horse, and looked warm and humanly determined. Thank heaven, thought she, and I feared he'd chide me all the way.

Silchester had its towering church and its mushroom caps of many roofs crammed below, and impoverished looking townsfolk in ragbag homespun. They'd had

Rupert through the town twice, and Hopton, and Ireton chasing. Some of the houses still reared their charcoal rafters to the sky where they'd been torched. The lawyer and the lady in black and the two serving men looked about them, and counted themselves lucky they lived in their backwater. Aeneas's uncle, the man who'd concealed Thunderer in his kitchen, had dwelt out of town in a stone edifice which had resisted tampering. Mary Florida had never set eyes upon it, for it was sold now, and no more rough hooves trampled the crockery. Aeneas had let his man-of-business deal with it, of course; no chance of his going forth, in warfare. She had wondered if she should foist herself on that man-of-business, but he was not vital except to furnish her excuse for coming to Silchester. Pettijohn was fatigued, and it would be better to accompany him straightway to whatever inn looked decent, that he might rest him. In the morning they'd inquire for the whereabouts of Pragg, and find whether he be quick or dead. They had an address in Sheep Street, and there in the morning duly fronted a pair of columns with greyhounds atop, guarding a flagstone walk to six shallow steps and a tall door. It was not the venerable gentleman they sought who met them, though. Pettijohn gave Mary Florida his arm and they advanced decorously up the path, both somewhat on their guard.

They were nearly bowled over by a rush and clatter caused by a stout small child with an iron-bound hoop. The child, a self-possessed maiden of six or so, fetched up smartly and gave stare for stare to Mary Florida. And Mary Florida was hard put not to smile, for the formidable little thing had the look of a dowager, so firm her chin, so double its undercliff. She would not lightly have bidden it to bed.

"My dear," mooed Pettijohn downwards, "we would trouble you to fetch your parent."

"Pray accompany me," squeaked the infant, abandoning the hoop, and with determined tread marched up to that great door and pushed, and gained admittance for all three. Her father, presumably, came, and he was a good-looking stern young man, with a cleft chin, wearing sober black like a Puritan. He was a Puritan. Mary Florida wished she were in quieter lace.

Pettijohn was explaining, in avuncular tones. He was the executor, needing to prove a will: a simple enquiry, if he might presume? They were let into a formal chamber and placed on upright chairs whilst politenesses were exchanged. Mary Florida twined her ankles against the barley sugar twists, and felt her heart painfully hopping up and down. What was this Puritan Adonis saying?

"Father'll be pleased to help, if he can, he's in the

garden – I'll give him a hail."

After an extended pause, like a century, a hale pewter-haired version of the young man strode in, with lead-grey eyes and an expression of enquiry therein.

"Matthias Pragg, at your service, sir," he inclined his nod to the lawyer, and on hearing the man's name Mary Florida's pulse quickened like a parade-ground drum.

But no, it couldn't be, she realised. He was yet in middle life. He was of a godson's age. The reality of time's passage reared in her breast like a phoenix, wings flapping. He was …

"If you will forgive the enquiry, sir, is your father yet living?" enquired Pettijohn, reverential as a Judge.

"Grandfather's been dead these twenty years," answered the younger man, and his begetter at his elbow nodded. After a score of years grief had faded. Mary Florida and Pettijohn, strangers united by the circumstance, now shot red-hot glances one to the other. Dead! Said the look, and we can prove it.

Chapter XIV

What might Mary Florida do, chained to the elderly lawyer who had no intention to travel back home till the morning? She was forced to kick her heels and wait to deliver the vital news that the Pragg household contained the quick who were not named in the will, and the dead, for whom the great bequest came too late. Mary Florida recognised she was for the hard path of waiting while time crawled by.

"Get me an early night," Pettijohn declared, "so we can be off early in the cool of the day. You'll be pleased, Mistress, that we took the bird in our tree so sweetly."

He was as fixed as the Rock of Gibraltar, the crumbs of gooseberry pie scattered round his empty platter. He was pleased that the Dragon Inn was such a decorous, well-run establishment, and its cook had a feather hand with pastry. Mary Florida made a change from his matronly wife and lumpy daughters, so he was only now ready to rise from table, quite sleepy from the splashing of wine from jug into tankard, and smiling a little upturned crescent, supported by the pink pear cheeks. He had no legal knots of 'on the one hand, or on the other hand', to irk his dreams. He yawned, apologising for sitting on while the candles brightened and twilight closed in.

"I have not often enjoyed such charming company," he patted Mary Florida's unrestful hand, and bid her sweet dreams.

He left her as though she were a ewe lamb at her door and clumped off to his bed in a room round the corner; she saw his substantial outline depart in the halo from his candle, and that was that. Oh, this is jail, thought Mary Florida. We can't go till morning, I'm in for this long night awake. 'Tis too late to walk abroad, even if I told Piers and Jesse to accompany me. I am here in a strange town, the townsfolk in straits, and the flow of the times shifting to a new river of Parliament supporters. So there was nothing for it but to shut herself in the Dragon's homely bedchamber, she a powder-keg within, telling herself patience was virtuous, and by heaven, Black House had its true master. Good news could wait. Doesn't happiness keep? The funeral was done, the will was read, and let's assume the other godsons were packing up today, John fuming the while. She was almightily glad she'd given him the slip, or they'd all have followed him over here in a regiment, had they realised the absent Pragg had outlasted the benefit of his term on the planet, that he wasn't a godchild at all. Thus leaving John target of his ill-wishers.

*

John, following her train of thought, made as much use of his mare Hetty to follow her hoofmarks as he ever would, and he got into Silchester late that day. Sheep Street the second time received a visitor with courtesy, and Blackavise exercised restraint to keep his good fortune quiet when he discovered the artist Matthias Pragg was no more.

Pragg's middle-aged son, well-favoured grandson and this fat little hope of the future in her cap and bib and tucker, struck Blackavise's sense of humour inopportunely. They were all admirable, strait-laced and sober, but not such as he could offer a folder of naughty drawings, as a memento.

"I am most obliged to you, sirs," said he, serious as they.

"Your lawyer hath put up at the Dragon Inn," quoth

the younger Pragg.

He was probably praying he would find no more strangers on his doorstep; John recognised the tone. Just so had he indicated to his bothersome, Gerard, and to Radlett, the Lyons, that he did not feel personally obliged to lodge them: get thee to the nearest hostelry! Brave their fleas. He gravely hatted out of their lives.

"I think you'll find them well lodged, 'tis a decent inn," called the middle Pragg after him.

"Them?" queried Blackavise, startled. He'd left Alan in Pettijohn's office, hadn't he?

"Your lawyer brought a lady with him, we supposed her to be a beneficiary."

"Thank you," exclaimed Blackavise, "I hold out hope of that."

He fled back into the market square and braved the bristly black hat and shawls of a righteous goodwife putting her cat out, who directed him towards the Dragon Inn down a side street. Hetty trod the cobbles. Here was the inn sign, swinging and creaking over his head, St George thrusting at a small put-upon red dragon. Then he found he couldn't nerve himself to go in. He took Hetty into the inn's stable yard and had her looked to in a commodious box all to herself; and paid the man, and wondered how he could get himself in and announced, late as it had got, in the circumstances.

Yellow upper windows indicated bedroom candles. Above the windows, above the crouch of the roof, tints of darkness were washing deeper in a crocus colour, with a sliver of moon. John marched into the Dragon Inn, thinking to announce the name St George. But that wouldn't do the trick. And the Dragon landlord looked a polite, serious man, not ripe for slaughter, when John came upon him in the act of taking off his apron for the day.

"Ar, we got Master Pettijohn lodging, he retoired an hour back," said the innkeeper, country voiced, "made a good supper, first though."

"And Mistress Lacey? Retired also?"

"She have, sir."

"Oh, that's all right," he said, "Tell her ..."

*

Mary Florida still in her ruffled petticoats was removing a pearl earring, and her back hair was down on her shoulders, when the servant tapped.

"Master Lacey's here, M'am."

She dropped the earring, her pulse raced. The earring rolled and rattled, as the room evaporated all but the rising door-latch.

"Forgive me," said John Blackavise, "I'd have

297

swarmed up the ivy, but there is none."

So she was shut in with a husband who was across the threshold in a single stride, closed the door and turned the key behind him. The moment had passed when an outcry would have alarmed the servant by protesting that this was no spouse of hers. How could she escape? Did she want to? It was too late now. The fact that he had calmly come in and penned the two of them in was all she could register. Speech was gone. Not with John, apparently, who asserted himself by leaning on the doorpost, at ease, poised to open his campaign of amorous intent.

"I've been testing the waters of this curious town," said he conversationally, "'tis full of Puritan beldames, yet they still boast a trollop or two amongst them who the twice propositioned me as I walked up. I suppose custom hath fallen away, what with the Godly nature of the day. I walked up from Pragg gate. Is this your pearl beneath my foot? Here, take it before it is trampled. Most certainly, I said Master Lacey, since I am desperate to see thee."

Mary Florida received the pearl as if it might bite her.

"Now," he said, "we each know how matters stand. First, I am a fool to think you had fled on hearing I had not inherited Black House. You braved much to ginger up old Pettijohn, to get you here. This penetrated my dull wits. I asked myself, what could it mean?"

"I bethought me," she managed to reply, "that old godmother of yours couldn't have stood sponsor to the man who parades himself in the lewd drawings. He must have matched her years, and today be either very old or very dead."

He approved the lightness of her approach. "Indeed, I followed the same trail, having been beset by godchildren who had no idea how to react to the news that I had not in fact wiped their eye. Thus far you are ahead of me, and also I am probably slower witted."

"We were not wrong," Mary Florida mouthed. She would have been audible, but her energies were exhausted by the sight of John Blackavise leaning his shoulders as an additional barrier against her door. Rouse yourself, cried Mary Florida inwardly. Why don't you shout Help? Because I want him, since the day I saw him, half drowned, carried in like wounded Acteon hurt by hounds.

"Did you consider that I only cared for you if you inherited Black House?" she asked, fiddling with the pearl at her ear.

"No. I feared it was me who might be shallow when I was demoted in favour of this unknown man. But I wanted to brandish the house so you would take me seriously. The thought of subjecting you to my son and his sad sack of a wife in Sussex holds no appeal for me, or if I may say so, for you."

"I understand that. I worked that out on my own."

He found himself admiring her fortitude under fire.

"Nor will I play the role of Aeneas," he told her, "I am not for strutting him in any play. I am not for representing myself by stage tricks, behind a faceless mask and silks and curl paper. But I am for you becoming Blackavise, and I've come to complete what we have essayed."

He turned his dark eyes upon her, and she said, "Show me."

This was the moment, and he likened her presence to that of a feathery, exotic bird with turquoise-coloured eyes. Now the bird was singing and had become a nightingale.

"Mary Florida, since you were pleased to grant me so high an honour when you returned my kiss, pray let the two of us prove the pleasures and delights." He was not prepared to fawn over her, nor would he beg or cajole. He crossed the room, assumed his place on the edge of the bed before shrugging off his short coat, his full-sleeved linen shirt and his heavy riding boots. His mane of tabby brown and silver fell across his bare shoulders. With a shock she saw the power of his muscles, the firm carapace broadly made, a great contrast from Aeneas poring over his collection of pretty Dutch glass pictures in the safety of his parlour.

John looked back at Mary Florida. "Join me, my love," he said, and extended a broad hand to invite her to come closer, the light of anticipated pleasure in his dark blue eyes. She moved towards him, her petticoats rustling, until he was near enough to touch her. She let him untie her petticoat ribbons, undo her earrings and place them with a chink next to the candle on its pewter saucer. When he had pulled the last ribbon he kissed her full on the mouth and encircled her body in his strong man's arms, feeling the warmth of unclothed Mary Florida against him.

"Thank heavens you are no longer constrained. I hate stays," said Blackavise truthfully, ravished by the sensation of her young breasts on his skin, "nothing's sweeter than this. You must have guessed how much passion I have always felt for you. God knows, you've had me tied in knots." He was distraught, but wholehearted. Since that far off day in the lawyer's office when he first learned that a Beauty and her husband had moved into Aynescote he had felt impelled to test the truth of the gossip. Too often in the backwater of restricted social circles, any woman who was free of pockmarks was called a beauty. Having his particular Beauty naked in his arms at last, had he been armed with

a Golden Apple in his hand, he would have awarded it
to her there and then. Mary Florida was pink and ivory
and smooth as the goddess Venus from a painting. His
breeches might be lying dead and lifeless on the floor,
but had he ever felt more certain he was alive than the
moment Mary Florida responded to his caresses? In the
amber and shadowy light of the candle he put his arm
beneath the small of her back and she arched her body
as if she were that loveliest of goddesses rising from the
sea-foam. In this new ocean he sucked her rose pink
nipples. She ought to have blushed, but Mary Florida,
roused, had sharp little teeth and she bent and bit his
shoulder.

"What do I taste of?" he asked.

"Royalist," she told him.

Now you're ready, sweetheart, he thought. Aloud he
whispered, "Feel me."

And she knew him for all he was. John possessed his
Beauty, and she knew a pleasure which she had never
known existed.

Chapter XV

Joy and fulfilment was his. Mary Florida entwined in
his arms in the inn's soft feather bed had given not only
her heart but the promise of her ring finger. She would
accept him. He envisaged a whirligig of rushings and
dashings to Aynescote on his part, and an absurd wish
to run a flag up to signal his welcome every time she
trotted her riding horse into the courtyard outside Black
House. For the necessary interval of decency the lovers
would hide from the prying eyes of Bessie and Ginger.
He presumed they would have long suspected him of
making sheep's eyes at the lady, but had not reasoned
she would respond, she being the catch of the county.

This was the sudden doorway to the future. But in
the present, the dawn light in the morning came and was
unwelcome to John, who realised he had better be gone
from the inn bedchamber before the church clock next

beat the quarter. It wouldn't do for the good lawyer to glimpse him leaving her bedroom. A breakfast account of their separate journeys and the similar discovery of the demise of Pragg would do well enough to explain his arrival. He dreaded the unwelcome quarter to strike. As dawn rose, trumpetings of songbirds outvoiced the murmurs from the man and woman in the softness of the inn's best feather bed.

"I had no idea that reality could be this pleasurable," revealed Mary Florida against his willing ear. To hear such a thing gave him a thrill, which increased because then she added "Aeneas was but nothing compared to this."

Whatever the Bard had writ, comparison came in no way odorous to John. What an idiot Aeneas had been playing his damn-fool games.

"All men are not bastards," he declared, "I may be a bastard, but only, I do hope, in law. Your late husband was a real bastard, as we understood the word in the Royalist army. I hate to think he distressed you. Certainly I do assure you I am not for cavorting in skirts. I trust the only people I hurt were the King's enemies. I have nothing but love for you and my determination to offer you this as long as we are alive together." (And, he added feelingly to himself, I am even able to back up love and determination with the actual fact I have inherited Black House.)

The chime of the unfeeling bell sounded, and he swept her hair from his eyes, and made himself sit up against the pillows.

"I wonder where I threw my shirt, the white flag of surrender, Mary Florida, with which I yielded to thee."

"I thought it was for me to yield," she whispered.

There was the shirt, he twitched it, but she would not let him tent his strong man's torso until she bent her head and kissed him.

"There, upon thy heart," she told him," I give thee my surrender."

With these simple words she declared for a union between their estates and the future of their bonds in wedlock. She did not dare to harp on the prospect of happiness in case it was too much to ask of Fate.

"Should the good Lord permit," John told her, "I want to beget us a little daughter, like to thee. I believe in proving these pleasures, not one's nose in the book of poetry but the clasp of my arms enjoying your silky skin, Mary Florida."

The journey homeward took its course. Pettijohn allowed himself to be re-captured by his womenfolk, and his travelling companions had a happy parting from him at the steps to the repainted front door of his house, he backing away resounding with their thanks. He felt quite dashing, and younger from the success of his lawyer's mission. Then our hero and heroine set out for Black House, with Mary Florida in her nun's black, decorous and graceful on her riding horse, by his side. He began to think of the improvements they would bring to the big old house which he had lawfully inherited. He would brush aside the fleabites of telling old Radlett and Lyons and Gerard that they might now leave, and close the door after them as they left. But he would be kind, now; he could afford that much. He contemplated these pleasant prospects until the weary horses scrunched within sight of the oaken front portal of Black House. Here his dreaminess was stripped away as if a surprise attack had come upon him out upon army manoeuvres. Someone had nailed a dead cat to his door.

Mary Florida, horrified, hid her face in her hands, and at the sight John vaulted the hotfoot way down from Hetty, throwing his boot up and over her neck. As he landed with a clatter he felt sick and disgusted, feelings mastered by his fury at horrid shadows unwelcome on this sunniest of his days. First he ran to turn Mary Florida's horse so she did not front the sight where the poor tabby hung spread-eagled, its death-blood striping the wood. He'd seen far worse in the army, God knew – men, horses – but this innocent domestic creature, his godmother's companion? Were there darker undertones

306

yet, of witchcraft associations?

"Aaah," cried John Blackavise aloud, his happiness ripped from him like blossoms in a squall. I wanted respite, I wanted peace. Why have my enemies not given up? They are not done even yet! Why this enmity toward me, for even though the godchildren know full well the will did not favour them, it does not favour me, but Pragg?

He threw Hetty's reins over his wrist so he might lead Mary Florida's horse by the bridle and turn her from the sight of the bloodied animal when she took the hand from her eyes.

"Don't look, don't!"

"John, they mean to kill you, this is a warning to frighten you off."

They certainly have not lined up to give me a round of cheers, he thought bitterly.

"Then I must deny them that pleasure. Where's Bessie? Where are the girls and Ginger? Piers, attend your mistress." Mary Florida would be safe out in the bright day guarded by her brawny serving man.

"Jesse, come with me."

Why had he assumed the staff and the motley godsons he'd left at Black House would suddenly have become lap dogs by the naming of this stranger, Matthias Pragg, to disinherit him? Wait: although he knew Pragg was not living and could not displace him, as yet they did not. It was enough to make his head spin. One thing was certain. He, the inheritor of Black House, had an enemy lying in wait, be it whomsoever. And this house is mine, thought Blackavise grimly. I'm for keeping it. He strode for the kitchen. But here were Bessie and her girls armed with flat irons, at their homely tasks, to a faint smell of singeing. Was he mad? Had he imagined that cat? One glance at Jesse showed him that he had not. Was Bessie a witch, and had she called up the whole dance of all this with incantations and what-not? Had a spell on the cat gone wrong, or was she training up Ginger as a warlock?

"Bessie!"

"Glad to see you home, sir," said Bessie utterly normally. The steam from her weapon wreathed her cap and had caused her bit of front hair to go limp. "Can we ask, sir?"

"Ask what?" he responded, dense with problems.

"Be you the master of Black House, sir?"

"I survived Master Pragg," said he grimly, and she, simple soul that she was, smiled at him never heeding his tone. She was used to his roarings.

"Welcome, our master," said she, and the little wenches simpered and made him a bob, normal as the day.

Blackavise tried to regulate his wild eye, compose his features.

"Bessie, thank you, but not now! Tell me if you have been forth by the front door this afternoon? 'Tis important: when did you last use it?"

Bessie furrowed her brow, a rivulet of condensed steam coursed her cheek, she sped it with the back of her hand and concentrated on Blackavise standing before her.

"No sir, we'd no cause to, busy as we be to get th' ol' place straightened up. What's amiss, sir?"

Blackavise had interrupted her because of another horrid thought.

"Have my son and his wife got themselves hence?"

Was Simon, was poor Mistress Killjoy, in danger? He nearly went to shake poor Bessie, whose thought process, ever gentle, took time to achieve speech.

"O yes, sir, they left this very morn."

He breathed with relief.

"An' that Master Gerard got himself gone, he hath left a letter for thee. 'Tis his bedlinen, and poor Missus's, that we be ironing, making all fresh."

"Something nasty's happened, Bessie," John warned her, and put his hand on hers, "where's Ginger? I want you, and the girls, to go down the hill with Mistress Lacy, she's outside now. You are to lodge with her at

309

Aynescote till I have sorted matters out. Now don't create! You'll soon be back at your laundry."

"But, sir?"

"Do as I say. I'll see about it, then you shall all come back."

"What's come about?"

The maids were exchanging big eyes, Sarah with a wobbling lower lip, Plain Jane, poor soul, looking as if he intended to whip her. So he said, "Come along, my pretty ones," and he took Sarah's flat iron out of her fist and set it down for her, "some fool, I can but tell thee, hath done one of our poor cats to death and left her for a sign upon the door. That the sign was meant for me, is certain – there have been other signs, remember. I got me thrown in a ditch. And so forth. Well now, I have come into owning the house, someone mislikes it, mislikes me. I will wait and see if I can draw out the culprit who is responsible. And while I am about it, you will lodge safe, down the hill, with Piers, and Jesse here, to look to you."

"Oh," said three round mouths, and there was a bit of huddling together and twittering, with the irons cooling and the sheets creasing in the big workaday kitchen. And he put his arms round them and led them forth enfolded as best he could all three, Jesse clumping stoically behind. There in the late-day sun, with their shadows elongating, sat Piers on his nag and Mary Florida wilting. He hastened to them and requested what he had promised in the kitchen.

"May they come to you?"

"Of course," said she, "But …" She wanted to say, 'Don't leave me. Let me stay'.

He didn't want to hear the words – he guessed them, forming, and motioned her to bend to him, that he might speak low.

"Dear heart, I must draw out my enemy. I'm the only one who can fetch him out. I'm the …" he was going to say 'bait', but that'd not do," the magnet. So if I know your Piers and Jesse will keep you safe, I can deal with it." I hope I can, he thought seriously.

"I can't leave thee alone, in danger."

"I'm an army campaigner, remember. I would that Colonel Cromwell had shared thy views."

"O, John!"

Shh. They'll hear you. What matter if they did, in the circumstances.

"Keep Jesse."

He looked at the country boy, raised an eyebrow at him. "What d'you say, Jesse?"

"I'll do whatever you say, sir."

"Then return to Aynescote and look to the household. That'll be more help to me, than anything."

John looked to Mary Florida, and Jesse followed his glance. Mary Florida side-saddle on her horse was poised as though a statue above Blackavise, yet she trembled, and he knew she did.

None of my enemies will keep me from her, he vowed. I must protect her from all my troubles. Piers and Jesse can make sure that she is secure in Aynescote. I have to sort out my enemies for good and all. I am certain someone means to do me to death. Not quite sure why. I must find out.

"Now go," he urged, "and come up in the morning, boys, if I am not down to you." He needed them away, that he might have time to think.

Piers on his horse, Jesse hopping round with a foot in his stirrup remounting were too busy grappling with the idea of these events to speculate when John Blackavise, in parting from their mistress, put his lips to her hand. Not the formal, plant-a-butterfly an inch above the surface, but inwards, on the pulse at her wrist, and she had leaned down that he might do it.

*

He took the poor cat down, pitying it, and was done with watering Hetty in her stall, beginning on the bubble of waiting and waiting, when the missing Ginger came whistling up the yard with a fishing line and three troutlings hooked over his shoulder. Like his mother and the maids, he did not use the big front door used by Blackavise, his betters and the slayers of cats. He strolled in by the kitchen door, not in any way disturbed, and he was pleased to find his master had returned. Blackavise soon altered that. His succinct account of the state of affairs changed Ginger in the course of hearing it from a cheery greeting to an honest gawp, followed by shoulders-back resolution.

"I'm here, sir, that's two on our side."

John wondered who was on the side of the ill-wishers; he enquired this of Ginger out loud.

"Who do you think, sir?" parried Ginger, "all of them?"

I hope not, thought the object of disfavour. "I understand we've lost Gerard. He hath gone home and left us."

"Or is that a pretence, sir?"

"Who knows? He's left me a letter, for whatever that's worth, I must read it directly. I imagine his style is that if he intends me harm, he'll announce it. Nay, he'd have hit me over the head and be done with it. He's set for home all right. I feel it."

"Ought we to check the house through, sir, before dark?"

"I was on my way."

He shot the bolts to the doors to the outer world one by one. The front entrance still bore its horrid smears, and Ginger fired Blackavise a hot-eyed glance. His master nodded. "I've lowered their flag, boy." Inside, the house was slanted with westering sunbeams laid levelly; so normal. Blackavise even noticed that the topiary horse of clipped box still stood, stump-tailed when he let his eye range out from the cathedral chill of the dairy. Then he checked the window catches. Well, the outer world was still standing. It was surprising that the green-leaf ears of that topiary horse had not laid themselves flat back, after the draughty events blowing round Black House.

He turned, banging up the shutters. Before he made twilight come, the homely objects seemed to taunt him, ready for the routine now suspended. There were the dip-scoops, in graded sizes, hanging above the milk pans and pails. Bessie had set a good round cheese on green leaves, upon its platter on the cool tiles. Next to it were the wooden butter-presses she used on the yellow pats waiting for the household to have a calm meal again. Blackavise sighed, and ran up the darkened steps to the kitchen. It was still lit by sunset, and the linen baskets spewed forth snowy sheets and pillowslips, some smooth, some in wrinkled heaps. The flat irons stood cold and lifeless upon their stands, like the pattens which ladies wore to keep their feet dry above mud in the streets. The room felt undisturbed and deserted. He'd learned how to sniff out enemies waiting to send him off to Hades, when some Parliamentary zealot believed that heaven was saved for his own kind rather than that of Blackavise. He got Ginger to help him raise the flagstone ring so they could get a peep into the hidey-hole in the cellar below, where the spymaster had gone to ground. Casks and cobwebs dwelt there alone, unless there were mice. They let the big flagstone groan back and they stood dusting off their hands.

"Right. Now for the parlour and upstairs."

An empty house, lacking the unwell old lady for its heartbeat. In her chamber Bessie had stripped the bed of its linen and the tester of its drapes; the window was flung wide, letting in the outdoor wafts of Maytime. Blackavise half chid himself for reaching to shut the window, when sense and reason told him that unless his assailant would prove a bat, no-one could get in that way. He thought, deliriously, that if fate allowed it this would be his room and here he would lie night after night with Mary Florida. Everything seemed to float, and reality was suspended like those golden fish that hold time still, finning in the flow. Thus, his life.

"I think it is Lyons," he responded at last to Ginger,

"he chased me up in person, I dare say, only when his hired men failed to dent me. What do you think, boy?"

"Mebbe," said Ginger with little faith in his master's judgement, "or was it all of 'em?"

Blackavise would not look again to Ginger for cheer, but then they jumped at a banging from the cupboard, and he felt thoroughly reduced to Ginger's age and status, when investigation released the other tabby cat.

"Poor old Tib got shut in, then," Ginger ushered the animal toward the stair, and Blackavise laughed at himself ruefully when the cat raised a flagpole tail in acknowledgement.

"That one's safe, at least."

"I think the old party, Theo Radlett, was in on it. You heard some passage down at Aynescote, did you not, Ginger?"

"Yessir. That makes two of 'em."

And there's another godson hiding over the hill, let's not forget Corrydene who loves not my breeding.

"Why are they against thee, sir?" asked Ginger most politely, as if enquiring if Blackavise would take his bedroom candle yet.

The sparks from Blackavise's eye shamed the sunset. They fired at Ginger, who stood back a pace on impact.

"Damnation, boy! I am bastard born and I've taken this fine house from beneath their outstretched palm.

316

That's chapter and verse."

The old lady cared for thee, thought Ginger honestly.
"I hope they don't get 'ee, sir."

"That's handsome," cried John coming to himself
and he clapped Ginger on the shoulder and directed his
sparks more kindly. "Now seeing as you have thrown
your lot in with me, then we are for besting them."

He had a rudimentary strategy, and although he
would have preferred six troopers to support it, he had
been forced to recruit poor Ginger in his beardless state.
But so be it, and with Ginger's help he would set his
trap.

"When I am ready I mean to draw them to me. Let's
throw our eye around. I want a furnishing or two for my
design."

He must leave himself an escape route, and not paint
himself into a corner. His plan was to bring the enemy
to the upstairs hall, where the passages led off and the
stairs came up, with the further flight up to the attics and
a bolthole onto the leads. He needed a lantern, his horse
pistols, and patience.

"When I tell thee, boy, run for it. Give me thy word."

Whoever came, he'd tease upstairs from the floor
below. He left all he needed in readiness, and primed
Ginger with the essentials. Then he ran downstairs and
unbarred the single entry, the front door, so he would

not be crept on from behind. He didn't think his enemy
would resist the single firefly he left burning as a sign,
a dark lantern, with the cover hinged open. Twilight
was gathering helpfully out of doors. He occupied five
minutes in reading Gerard's screed by the last of the
twilight; sat him on the stairs, turning the page to the
lavender glim from the rising moon. It was brief.
'Thank you for the hospitality. Black House was not
destined for me. I remain, your obt. servant, F. G. Post
scriptum, Mistress Radlett knew your mother'.

Mistress Radlett?   Had she spoken from the
hereafter? He'd assumed the avuncular old gib cat had
no wife, but merely because he had failed to recall any
mention whatsoever of such a lady, it didn't mean he
never had one. No law about wives, or widows. He
should know that. Did he care? Not unless this was the
link which led to resentment, jealousy, and the rest of it.
Blackavise began to wonder if he should not have got
more sleep last night. It was still only early evening,
time for the first candles to have shrunk an inch, when
that extra sense he'd acquired in the army made his neck
hairs prickle. Starlings on the roof, or a servant stirring,
make as much noise as the scraping open of that front
door. There were leaf-rustle footmarks. Blackavise
could imagine the rapier dart of eyes left and right, the
chiselled features of Master Lyons. Only the one set of

318

treads, he thought. I wonder he didn't bring up his friend Theo to hold his hand. But Blackavise hadn't expected what came next. It was a woman's tremulous bird-cry. Who was it? Had it been Mary Florida, his every nerve-ending would have known. It was not Bessie's homely note. Was it a trap? Was this the goat staked to bring forth the tiger? He breathed in the shadows, willing that his outline cast by the moon might reach the bend in the stairs ahead of him, and itself grow eyes. But he judged the moon kind when, even as he wished, a cloud came and cut off his shadow self. Now it would not announce him, and he could creep to the corner of the stairs and let his own eye do the spying.

In the oblong of the open doorway to the wide world, and advanced a yard within it, he saw the outline of a woman, small within bundled garments, a cap, shawling, skirts, and beneath, the giveaway of two turned-out small flat feet. Blackavise never mistook a foot. It was Mistress Lyons, quite alone. Shelving his plan of enticement for the moment, he let her stand there and the second time call his name in a half breath undertone, then he ran straightways down and bagged her, the first captive of the campaign. She reminded him of a poor fowl that expects to have its throat wrung, with the jerking and flapping that went on with the fright he'd administered. But all he'd done was pinion her wrists together in his one strong hand and hold her with the other, once he had the portal safely shut and the bolt thrown to. He called Ginger to bring the lantern, and to hold it so the rays might illuminate the face of the lady who, he bethought him, had asked for him by name in a low voice and had not cried out in one louder, when he'd given her every cause to utter a good screech.

"You seek me, madam," said John Blackavise quietly, "I'd know why."

She flapped to a standstill and he unhanded her. Ginger angled the bright light at a slant, so she might look back at them, and she showed determined mouse-eyes, round and black. No-nonsense, said those eyes. We'll see, thought Blackavise.

"Matters have come to a pass," said she, "that I'm come to alert you. He thought he could warn you off, of course."

"Who? Your husband?"

"Don't interrupt. No, Theo. We had to come, in the end."

So Radlett had writ that letter, had he? The bastard attended keenly, for Mistress Lyons was unburdening herself of a cargo.

"My husband hath got himself into great debt, and he blames Theo for some investment, one of those doomed adventuring schemes. It sank with the ship, it foundered

320

and brought no hold of sea pearls home. Theo had said, we could not lose."

"People do."

"Then the conflict, and bad times."

Blackavise sought to circumvent a weary tale of all that. He could guess, and wanted her to come to the point.

"And where does Black House come into it? And me? And this?" he prompted.

"It came out that my husband and Theo shared old lady Blackavise as a godparent. The connection had long lapsed, for the two families discovered years ago that she wasn't what she, she claimed; had a past, and had been quietly forgotten."

Not by me, thought Blackavise.

"She was still alive, and presumed wealthy, it was a last throw, to get us here to gather favour and know her. Can I sit me down? I have rattled up the wood in the dark, and tied the nag up and came in straight."

He made her sit on the stairs, and stood over her.

"And why, pray, so vindictive towards me?"

"'Tis none of my doing," she said, "but my husband did not see why the godson he knew base born, should become rich."

"They wanted me to throw up the connection, fearing she would leave me wealthy?"

The shoe-button eyes blinked that he should be so understanding.

"Simple as that? They make me unwelcome, they threaten, and I run off?"

"Well, no, they discerned you were for sticking."

"So they hire some vagabonds, to try to drown me."

"Never mind about that now," said she with aggravating female logic, "I didn't come to discuss that."

Blackavise became riled.

"Then in the name of Hades what did bring you?"

"It is not right that they should hold your daughter."

My daughter? Great God, what is she saying?

"Who?" Did she mean Mary Florida?

"Your, Simon's, wife."

"Susan!" But, Susan had left with his son that morning.

"I am afraid," voiced the mouselet, and something in her tone made John believe her.

"Why would they want Susan? Where's my son?"

"They have him too."

"Why didn't you SAY SO?"

"You didn't ask me that; I was explaining. I couldn't let them hurt a woman. My husband seems not to be himself at present."

"Where are they?"

"He asked them in to the Three Tuns to drink with him as a farewell, as they journeyed away. I think he hath them upstairs as if for a private party but he won't let them leave."

"And he let you leave?" Was this all a ploy?

"No he did not, I ..." she broke into unlovely tears, and he recognised she had been brave to escape.

"Then sit you here, safe, and I will go about the matter."

Here he was, stuck in the mousehole with the cheese, and the cats were down the hill tormenting poor Mistress Killjoy and his son Simon, who had never been robust. The first thing to do seemed to be to separate Messrs Radlett and Lyons. Once he had done that, surely he could knock them off one and one: and liberate his family.

"You say, your husband seemed not himself. How seems old Radlett? Himself, or worse?"

"He seems in a great state, something against thee, which he had from Flynn Gerard."

That was a great help, thought Blackavise ironically: Gerard, even on departing, could be relied upon.

"With my husband everything is money," said the little woman earnestly.

Blackavise wondered if this was supposed to give him cheer.

"O good," he allowed himself, bitingly.

She couldn't read irony. But he was halfway out of doors, calling for Ginger, turning the key to lock her in. Ginger would have to bump down the hill side-saddle on her riding horse unless he looked sharp about it and set to unbuckling the girth, in the minute it took Blackavise to put saddle athwart Hetty in the dark, hay-smelling stall. He was glad of his preparations and the pair of horse-pistols readied; he rattled down the night-time wood whilst a vixen barked in the distance. The full-leaf twigs beat their wings against his face and stung him with their canings. Beneath the horses' feet rose leaf-mould smells, all very other to the walling up of himself inside Black House like a corpse in his tomb. Ah, action was better! Far better, and now it was imperative. He knew where his enemies were and he could call up reinforcements, since taking Piers and Jesse would not now jeopardise Mary Florida.

At Aynescote gate, three parts of the way to the Tuns, he sent Ginger in to fetch them. He had a sight of Ginger flapping his reins and flapping his inexpert heels like Sancho Panza, against the illuminated Aynescote windows. He himself was clicking his tongue to Hetty and tidily wheeling to go as fast and collectedly as possible to have a tilt at his windmill. Here in the circlet of trees beyond the Tuns he drew rein and looked at the outline of the inn. In the yard a wagon reared its shafts to the sky; there was a glim from the kitchen and upstairs someone was wasting candles, for one window was bright canary yellow.

There they are, he thought; I suppose they are expecting me. So let me move that cart a yard and get a leg up to the sill next to theirs. Let's hope the axle's dumb, I don't need a squealer. Blackavise employed his shoulder and with a haul on the shaft nearest him, the cart came about as if it were a ship under the tiller, and there he was below the window, taking two big steps up onto the wheel and then the wagon-side. A hand on the windowsill prevented his weight turning the balance into a see-saw, and then, seeing the casement had been obligingly left open, he swung himself in with a crash and a clatter, landing upon his feet to a satisfactory round of about-turns and rearings-back of the company there assembled, who had been facing the other way. Startled outcries were all stilled. Blackavise had tried and tested ere this the swift greeting of the steady gaze of the pistol he took from his belt. His eyes were less impersonal, for there was Simon looking far too young, and Susan with her hands tied up giving a sad foretaste of how she would look when old: a complexion of yesterday's pastry, all strained and lapsed downward, and her forehead showing two new furrow lines of anxiety.   There was the landlord, in his apron, shirtsleeves at half-mast, looking imploringly at Blackavise as if handing over his duties to another would set matters right.

One godson put up his arms. A toy pistol fell from the hand of Theo Radlett, who jumped back, away from the apparition of soldierly determination that had sprung at him from the window. Master Lyons however kept his head, and clapped his long-nosed pistol promptly to the head of Susan, who gasped and glared at Blackavise. In less harrowing circumstances he would have been glad to see she was still herself. But he'd played similar games in the last five years, and he was used to move and counter. He didn't let Lyons pause to keep the advantage, but virtually without thinking played one of the oldest tricks. His own pistol never wavered, and with his other hand he felt in his pocket.

"Here, Godson," he cried at Lyons, "take thy inheritance!" and threw King Charles's noble profile, gleaming, "Heads or tails?"

Of course the non-soldier's eye flicked upward with the eye-catcher, and of course the pistol wavered. Blackavise threw himself across the space between them, and discovered he had knocked Lyons off his feet and was now sitting upon him, the hand which had lately grasped the pistol spread flat on the oaken floorboards

326

as if still begging for that silver coin. Radlett ran for the door and Simon started after him. The landlord bent over the four-legged confusion of Blackavise dodging a rabbit-punch and turning Lyons over in a throw he'd learnt from those big Cornishmen he'd recruited. There was a loud crash, and Lyons had lost the breath and the will to argue further.

"Well done, sir," said the landlord, "I could do with 'ee on hiring-fair nights, when I've throwers-out."

"Are you hurt, Susan?" enquired Blackavise, putting the hair out of his eyes.

"What do you think?" responded she, "this is all your fault."

"Thou art as normal, then. I am relieved," declared Blackavise, his indigo glance registering relief; and then, even as he still let the round eye of his pistol regard his prisoner, he heard shouts from the yard outside. It was Ginger and the men from Aynescote. He hoped they were in time to bag up Radlett, if Simon had not managed to do it. Here came footsteps, and a two-tone squeak.

"Ginger, sir, an' ol' Piers and Jesse."

The door let in what seemed a small herd of boots to Blackavise, still sitting on a level with his charge on the floor. He hoisted himself and gave Aynescote's servants eye-for-eye, and Ginger a pleased nod.

"Didn't you trap our other rat?"

"Who, sir?"

"Radlett – but Simon may have …"

"I can prison this one up," the landlord tugged John's sleeve, "till we get magistrate to do it for us."

"O, yes," he had scarce bethought him, what next, "can you?"

" 'S a pleasure," said that good man, "and he ain't paid his reckoning, neither."

Simon, maiden's-blush pink and blowing, came back. "No, he slipped me. I'm sorry, Father."

Blackavise sat on his tongue to stop the reproach. He could have done with the easy mind of the man who'd taken all his prisoners. But he thought, one's caught and one retreating; that's not bad.

"What in God's name has been going on, Father?"

"Oh, good grief, boy. Not now!"

"I think you should tell us," Susan said, "I suppose this is some enmity of your war-mongering."

"No it is not," said he with spirit. "I've had better interchange with Parliament and Puritan, I'll have you know, Susan, in what I've heard termed This War Without an Enemy, than I have with some grudging fellows who didn't like that I inherited from my godmother and they did not. That's what it is, and all it is."

"What d'you mean?" Simon asked, "I thought you hadn't inherited? Some man, Prigg ..."

"Pragg. He's heard the last trumpet, and so far I have not. But it was money with you, Lyons, wasn't it? You must be far gone. But I was a stranger to you. Why think if you attack a stranger, it is less to your conscience, than had I been familiar?"

Lyons, winded, was still holding the shoulder upon which Blackavise had thrown him. He gave Blackavise dulled-rapier eyes. "I didn't hate thee in person. Nay; I wanted debts paid. That's not hatred," he smiled a very small smile, "that's expediency."

I'd have been just as dead, thought John, whether you hated me or not would have been immaterial.

"Nay, it is Theo that hates thee," Lyons informed him, and cackled.

Chapter XVI

He was an innocent, perhaps, that this stung. Shooing
Susan and his son towards Mary Florida's castle keep of
Aynescote, they shocked and frightened, if unharmed,
he found himself a ruffled ocean. That would not do,
for he had yet half the night's work unaccomplished.

"I never wish to endure the like of this again," said
his daughter-in-law, accepting his arm that she might
thud down off the riding horse Piers had given up to her,
"I was terrified."

Blackavise fought the absurd urge to utter a truth,
only narrowly beaten back by common sense; he'd
nearly said, I wager Simon is, most nights. He'd not
win by side-tracking himself. This was time for single-
minded attention. Upon Theo Radlett, wandering the
wood, riding Jesse's horse; so Jesse, Piers and Simon
had perforce to walk the way to Aynescote. He should

have given Simon the ride, and made Susan walk. Nay, remember, she's had a pistol at her temple. That's penance enough. He checked round with his night-hawk eye. He'd ever been an owl in the dark. Well, he'd lost no stragglers, not even Ginger, who was thoughtfully hitching Mistress Lyons's nag to a ring in the Aynescote wall next the mounting-block, and about to do the same for Hetty, who looked round at him enquiringly for a haynet. No-one's routine was sacred, not tonight.

"Come Susan, my boy,"

He herded them without ceremony in at the porch. They had not visited the big house before, and stood rafted on the shiny floorboard sea of the hall as if for once looking to him for guidance. That door hadn't been barred. Fierce because of a hundred fears, he strode towards Mary Florida, his face set.

"Why was that door unlocked?"

Dorcas and her mistress had to hear the soldier's tone; but Mary Florida, large eyed, stood up to him and raised her chin.

"'Twas fast, until we recognised it was you in the lantern light. I put the bar up myself when the men left and I only released it this minute."

"Good, good," he said tersely.

She visibly bit her lip, succumbed to panic at the

sight of Susan and John Blackavise's adult son standing there, invaders in her home. Messages flagged down her glance. Please explain, please speak.

"Sweetheart," burst out John toward her, repentant of his fierceness, and the explosive force within him had him take three strides and clasp her hands to his heart. Thus was the mine of his secret blown high, as if into the clear blue sky when Rupert had blown the breach at Lichfield.

The wall of secrecy was detonated as such a relief to the two principals that they clung hand on hand, united, proud, and then realising what they'd revealed, turned as one to the others. There was Ginger hopping up and down in a silly grin, and Jesse and Piers taking refuge in immediate eyes on the floor, but Simon, poor soul, looked as if he'd caught them in flagrante.

"So this is what's been going on," remarked Susan.

"Good grief, Father. Er, well done."

Sunrise burst on John Blackavise. He might have an enemy bagged at the Tuns, and another cherishing adamantine hatred for him loose in the wood, but if Simon and he could clap each other on the shoulder as now they were doing, he rejoiced.

"I've caught the Queen of Sheba, boy."

Which allusion had Mary Florida lost, but she saw the two men smiling, and relief swallowed her, all but the jewelled eyes. Susan felt the defection of all present to the cause of sentiment. Here she was in the act of opening her mouth to cry folly, but the tongue in her mouth turned to stone and made her dumb because of this mummers' show of everyone apeing pleasure. 'For Heaven's sake,' quoth Susan inwardly, 'you have all gone mad, but me'. She saw clearly that her ground was lost, her allies had deserted, and she was marooned in the house of this creature presently holding hands with her father-in-law as if all that was lacking was a flourish of trumpets. She found her voice.

"This is no time for that, when the unspeakable Theo Radlett is dancing about outside, waiting to follow his friend and put pistol to someone's head. Mine, probably. Father, you should see about that matter, and forthwith."

"Thou'rt right," acknowledged Blackavise. "Look to yourselves, put the bar back up at the door, and let me be off to see to the trouble. Susan will enlighten you as to the ordeal that man Lyons put her to in the meanwhile."

He lowered his tone from this general address and spoke into the ruffles guarding Mary Florida's left ear.

"I licence you to turn a firearm upon Mistress Susan, should you find need. Don't wait for old Radlett to do it. I'm for drawing him up to Black House, 'tis me he is after. We've already bagged Lyons."

"How?"

"I threw him for daring Mrs Killjoy's ear with that pistol of his."

"Did you? Well done!"

"She's had a tough evening. Being grateful to me comes as a hair shirt. Make her a cordial."

"I will." She clasped his hand, "Don't be so matter-of-fact; I am affrighted."

"I love thee, that's armour plate."

He sundered, all but the glance, and retreated keeping it, as if he backed out before royalty; thus, she diminished while the eye contact held. He reached the door.

"Ginger?"

"I'm for thee," said the boy, "Black House it is, sir."

"Send Jesse and Piers with the daylight. No argument: I want them to stay here, keep all safe, don't argue! Let's be away."

"This is all foolishness," quoth Susan.

His only real fear was that Radlett would ambush them in the wood and try to shoot a hole in him, so he took Ginger and himself roundabout, and walked the horses up the garden through the silent topiary outworks. He looked to see that the ramparts of Black House lived up to their name, a bastion of darkness.

Mistress Lyons could not have had the mouse courage to fiddle with a tinderbox even if she'd been able to put hand to one, or a candle.

He guided the horses into their stall, safe with the strawy bedding and the hay nets ready to blow into. Then with the sprite at his side with the lantern, he sped round the building and entered his own front door. He'd scrub the blood-stripes away in the morning. Always supposing his were not ready to join them.

"Mistress Lyons? Thou art no lioness, I see. Yes, we are returned, and thy dear is not a-roaring. But we have Theo yet to deal with, and therefore, I am sorry, but you must go in the little room here, without candle, and I am going to lock the door to protect thee."

He implacably trampled her therein, deaf to warblings, and that was that. Now to the unfinished business: he'd had it all planned. Well, he could temper it a little now, with one caller expected, not two. He re-rehearsed Ginger, for events had moved since he'd told him what to do.

"I 'ent forgot, sir."

"Ready yourself."

He thought he'd brought everything he needed from that attic storehouse. He placed his firefly, the lantern with its door open, on the hook at the front entrance, then its companion on the little table in the upstairs hall at the head of the stairs. It would be a beacon to draw anyone up who stood below. Should he have gagged Mistress Lyons? He'd not relish the doing of it. Too late, now. He'd laid out his bait here, and he wouldn't interfere while – good gracious, was this Mr Footsteps already? He'd been waiting but the half hour. Ginger was hidden round the corner of the stairs leading up to the attics, and John was frozen to the crack between the door and its hinge, his eye to the gap. He discerned an approaching candle. Radlett had taken the lantern down from its hook at the entrance, and therefore had one hand occupied holding it. John needed Ginger to play his part on cue, or he would lose the moment. But he must lurk, and this close. The flight of stairs creaked, as if the old house complained. Here came Theo Radlett, large as life, though smaller than his shadow which forewarned John. The actual man followed the exaggerated outline on the boarded floor. He was looking about him, the glow of the candlelight catching the pink of his complexion and the halo of white fluff on his head. He was checking to see if the rightful owner of Black House was about to jump on him, as if he were merely about a stroll in the garden and checked for wasps. What had Lyons repeated? 'He hates thee'. It was a personal issue, though not on John's side, but he wanted to find out why. Radlett soft-footed to the other lantern and the table upon which it stood, and he looked down at the objects set there. Perhaps I've tried to be too clever, thought John. But no; he's taken the bait. Radlett had been hovering, he picked up the stool John had left overturned to indicate his own hasty departure, and he sat down upon it. He had a touch and a fiddle, like a miser drawn to gold; and then he laid down his own, single pistol (the companion to that which he had left on the Three Tuns floor), for he saw he might augment his weapon with the very flintlock placed there by Blackavise, who had been wont to discharge it at the soldiers of Parliament.

John saw its familiar chasings gleam in the close-set candlelight, saw Radlett smile affectionately upon it and begin the out-of-practice labour of a sit-at-home, fiddling to load it. Blackavise had laid out the powder-flask the little lead spheres, all the paraphernalia. He was glad to feel his second pistol snug at his belt. Now, Ginger, do your trick. Do it. Where was he? Ah: a face appeared round the staircase corner, startling in the lantern light. It was all nose with dangling colours at either side. Because Ginger was hanging on to the banister with his left hand behind him, peeping round the corner of the staircase like a gargoyle, the mask-face did not appear to be connected to a body: it looked sinister in the blink of the moment. Radlett jerked his head up, Ginger retracted, and the staircase was as blank as hitherto. Radlett, after two looks transfixed, dropped his eyes to check the readiness of the new pistol. He's not used to safeguarding life by drill, that's clear, thought Blackavise, who could perform the ritual in the dark. Now it was his turn. He pulled on his mask, a grinning harlequin, leaned on his door a little, and tapped twice on the panel to be sure Radlett looked round, as well as to give Ginger his next cue. Here came Ginger tossing his streamer-ears, vermilion and blue. Radlett stood up bemused, and the full-face towards John became a profile as Ginger obtruded and Radlett turned to eye him.

"Get away, get away!" cried Radlett, and he started up the stairs toward the smaller will-o'-the-wisp and the gleam of Ginger's own lantern set above. He left the table laid as if for a duellists' dinner, with the two pistols and the spare bullets and powder-flask for a cruet. Blackavise watched him vacillate, then dive for his own familiar pistol, nearest to hand. This had given time for Ginger to dash away and get him hid. John stepped forward hastily once Radlett tackled the stairs, to remove the bullet which Radlett had so painstakingly loaded into the other pistol. He replaced that weapon as it had been left and cats'-paw footed it down the passage to the servants' door, which led to the ladder upstairs.

"Wrong way, Theo," he shouted.

He was very glad indeed that Radlett had no soldier's instinct. Here he came back down in a disorganised manner, waving the maw of his pistol like a pointer at a blackboard.

"I wish to talk to thee," Blackavise told him firmly. Judging that the moment had come, stood there to be seen and recognised, held the shield of the stout door, poised himself to back off, and threw it, just as he'd planned, so when Radlett's pistol spoke it spoiled the door panels. Blackavise had to take on trust that his enemy would now snatch up the other pistol, the one that he had emptied. He ran up the Jacob's ladder to the broad plain of the top storey, where the garlanding of old bolts of cloth and the chests of masquerade trappings, all Black House's yesterdays, were placed to watch and listen with him. What next? A dusty curtain boiled, and out popped Ginger, mask now round his neck and his big eyes urgent upon Blackavise.

"I heard the bang – did he miss thee?"

"He hath shot the servants 'door stone dead. It's off its hinges. Not me."

"Did it work?"

"Yes, he hath now the unloaded pistol, and I have the ball snug,"

"Where's ol' Radlett now?"

"We'll wait and find out. Back under your curtain, boy," He handed his own pistol to Ginger. "Use your judgement."

Steps were advancing. John picked up Ginger's lantern, let it point where it would light his own face and set it down, poised to turn as if startled. Radlett was delighted to have taken Blackavise unawares.

"Do not move!"

"You have me," pretended John, and raised both hands in the gesture to comfort his adversary. He stood there exhilarated in the moment; he was about to take his enemy Radlett prisoner, confident in his empty pistol, and rooted to the spot within negotiation distance. John could do whatever he wished, as he had unloaded the other man's weapon. And Radlett didn't know it. Let's tease him out a little. Let him boast at me.

"What's to do, Theo?" he asked and tried to sound apprehensive.

"Of all people, you ask me that? For you surely do know." Radlett shook his dandelion-head of white hair. His avuncular countenance in the theatrical mixture of candlelight and shadows gave Blackavise the creepy sensation that he beheld a man in a weird state of mind. The memory of the dead cat returned. Hitherto he hadn't seen the give-away gleam in Radlett's eyes. It was the reverse of Ginger hiding normality under the mask, whereas Radlett's false face, built in, had seemed normal. It had slipped.

Blackavise spoke. "I've inherited everything from our godmother, Theo, and there's naught you can do about that; it goes to Simon after me, even if you shoot me dead," he made his expression assume apprehension, he shrank away a little, and he was aware Radlett enjoyed that. Let's try further. Could he be pathetic?

"In this conflict that has been called a War without an Enemy, I lived by that description so far as I might," Blackavise heard himself say in hangdog tones, "I have an enemy, Theo. Tell me why."

Got him: Radlett was ready to enjoy telling him, relaxing a bit, caressing the pistol.

"I've been waiting, Blackavise; I thought you'd run away."

Not even the New Model Army had made that assumption, thought Blackavise, making stern clampings-down on his normal attitude to insult. "I might have," he made himself say downheartedly, "but why did you want to be rid of me? Now you've got me, you can face me with the truth."

Why did Radlett's smile now seem sinister? 'Tis a pistol with no shot, remember. Blackavise allowed

himself to shrink back upon the big chest, closed shut
upon its folders of lewd drawings and ostrich pluckings,
and sat down upon it at if overcome by weakness. The
chest creaked, protesting at his strength.

Theo rolled his tongue round his pink lips as if
anticipating   dinner.   "You've   done   me   harm,
Blackavise,"   said he.   The pistol made nods of
agreement.

"Have I? Not by my deeds, nor yet by soldiering,
surely?"

"By your life."

That was a nasty phrase. "However mean you?"

"You call me sir!" cried Radlett unexpectedly.

Blackavise saw the curtain containing Ginger sigh,
as if feeling an unusual draught. "What mean you,
'sir'?"

"I am your better. So's Ann."

Who the devil was Ann? Wait! Gerard's letter.
What was that cryptic remark: 'Mistress Radlett knew
your mother'. "Is Ann your lady wife?"

"You know damned well."

He didn't, but an old cobweb brushed his face, the
spider in it, his past: was this John Nameless come to
haunt him? What had his mother done, upon the
business of begetting him? Was it that? Genuinely
disconcerted, he mentally retreated to regroup.

"I'm sorry," he heard his voice in untypical humility, "what have I done?"

"You dare ask me that? You pretend not to know? You have a pretty legacy, Blackavise."

"I really have no idea what your drift is, if you don't mean Black House."

"I do not mean Black House, left you by a scandalous old woman I care naught for."

He meant that, therefore it was Lyons on his own with the debts. So they had made an unholy alliance; but what was the cause of Radlett's sore hide? What next?

"I hate thee, Blackavise, for what you did to my wife."

"I have never clapped eye on this Ann of yours," bellowed Blackavise, restored to normal outcry, forgetting to ape fear.

Unfortunately this roar of his provoked Theo to laugh and sneer together, and the slippery light that wasn't a smile in showed in his eyes. He'd stirred up the old fool this time, observed John, and irrationally, felt his attention drawn to that pistol in Theo's grasp. Twenty feet remained between them. Should I rush the madman, before he could shoot me? But he can't shoot me, don't turn foolish.

"Tell me what I ever did to her." He was intrigued

now.

"I blame thy mother who begot thee," cried Radlett suddenly.

Well, yes, a lot of people had. But why Radlett, particularly?

"Your father," began John's enemy.

Here came news, and Blackavise stood up off the oak chest.

"Your advent ruined the life of my wife, Ann." Radlett told him, raised the pistol, aimed and shot Blackavise for dead.

Chapter XVII

Three people received a profound shock at the crash of powder igniting. John had oft enough been in the position of danger when heat of skirmish had presented scenes when kill or be killed (save a mis-fire) had complete hold. He stood upon his two feet marvelling that his illusion of safety had been real, for all he'd set it up. The crash had near deafened him, his ears rang in the confined space. Radlett, on seeing his enemy alive, and impervious, stood aghast. Ginger fought his way from his curtain and clapped his loaded weapon wildly to Radlett's cranium. The two principals locked eyes.

"Thou art the devil's tool!" cried Radlett, looking in vain for the bullet hole in John's body linen.

"No, I merely removed the ball."

And Radlett had sufficient sanity left to turn beadily, shiftily guilty, caught out. Downstairs they could hear

Mistress Lyons in the grip of hysterics. John produced the ball from his pocket and grimly displayed it.

"Now you have shot me, do you feel better about yourself?"

Radlett put his hands up as if to ward off the devil. Ginger and the pistol shadowed him, the boy with eyes as big as a hare's in the crisis. But the instant of the bang had punctured the fantasy Radlett had allowed to grow upon him. He had been forced to accept the enormity of what he had meant to do, and that this deed had been denied him. John could tell the difference between Radlett's warped intention gnawing at him under his smiles and rosy cheeks, and the sudden cold dose of reality. The bang of the pistol should have rid him of the bastard he hated. At least he hasn't my corpse to explain away, thought John. But that is no thanks to Radlett's urge to shoot to kill me. John felt as if he himself were the test for strength that was routinely applied to body armour. He'd formed a habit of touching the impress on his breastplate to reassure himself that he should be proof against the Parliament.

"Theo," said he, "what you're telling me, is that my father," (odd word, that, on his lips) "spoilt the chances of who? Ann? Who is wife to thee?"

"Nay."

Good God, were they at dreamland again? "What,

346

then?" cried exasperated John.

Ginger, prompted, gestured with the one loaded pistol, and Radlett fidgeted the gleam in his eye to and fro.

"Nay, she was. Was wife to me. She died."

Oh heavens. Blackavise, having found a link to his background, had in the blink a parting; his heart heaved, sank and readjusted.

"But what you tell me is, that she suffered by my entering the world? Ginger, I'll take that pistol." His own mother had suffered; but he could not work out who this Anny had been as yet. He got the collapsing miscreant into a chair, dust rose, and Blackavise sent darts down his glare to penetrate this cloud.

"What do you think?" snapped Radlett, "the family suffered; they had probity, they had standing, and then when your father was on the altar steps to marry Ann, he was exposed as a seducer. Your father had been betrothed to poor Ann, naturally that put a stop to the marriage she had wanted." He subsided with a grimace. "Word was noised abroad. Ann never had another prospect. I eventually became a substitute."

So the memory of the lost suitor had clung. Assuredly John's begetter's way with women had not been matched by Radlett, to whom, Blackavise surmised, she had sunk as a last resort. Perhaps comparisons had been voiced. It would account for the comparison's bastard offspring being a thorn in the Radlett marital flesh, even offstage and unknowing.

"I fail to see that this is my fault."

"The family suffered. What God-fearing household would not? Oh, there was one good thing came from the interference of old Mistress Blackavise."

Sarcasm, thought John, I ever mislike it.

"One good thing?" he enquired, seething.

"She removed thee three counties hence up here." Radlett smirked, in parody of his old-avuncular performance.

"I dare say I benefited from the cleaner air," Blackavise battened himself down.

"Of course word got about, then they couldn't get up a good match for Ann."

Radlett had not relished having to live with being scraped up as second best.

"Ours was a Godly household, the background to the way we lived. The shame, the disgrace of your begetting, blighted our lives. Before Ann was to be wed came the shock of your bastard arrival, sired by the bridegroom. The horrified family called the wedding off. For some reason Ann pined for that ungodly man whilst we were wed. I had to endure those years. I believe we scarce exchanged a word, daily, save before company."

Radlett's wife had wanted to marry John's father. By God, she took a mean revenge, thought John; think of living like that. So his long-lost progenitor had a near escape from this Ann, and then vanished, John knew not whither. He concluded that Ann and her unwanted second-best husband Radlett had deserved each other. Radlett had not finished.

"That disgraceful old creature our godmother, had to befriend your mother, that Jezebel, and stood sponsor to you, the bastard brat," Radlett spat out.

Blackavise had not considered his mother as a Jezebel: his parting from her as a six-year-old, holding his godmother's hand at the deathbed, rose painfully before him. Her poor face had been unpainted and as anemone white as the pillow. Sinning had not suited her, he reflected, unlike his godmother. Life was unfair.

"I was glad when Mistress Blackavise's true nature got noised about. No better than thy mother, Blackavise."

"So let us come to it. Art thou of the opinion those peccadilloes gave thee right to kill me?" demanded John, infuriated.

Radlett blinked. He grew pink and white and baleful.

"It came upon me," he said, "I could not take, that we were fellow godsons. Anny resented thy bastard existence."

I suppose she would, thought John, and it saddened him. He vowed never to take to resentment, the canker of life.

"So you intended to kill me."

"I didn't consider it in that light. I wanted thee gone."

"Such is life," growled John, "so you took steps, reached the tipping point? Didn't want to do it yourself, not to begin with, so you hired the nearest deserters to shove me in that ditch. Yes Theo, such is life; there's many I would wish, er, gone. But 'tis no part of our brief to act on the desire. That, I daresay, is the difference between us."

Before him, squashed in the chair, crouched the punctured pink of failure and something other. He was unhinged. Blackavise shuddered. The mixture before him in Radlett was, presumably partly being sorry at being caught and a portion of pride that he'd shot to kill and been a hero with a pistol even if it had no bullets. He had provoked Radlett, of course, to determine if matters were so far gone as that. He'd had to know if his adversary would do murder. Had Radlett baulked at this point, if sense, reason, had prevailed, John could have forgiven some of it, for all that his childhood Nameless state cut deep. That circumstance had stalked years of his life in hard reality. He had found a hard answer in that crash of powder igniting, so close and elemental.

I had a horrible feeling it *had* killed me, yet I breathe, I feel life; relief liberates me, he told himself. The past weeks' worry, of look-behind-me uncertainty, the taste of puddle water in that damn ditch, drops behind me.

"Ginger, is that dawn breaking?"

The windows enclosed lozenges now of deep, pure blue. He heard the birds. Mistress Lyons had gone quiet again. Jesse and Piers would not be long away. When they came, he handed over his house guest and sent them to join Master Lyons. Then, the house silent, he sent Ginger gummy-eyed to bed, strode round Black House and threw the windows wide, every one. He took a pail and a stiff brush and he scrubbed his own front door as if he were a washerwoman until the wood was clean.

"Goodbye to the dung-hill of the world," said John Blackavise aloud, and weary as he was, turned his footsteps into the new-aired garden and stood there in the dew, communing his thoughts and his grasp of life to the dock-tailed horse. But the day was advancing, allowing every groundling who wished to attend the curtain-fall at the play to find the path to Black House and gather in John's parlour. Simon, the rector, neighbours, Aynescote's household staff, Bessie, Bessie's girls, all frantic that they had been party to the goings-on, or worse, had missed them, formed a guard of honour round John, variously pop-eyed, begging details, or concerned for his health. Ginger, normal as a sparrow, hopped about wearing his livery jacket as if promoted to steward. John found his presence a relief, as if the world with Ginger in it would revolve as usual. Simon kept begging him to sit down. But one look at his son told him it was Simon who needed the rest.

"I'm well, boy! And breathing. Look at me. Didn't Susan tell you, I'd be tough as troopers' old boots, no matter what?"

"She did give something of that opinion," admitted Simon, stooping his high shoulders as he turned to check if she were within earshot. "I'm very sorry at this business, Father, it must have been most painful for you."

"You were worried," suggested Blackavise with a lift of his chin, "without her permission, too. There's hope for you yet, boy."

Whoever had sent for the physician?

"Go away, if you have plans to leech me!" bellowed Blackavise, "If not, join us, do, and let us all be friends together this day. I'll tap a good cask, or something."

Mary Florida came up on her riding horse.

Curiously, the sight of her had quietened John's spirits, as if he had newly met her and was best-behaving. The dark night had come and passed, and now the herd of amazed well-wishers held them apart as if they were upon the two banks of the Red Sea, with the Israelites between. He tried to catch her eye, but the shuttle of looks between them snagged its thread when Bessie's girls got in the way pouring the jugs of claret wine, and then the Rector wanted to praise God for delivering him.

"Thank you," responded Blackavise, recognising he was sanctioned this once by clergy, "Simon, if I give thee a sovereign piece, or a sixpence, or after what I have been through, tuppence, will you get them all gone? Give them the idea, say I'm weary, been up all night, that drift. Take Susan back to Aynescote."

"You don't mean get them *all* gone, Father."

"No. Thank you, Simon."

Half hallucinating, weary, despite the lift of circumstances, John watched them ebbing away, saw Simon manage it quite cleverly; he suffered a smile to cling to his lips and he mouthed a suitable thank you, to everyone, and then he thought she'd gone, too. His own parlour door tickled shut behind the last of his friends and he was stranded like a savage on a desert island, with the clock stopped, before she came. The door wavered as if through a candle flame, yet this was broad day. A cloud obtruded, and it was coloured frog green. Her skirt, thus she, was advancing. The void of loneliness vanished because she hadn't left Black House with the visitors. Love was armour plate, he'd said, parting from her. Well, he felt as unprotected as if breastplate, buff coat, all, were stripped from him and the wretched blind boy was firing his dart at him again. That urchin had made the hole in him that his enemy had failed to do. His heart, unprotected, smote him.

"Have you left a kerchief, Mary Florida?"

"I think I must have, since I told Susan so. After which, until I heard the horses tramp away, I waited, counting the stars on that painted screen in the passage; there are thirty four."

"Did you in truth say that to Susan?"

"For sure I did, and to prove it my kerchief sits there on the tray of your wooden black boy."

He looked, it did: the ebony boy had covered his fruit with it, as if he were the joker hiding his white rabbit. She saw him tired and tense.

"I had trouble catching thine eye, in this roomful of people," said she, "no wonder, now I am close to thee – *can* you see out of those eyes?"

"Something, lady. You've thrown off the mourning far too early."

"I didn't want to come up as if I was wearing it for

thee."

"What a good thought. Now, what's amiss with my eye?"

"'Tis the stripe of the rainbow."

"That's uncomplimentary. What's it show? Red and yellow?"

"Merely a touch. Your iris remains deep blue, just as always. But there are also indigo rings neatly matching beneath each eye. You had fair cause to spend last night a touch sleepless."

At last she was close enough to discern these giveaway details. He indicated the window seat and she sank in the waves of frog green, his favourite. The tides of silk lapped his knee when he joined her.

"You were saying, you did not want to wear mourning for me."

"Tell me the whole story of last night," said she dissembling, and turned pretending to caress the little wooden boy at her elbow.

"Methought you had the entire tale already, with embellishment from Ginger."

"There's more to it, surely?"

Blackavise ran his fingers through his waterfall of hair. He considered her eyes to be more the green side of turquoise this day, from the gown. Ah, she hadn't wanted to wear black for me. She isn't going to. No, he was living, kicking, and here she was, wearing the cheerful tint of frog.

Mary Florida, well aware she had emerged from life as a lamb in a bower into a world of untrustworthy godsons, wanted to know what more had John to tell her. He was boiling up. She watched him rise to his feet, rally, square his broad shoulders, spread his hands.

"What transpired is that I teased out my enemy, so I might discover if he could shoot me, or if his mislike was not up to doing the deed. I'd unloaded his pistol by a trick. He did shoot me, I heard the crack, felt the powder blast, I swear I nearly felt the draught. But the moment he did it, that crack! That wasn't like the army. Out soldiering, by my deeds, I stood to die. But that was not a personal animosity. Here, I had an enemy. He hated me for my bastard past."

He couldn't avoid re-living it as he told her, saw anew the pistol's round mouth when he grasped that Radlett would do it.

"He tensed his hand. So here was the moment he would sunder my life. I was stunned, for I didn't believe he had it in him to fire the thing. It is as well I took the precaution. His ball couldn't kill me whilst in my pocket. The doomsday crack came. I was stunned. I was liberated. There's my tale, Mary Florida."

"Liberated?"

"I felt he'd killed my past. It cut the old traces of the wagon of despair."

"You carried that?"

"Perhaps I had not realised the weight of the cargo. John Nameless himself, and then, my poor wife who was long invalid after Simon, and he, he's like her, it hurts to see him not as strong as me. But this has come from dawn cracking over my head and I'm alive to see it; I survey this, it is a new day."

"'Tis true," murmured Mary Florida, "and let us say it brought sunrise."

"This is mighty welcome to me."

"Inner events came upon you," she told him, "they were the real surprise. People see the outer show, as they saw you today telling matter-of-factly that you disarmed Radlett who'd tried to kill you. But there was an undertow, of your feelings beneath."

When she'd been distressed, he'd talked to her. Now he heard Mary Florida's voice and it was his turn to listen.

"Inner events came on me, too." she was explaining, "Do you remember standing in Aynescote hall? Not on your first entry, when you were carried in prone. But the next time, on your own two feet, you dropped an alarm upon me, causing both pain and surprise, and pleasure. I did not expect such a jolt."

"Did I do all that?" he was surprised, "did I in truth do so much?"

"You are a powerful force."

"Perhaps Theo Radlett did shoot me dead and I am a cadaver imagining this."

"Nay, we neither sleep, nor are we feverish."

"Then, tell me why you've put me through this wait all morning? For sure I bade you remain locked in with Piers and Jesse to look to you, but why this day of days would you choose to obey me? I'd counted you'd be up here at daybreak, but I have to wait until you get conveyed up here in a herd with every member of my household and yours."

"And the rector."

"Don't laugh at me. Where did you accumulate him from? He actually prayed for me most cheerfully, which is more than Susan does."

"He was passing as we left; he was inescapable."

"Can you wonder, when 'tis a simple matter of riding up the hill to discover if I be still breathing, you gather up dozens of souls, yes including the Rector, wheresoever you claim to have found him, to be of our number, can you wonder that I am distraught, without thee to myself?"

This, from the stern soldier who now stood hand to hand with her, and they smiling.

"They've gone now," said Mary Florida. Her heart sang with the birds.

The pain and pleasure of wanting came to him. It was mid-afternoon.

"Go upstairs," he said. "Wait for me. Be Venus."